"Author Tracey Bateman's ability to 'tell it like we think it' is remarkable. I laughed out loud; I shed a few tears; I related, I cheered, and was touched...A perfect blend of mayhem, marvel, and ministry. Write on, Bateman! I'm hooked on Claire, who is my kind of a real woman!"

—Charlene Ann Baumbich, speaker, humorist, and
author of the Dearest Dorothy series

"Claire takes an honest look at what it feels like to be divorced, a single mom, and a Christian. Her family, her choices, and her lessons will inspire you and linger long after you put the book down."

—Susan May Warren, award-winning author of *Flee the Night*

"Whether you're eighteen or eighty, you will find something to love about Claire! She is every girl, and I loved sharing in her life, and can't wait to see her again. Tracey Bateman is a wonderful snappy voice in women's fiction."

—Kristin Billerbeck, author of *What a Girl Wants*
and *She's All That*

Leave It to
Claire

Tracey Bateman

WARNER
Faith®

New York   Boston   Nashville

Warner Faith
Time Warner Book Group
1271 Avenue of the Americas, New York, NY 10020
Visit our Web site at www.warnerfaith.com.

Printed in the United States of America
First Warner Books printing: January 2006
10 9 8 7 6 5 4 3 2 1

Library of Congress Cataloging-in-Publication Data
Bateman, Tracey Victoria.
  Leave it to Claire / Tracey Bateman.
      p. cm.
  ISBN-13: 978-0-446-69608-1
  ISBN-10: 0-446-69608-0
  1. Women novelists—Fiction. 2. Fiction—Authorship—Fiction. I. Title.
  PS3602.A854L43 2006
  813'.6—dc22   2005023523

To my amazing family,
who loves, supports, and puts up with
a full-time writer for a wife and mother.

Acknowledgments

Rusty, I love you so much. You promised God in the early days of our relationship that you would let Him love me through you. I know it hasn't always been easy, but in seventeen years you've never gone back on your word to Him. I feel God's smile in yours, His faithfulness in your faithfulness; I feel His tenderness in your soft words, His unwavering and unconditional acceptance and support every time you assure me that I am worth loving. I look forward to spending the rest of my days with you.

Cat, we know you are not the daughter depicted in the pages of this book. Thank you for letting me write her even though you knew people would assume she's you. You amaze me every day. Your constant drive to serve God better inspires me. At not quite sixteen, you're already beginning to learn excellence in ministry by running the soundboard for the youth band. I'm so proud of you.

Michael, you're my laughter. You're growing into such a fantastic and talented young man. I don't know what I would have done without your help while your dad was serving in Kuwait. You stepped up and became the man of the house in so many ways. Enjoy the rest of your childhood, son. Learn new skateboard tricks, play on the basketball team, and have fun with friends. You deserve it.

Stevan, my musician, my worshiper. Every time you sit at

the piano, I'm blown away by your gift. At eleven years old, you're already amazing. You have a love for God and insights that constantly challenge and delight me. I can't wait to see what God has planned for your life.

Will, my prayer warrior. The seven-year-old boy who refuses to let his feet touch the floor in the morning until he's taken a minute to pray. Every time I think of your precious face, my heart melts a little. As much as it touches me to see tears well up in your eyes when you hear the song "Here I Am to Worship," I can only imagine how it moves the heart of Jesus. Stay tender, baby, and let God direct your life.

Thanks to Chris Lynxwiler, Debra Ulrick, and Bonnie Burman for reading this book before I turned it in, and especially for laughing and crying in the right places.

To my editor, Leslie Peterson, thanks for encouraging me to dive deeper to true excellence. You're an answer to prayer.

Special thanks to my agent, Steve Laube. You are a pure gift from the Lord. Thanks for believing in me, supporting me, and partnering with me in this ministry-career. You are the best.

Leave It to
Claire

1

When I'm sitting in front of the computer, time means nothing to me. Whether I'm staring blindly at the screen, praying without ceasing as I beg God to take away writer's block, or whether I'm on a roll, burning up my keyboard as the words pour forth—like I just won an Oscar and this is my list of people to thank. I completely lose my sense of time and space and go on and on, oblivious to the orchestra playing "Get off the stage!" Or in this case, oblivious to the fact that my daughter is about to go ballistic because I forgot she needed a ride. Like five minutes ago.

"Come on, Mom! If you don't get down here, I'm going to miss kickoff."

I picture Ari downstairs in her cheerleading outfit, and I feel anxiety building. I don't want to be the one to make her late. I'd never, ever hear the end of it.

"Hang on!" I call down, hoping to buy a little time. "Just a couple more minutes, and I'm all yours."

After two full days of writer's block, I'm finally on a roll. The characters in my latest novel opened up to me today and started living out the story faster than I could type.

"Time's ticking away, Ma. Are you coming?"

Sheesh. What does "Hang on" mean?

My jaw clenches. Interruptions drive me crazy. Especially

now, when my hunky, albeit reluctant, hero Blaine Tyler is making his long-awaited move.

My novel—which, really, should have been on my editor's desk two weeks ago—is finally wrapping up. The romance is coming together just like every romance should (only I was starting to worry that this one wouldn't). And Ari is worried about kickoff?

In a few well-placed words, Esmeralda is going to get the kiss of a lifetime. Her toes will curl, her pulse will race, she'll feel things in her stomach she's never felt before—although if I were Esmeralda, I would have stopped waiting for Blaine a long time ago and either made the first move myself or started dating Raoul, the pool guy. But that's just me. My faithful readers want that happy ending, and Blaine's the one with the steady job, so . . .

"Mo-om."

"Sheesh. Okay, already," I yell down to my impatient offspring. "And we do not raise our voices in this house, young lady!"

Duty calls.

I push away from my desk, rereading the last sentence as I stand. How can I bear to leave them like this? Blaine's hand cups Esmeralda's flushed cheek as he lovingly moves in for the . . .

"Fine, Mom. I'll walk."

Never thought I'd say this, but I can't wait until that girl gets her driver's license.

I sigh. Yeah, I really do, just like a breathy character in one of my novels. I punch Ctrl+S to save my work. Blaine's waited this long, I guess he can hold that pucker for twenty more minutes until I get back. Then I'm wrapping up this last draft, taking two days—tops—to read over all four hundred manuscript pages, and off it goes to my longsuffering editor.

I'm still muttering as I slide my feet into leopard-spotted slippers and yank my jacket from the coatrack. I jerk down the stairs, every inch the martyr, and find my daughter in the kitchen, pacing like a caged dog. She pauses mid-step and stares, her eyes alight with horror—like she's Janet Leigh and the shower curtain just opened.

What?

"Mo-ther." She gives me an exasperated huff to show me she *cannot* believe how few brains—if any—I actually have. "Please tell me you're not going to wear that."

I look down at my outfit. A pair of SpongeBob SquarePants loungies that I slept in last night and a five-year-old faded blue long-john shirt my ex left when he moved out.

Okay, she might have a tiny point. But that teenage expression of utter disdain is just begging to be wiped off her face. I grin. "What's the problem?" Sometimes I just can't help myself.

Rolling her eyes, she huffs to the door. "Fine, but just drop me off in front of the school. No, at the side, okay?"

"Fine." I sling my purse over my shoulder. The strap immediately starts to slide. I end up dangling it from the crook of my elbow. I hate that. I'm turning into my mother. Before long, I'll have blue hair and false teeth and be calling everyone "honey." It's okay for her. But I'm not ready for the association. People already tell me how much I look like my mom—like that's supposed to be a compliment. I'm so glad they think I could be a twin to a seventy-year-old.

No woman under forty, especially me, wants to believe she's going to look like her mother one day. But denial notwithstanding, every time I pass a mirror, I say hi to Mom.

Ari gives me another once-over (clueless to the fact that in twenty years she's me). I snatch the keys from the counter. She rolls her eyes again. This time at the slippers. But at the end of a great writing day, I'm way past caring what a fifteen-year-old considers acceptable attire.

On me, anyway.

I do, however, care what she considers acceptable on her own body. And I think we've just hit an impasse. I'm looking at a good two inches of skin between the bottom of her shirt and the top of her cheerleading skirt. Mentally, I fast forward thirty minutes to when her arms (and consequently her shirt) will lift during a "Go, fight, team" cheer. Yeah, I'm thinking, no way, José.

I know she gets the picture, because her face goes red, and her eyes are way too wide. Deliberate innocence. *Soooo* not going to work.

I lift one eyebrow and dip my chin ever so slightly. "Did your shirt shrink?" Oh, that was clever. She scowls.

"Don't give me a hard time, Mom. Please? I know belly shirts aren't exactly in the rulebook, but these are standard issue for home games now. We're dancing at halftime."

Amazing how a kid's tone can go from "You're too stupid to live" to "I wuv you, Mommy" in a matter of seconds.

I feel myself caving. In my mind's eye, I see her very first itty-bitty finger-paint handprint and I want to give in. Then my gaze sweeps her in another once-over. Okay, she did *not* have that body in preschool.

I fold my arms across my—*ahem*—ample chest, bracing for World War VI (III, IV, and V have come and gone since puberty hit). My daughter is not going to dress like the latest teenybopper pop diva. Not in my lifetime. "Hmm. Let's go back to the 'I-know-belly-shirts-aren't-exactly-in-the-rulebook' part."

She can't exactly argue with that now, can she? I smile. But only on the inside. No use flaunting my rapier wit when she's on the losing end of the argument.

She's not smiling at all—not on the outside, and I'd bet not on the inside either. The girl has no sense of humor anymore.

"Mother . . . if I don't wear the shirt, I can't dance tonight."

"Then I guess I might as well get back to my computer." I shrug and move like I'm headed to the stairs. Totally calling her bluff.

"I'm on the third row of the pyramid!"

"Then they'd better let you dance fully clothed, or it's going to be a lopsided pyramid." I grin at the image. But again, she's not thinking it's funny.

"Fine, Mother," she bites out. "I'm going upstairs to change."

I nod, sending her a "good choice" look. She rolls her eyes again.

Oh, yeah. High five, me. I am way too cool to be pushing forty.

I'm liking the outcome of this little blip in the road, and it appears all will be smooth riding until Ari turns back around and gives me that look—the one every teenage girl begins to acquire around age thirteen and has down to a science by the time she graduates from high school. Only, my daughter has it down pat at the tender age of fifteen, and I can tell things are about to get ugly.

"I can't believe you're criticizing my cheerleading outfit when you're planning to go out in public like *that*."

See, the great thing about being a published writer is that I can stay home in my jammies all day if the muse is hot on my shoulder. Usually no one cares—unless it's six-thirty and I forgot to get dressed and my daughter is mortified to be seen with me. But the thing is, I *am* the mom and she isn't going to get away with talking to me like that.

I open my mouth to tell her so, but she cuts me off. "I'm sorry I was rude. I'm going to change."

Score one for her. Can't help but grin at the clever way she avoided being grounded. And she *did* sort of apologize, although her sincerity is highly in question.

Besides, it's hard to think about holding a grudge when I'm staring at five slices of leftover pepperoni pizza sitting in the box from dinner. Ari was supposed to put those away. Hmm. My mood is starting to improve just looking at the grease spots on the box, and I'm not sure if I should yell at my daughter for disobeying a direct order or thank her for not doing it.

I look at the box. Look away. I'm dieting. I drum my fingers along the countertop, trying to ignore the little crispy edges of slightly overcooked pepperoni.

To divert my attention, I envision my scene with Blaine and Esmeralda. The raven-haired beauty waits breathlessly, heart pounding as Blaine moves in for a bite— A bite? Oh, brother. What, is Blaine a vampire now?

Pizza is the thorn in my side. Every excess inch of my side. Suddenly, I can smell pepperoni. And it smells so good.

Walk away from the pizza, I tell myself in no uncertain terms.

I start to, but the power of the cheesy, tomatoey, crusty pie is too strong. I spring back like an extra-large rubber band.

I snatch a slice and bring it to my mouth, my eyes shifting about like one of those tattered, starving people in an apocalyptic B-movie. You know, the ones squatting next to a building eating the last rat on the face of the earth before anyone else can get it? That's me. Sad thing is, even that image doesn't make the pizza less appealing. I'm so weak.

"All right, I changed. Let's go."

I jump, guilty as sin, at the sound of my daughter's voice, and drop the goods back into the box. Only one bite gone. Oh, sure, she decides to hurry for the first time in her life. Two more minutes and I would have scarfed that slice down plus another one.

Probably just as well. Who needs a bazillion calories anyway?

"Okay, kiddo," I say, following her through the kitchen and out the garage door. "Sorry about the SpongeBob pants, but come on, you should read the great stuff I wrote today. Five thousand words of sheer magic."

"I'm happy for ya," she practically snarls.

It's funny how I find the well-placed acerbic remark rather amusing and occasionally brilliant, coming from me. Coming from my sarcastically-inclined offspring, it just burns me up. Is that a double standard?

"Hey, watch yourself or forget the game. I'm trying to be

civil here. And you're not at the top of my happy list tonight as it is."

"Sorry," she mutters in an un-sorry tone.

Within minutes, we pull through the circular drive in front of Jefferson High School, amid a crowd of teenagers shouting and tossing cups of water on one another just outside the gym. A band member in full uniform jumps out of the way in time to avoid getting his tuba soaked.

Ari reaches with purpose for the handle. Her jerky movements clue me in to her displeasure. Somehow I've completely forgotten to drop her off at the side of the school as promised. I can tell she's seething at the injustice of being forced to step out of her mother's van in front of the building.

I shrug. "Oops. Well, at least you're not late for kickoff."

She opens the door and slams it shut without a good-bye, "Thanks for the ride," anything. Resentment cranks inside me as I watch her sashay off toward the building where her half-naked cheerleader friends are packed together like canned fish.

Cool canned fish. There's something satisfying to me about my daughter being one of the cool kids. Rationally, I know that's just stupid, but I can't help but live vicariously through her. I was always in the nerd click. Fodder for cheerleader terrorism. And come on, who doesn't secretly wish to be one of the beautiful people? My Ari is a natural beauty and has a confidence about her that induces her peers to clamor about waiting for her to notice.

Only, at this moment, she's oblivious to her little entourage, because I have her full attention—and the full force of her glare. Apparently I haven't driven away quickly enough to suit her, because she sends me an exaggerated wave.

Sometimes it just burns me up how insignificant I become to my daughter once I've done her bidding. Tonight it really gets to me, especially since I left a perfectly yummy kiss scene and an equally yummy pizza to bring her to the game.

The injustice of it all hits me smack in the middle of my forehead like a suction arrow. In an impulsive moment, I roll down the passenger-side window. "Ari, honey," I call, louder than necessary and in a tone that's just a notch above my normal pitch. I have every intention of making her walk back to the minivan and kiss me good-bye in front of all these people. The little stinker. I remember when she cried every time I dropped her off at school. Okay, so she was five, but still. When did she stop loving me?

Quickly, she turns around and slinks back to the minivan, trying desperately not to be noticed. Only problem with that is the whole popularity thing. Everyone knows her, so when someone calls "Ari" like I just did, kids stare.

However, I'm regretting my rash decision to put her in her place. Because not only are they staring at her, now they're looking at me. My hair isn't brushed, and there's not a speck of makeup on my face. Instinctively, I check out my reflection in the rearview mirror. Big mistake!

"Mo-ther," she hisses. "You're humiliating me."

Suddenly needing to get out of there quick, I take pity on us both. "You forgot to tell me what time to pick you up," I say, as a way of covering up the fact that I was about to purposely embarrass her and ended up embarrassing myself instead. My mother would call that poetic justice.

"I have my cell phone. I'll call you when the game's over."
She walks away, leaving me to stare after her.

Shoot. Why does she always get the last word?

I see her group of followers pointing at me and whispering among themselves. Okay, they're probably looking and admiring her, and most likely haven't even noticed me, but when you have the kind of self-esteem I have, laughing kids translate to "laughing at me" kids. That's the way I feel if anyone is cracking a joke anywhere in the vicinity, and I'm not in on it.

It's something I've dealt with since I was a kid. Full of myself one second, down on myself the next. I probably need therapy. I hear Dr. Phil has a diet book out now. Maybe I should read it and kill two birds with one stone. Get my head and my behind shrunk for one low price of $19.99.

I'm about to pull out of the drive, seriously considering making a detour to Wal-Mart's book aisle on the way home, when I see a woman walking toward me, waving and mouthing, "Stop." I'd love to pretend I don't see her, but eye contact has already happened. Besides, I recognize her as the mother of one of Ari's friends. Linda Myers. She and her husband are new to my church.

That's the thing about living in a small town. Acquaintanceships go beyond work, school, or church. Usually there are at least two common structured organizations in your life to connect you to someone. The sad thing is that Linda and I have daughters who are best friends and a church in common, and I have never taken the time to get to know her on a personal level.

As she approaches, I notice she's wearing a yellow-and-black GO YELLOWJACKETS T-shirt tucked into a pair of button-fly Levis. She looks how I wish I looked. I haven't tucked in a shirt on purpose in a good five years. She reaches the van and I realize she's even prettier than I remember from seeing her across the church. Auburn hair and enormous green eyes give her a romance-heroine beauty. And they say no one really looks like that. Wait until I tell my skeptical editor. Still, I'd rather eat dirt than have to talk to this woman and pretend I don't care if I'm wearing SpongeBob jammie bottoms.

A bright smile is splitting her beautifully made-up face and I wish I could crawl under the seat. Instead, I press the button and roll down the window.

"Hi," she says. "You're not staying for the first game of the season?"

I stare blankly. *Shoot*. I should have.

"I'm uh . . . on deadline." I give her a you-know-how-it-is smile, although we both know she doesn't. For some reason, I really hope she won't think little of me for being a horrible mother and not supporting my cheerleader daughter like she supports hers.

"I understand," she says. "I'm so sorry to bother you."

"It's okay." I continue to smile tightly, hoping this is the end of the conversation.

No such luck.

She leans against my van and I start worrying that she's going to get a ton of dust down the front of her. When was the last time I had this thing at the car wash?

She pulls me from the question with her next sentence. "I hope you don't think this is inappropriate of me, but . . ."

Oh, brother. Here it comes. *"I'm a member of Weight Watchers . . . Low Carbers . . . Weigh Down . . ."* You name it, I've heard it. Well-meaning ladies who honestly feel that inviting me to a weight-loss class is just the thing. After all, I have such a pretty face.

My defenses are rising and I want to cut her off before she even has a chance to say anything. Instead, I take the less-than-truthful-but-necessary-for-my-reputation approach. "No, you're not bothering me at all."

Not so friendly as to invite conversation, but not so rude that she can spread the word about what a snob the published author is.

Instead of getting to the point, she clears her throat and looks toward the building. "I notice you didn't let her wear the crop top." She inclines her head toward the group of cheerleaders still milling around the doorway to the gym.

I relish the approval in this virtual stranger's face and give a superior laugh at her observation. "Not in my lifetime."

She nods in agreement, and again I'm feeling an unusual sense of camaraderie with this stranger. "Trish threw a fit, but I told her either she could wear the old top or they could have a crooked pyramid."

I give a weak laugh. It's the best I can do. Funny how you think you're the only one with quick wit—your one claim to self-worth—only to find there's a Linda Myers in town who is not only beautiful *but* thinks up the exact same jokes. How can that be fair?

"Anyway," Trish's mom is saying, "I'm so glad I caught you. I've tried to call several times but can never seem to get an answer."

Not that I'd tell her this, but that's largely because I never answer my phone. As a matter of fact, it stays unplugged most of the time. Drives my mom perfectly nuts. But it's the only way I can write without being interrupted every fifteen minutes. People inevitably believe if I'm home, I'm available. That's the drawback to working at home.

I don't unplug the phone to be hateful; it's a matter of self-preservation. Gotta meet those deadlines or we'll be eating government cheese.

Still, this lady isn't one of my regular callers and I really don't have a good reason to hold a grudge against her for something other people do. Besides, she seems sort of sweet and genuine. So I smile for real. "I'm so sorry I missed your calls. What can I do for you?"

"It was nothing, really. I just . . . Mainly I wanted to thank you for your last book. *Tobey's Choice.*"

Well, then . . . Maybe I should give her my cell phone number, because if we're going to talk about my books I can talk all night.

Only, she has tears streaming down her face. I feel this is more than an average fan gusher. I sense the Holy Spirit leading me to be still and listen. To get over myself for once. This is not all about me. Sufficiently chastised, I get a grip and cover the hand she has placed on the halfway-down window. "I'm so glad you enjoyed the book," I say, in order to encourage her to continue.

She gulps. "I—I could so relate to her. My husband did the same . . . Well, reading your book gave me the strength to confront him. God is healing our marriage and I want to thank you for listening to Him and writing what I needed to hear."

Tears fill my eyes. I say a little prayer aloud right there in the circle drive of Jefferson High School, heedless of the watchers. God has performed a miracle.

Moments later I leave the school behind, all thoughts of

Dr. Phil pushed firmly to somewhere in the back of my mind. Who needs that guy when God is in the office?

I drive home on autopilot. Humbled. Thoughtful.

Feeling like an utter hypocrite.

Tobey's Choice. My book about forgiveness. My heroine's cheating husband didn't deserve a second chance. I wanted to kill him off—after Tobey did the right thing and forgave the weasel, of course. But my editor insisted the ending be rewritten so that their marriage was saved. No horrible death scene—and boy, did I have a good one. I was mad, but I gave in.

Now I'm glad I did.

2

mazing how lukewarm pizza loses its appeal after you find out your book just saved a marriage. I float into the house on a cloud of "Wow, God, did You really use little ol' me?"

I'm refocused on the ministry of writing. The power of God flowing through the written word. With the kids at my ex-husband's tonight (except Ari, who will go over in the morning), I have all night to finish my book. I practically fly up the steps to my office, anxious to let Blaine finish his kiss.

Okay, so I know kissing isn't necessarily a powerful ministry tool, but even in a Christian romance novel, the last embrace is still the big finish. And good grief, Christians kiss, too—or they would if the right guy would just show up, already.

Great, now I'm depressed.

The phone rings just as I position my fingers on the keyboard. But I can't complain this time; I don't turn the ringer off or unplug from the jack when my kids are at their dad's. You never know when the cell phone might go dead or something. I need backup.

We have three phone lines in the house—one in my office (I used to use it for dial-up before wireless. Thank You,

God, for inspiring that one), one in the kitchen, and another in Ari's room. And Ari and I each own a cell.

I answer the ringing, and my ten-year-old son's voice washes all over me like a warm rain. "Hi, Mom."

My Shawny. The child who makes me exhale. I love all of my kids the same. Honest. But Shawn is the one who gets me. He always notices when I lose ten pounds. Never mentions when I gain it back. He loves music the way I do. And loves to come to my office and sit quietly just to be near me. And no, he's not a wimp like my older son says. He's just sensitive. And sweet. There's nothing wrong with that.

Kicking off my fuzzy slippers, I smile and lean back in my black-leather desk chair. "Hi, angel baby. Having fun? Did Dad pick you up on time?"

"Yeah, he was sitting right there in the car when I came out of the school."

I know a question like that might sound moot since Rick obviously got the kid home safe and sound, but my irresponsible ex *did* arrive at the school late once, and no one was left but the janitors and my four kids. It scared me half to death when I found out about it the next day. Hindsight fear can be just as bad as on-the-spot fear. Especially where your kids are concerned. Thinking about what *could* have been has kept me awake more than one night.

"Guess what?" Shawn asks, bringing me back from the black hole of what-ifs.

"What?"

"Daddy took us to eat pizza."

Pizza. Now I'm thinking about that box on the counter again.

"That's what we ate, too."

He hesitates, probably trying to come up with something to say. "I miss you, Mommy."

I melt like microwaved butter. "I miss you, too, Shawn."

"I like going for pizza with you better."

Oh, baby, my heart cries. Don't try to fix me.

"Honey, I'm sure you like going with both of us, don't you?"

He doesn't answer right away, and I know I've hurt his feelings. He was just trying to make me feel special. He's sensitive that way—my ten-year-old boy. But I have to make him understand that he doesn't have to choose. I'm not threatened by his love for his dad. Not much, anyway.

"You know what? When you come home on Sunday, I'll take you out for pizza again, how's that sound?"

"Great! I gotta go take a bath now. Darcy says I smell like a pig farm. It was only a joke, though. She wasn't being mean or anything."

"I know." I *am*, however, threatened by his affection for Darcy, his new stepmother. A woman ten years my junior. And a good fifty pounds lighter. "Be good and have fun."

"Okay. Here's Tank."

I can tell by the muffled argument on the other end of the line that the last thing Tank wants to do is talk to me.

My thirteen-year-old, Tommy, has recently changed his name to Tank and wants a lip ring. I'll humor him with the name, but he can just forget about the hole in his lip. I shudder just thinking about it. Last night we had a very long and loud "discussion" about the subject, ending with my telling him to go to his room and think about the effects of piercing—such as lockjaw from rusty needles, or worse. He stomped off, but not before expressing his opinion of my mothering skills and informing me of his well-thought-out decision to never speak to me again. He did, however, allow me to fry him two eggs (over easy—not too runny, not too hard) this morning, and a couple of slices of bacon. Sweet of him, huh? Thinking back on it, I probably should have made him eat oatmeal.

"What up, Dogg?" he asks.

Dogg? "Yeah, that's not going to work. Try again."

I hear him say, "Whatever" under his breath, but he loses a bit of the attitude before coming back to the conversation. "What's up, Mom?"

"Just got back from dropping Ari at the game. How come you're not going?"

"Football's stupid."

"You didn't think so last year." Or the other twelve years of his life.

"Things change."

Yeah, they sure do. Like last year his dad got remarried. Rick and I have been divorced for five years, and I honestly thought the kids had dealt with it. But when he announced his engagement to Darcy, I realized by the outcry that they'd honestly believed we'd get back together someday.

By the time the wedding took place, my son's personality had done a one-eighty. He looks different, acts different, hangs out with a different crowd. And I don't mean "different" just because they're not the same kids. I mean "different" as in weird. All this Goth black look. It's creepy, and I don't like my kid being one of them. I want back the clean-cut child I once knew. It's what I'm pushing for. "Well, maybe you'll go to Homecoming."

"I doubt it. Later, dude, I gotta go."

"Then put Jakey on the phone, will you? And don't call me dude." I'm stinging a little from his take-me-or-leave-me attitude. He doesn't say good-bye, just drops the phone (I guess he dropped it anyway, judging from the clatter in my ear). "Hey brat," he yells, and I swear he does it just so I can hear him call Jakey a brat without being able to fuss at him for doing it. "Mom wants to talk to you."

"Okay, I'll be there when I finish this round," my six-year-old calls back.

"Whatever, dude. You're the one she's gonna yell at."

I want to shake the phone. Jakey is addicted to video games. Day and night, that's all he thinks about. But I thought he'd at least want to tell me good night.

I wait. I glance at the clock and wait some more. Irritation creeps through my veins. Those kids! I'm definitely having a talk with Tommy about his phone etiquette. And I'm cutting Jakey off from Nintendo. Totally! Just as soon as I get this book off to my editor.

A minute later I realize no one remembers I'm on the phone. I'm just about to hang up when I hear Darcy say (in a testy tone that raises my hackles), "Who left the phone on the floor?" She drops her volume and mutters, "I swear, those kids."

My maternal indignation rises. Who is she to say "those kids" about my kids? She should be so lucky to someday have kids as great as mine!

The phone clicks off, and I sit there holding the receiver in my hand, looking like a dope, before I finally press the off button.

Kids. They never live up to the idealistic expectations young parents have. When that first precious offspring, that flesh of your flesh, comes along, all you can do is ooh and ahh and dream of its future. You are determined that you will not make the mistakes of generations past. Oh no. The family curses stop right here.

You kiss all ten toes and all ten fingers of your tiny, sleeping miracle and think nothing about this wonderful creature could possibly induce you to raise your voice, bang your head against the wall, or run crying into the bathroom for ten minutes of peace—like your own mother did on occasion when you were growing up.

Yeah, then a week later, you realize it's time to amend your lofty ideals from envisioning your prideful self attending your son's—or better yet, daughter's—presidential inauguration to simply making it through one more week with no sleep, no time for a shower, and for-the-love-of-Pete-will-those-stitches-ever-stop-itching?

By the time two weeks have gone by, you've adjusted somewhat to the foggy lack of sleep, and your mind turns to other things—like getting out of the house, which by now has the distinct odor of the not-so-cuddly things babies can smell like.

You burn the maternity rags and head for the prebaby wardrobe. Then moments later you sit on the floor and sob as reality bites you on your size 18 rear end. After nine months of dreaming of wearing the size 8 (okay, size 10) jeans again, you realize you didn't miraculously shed the fifty-five pounds you gained while carrying a seven-pound baby. But being the trouper you are, you wipe away the tears and cuddle your infant close and try to convince yourself that she's worth every busted-out zipper, all the hours of labor, and yes, even the cellulite and stretch marks (although that doesn't stop you from slathering gobs of cocoa butter on your stomach and thighs just in case it really does cause them to fade—which it doesn't).

I stare at the phone, reliving that so-called conversation with my boys, not so sure they're worth it after all. Swallowing down a lump of disappointment, I stare at the screen, fully aware that Blaine is still mid-pucker and Esmeralda is most likely about to get fed up with him and make a pass at Raoul. I want to help them out, but all the fire to write God's masterpiece has fled.

Suddenly, the weirdest feeling overtakes me: I want my mother.

Apologetically, I glance at the computer screen, mentally asking Blaine to be patient for just a little while longer. I will get to that kiss, but first things first.

Mom picks up in two rings. She must be sitting in her recliner with the cordless in her lap. She does that so she doesn't have to get up during her TV shows if someone calls. I told her she should just turn off the phone during her programs and check her voice mail afterward. Pointedly, she said it was rude to turn off your phone unless you were going to sleep. Ouch.

"Hi, Mom."

"What's wrong, honey?" I hear the TV volume go from blasting to mute in a millisecond. Mom can always tell when I'm distressed. Guilt sort of wiggles through me when I remember that I had the phone unplugged all day. What if she had fallen and couldn't get up? Or what if a robber had broken in and tied her up and left her on the floor?

"I just wanted to make sure you were okay," I say. It's a little lie. I really only called to talk about me and my feelings. But now that I hear her voice, I do care. As long as she makes it quick so we can get to my dilemma.

"Oh, I'm fine. Joan and I went to the Center." (Translation: old-folks hangout.) I think the only reason Mom goes is because she's the youngest person there by a good six years, looks even younger, and has all the old men drooling over her.

"Josie cheated at bridge, so we decided not to let her play anymore."

"Josie cheats every week, and you always say the same thing until you need another player."

"Well, today was the straw that broke the camel's back. She won the penny pile, and that's practically the same thing as stealing. So why did you really call? Are the kids okay?"

"Yes. It's Friday. They're at Rick's."

"Oh, that's right. Why aren't you writing? That editor of yours isn't going to wait forever without docking your pay."

Mother knows way too much about the process. I roll my eyes (which I'd never have the guts to do in person). "I wrote a lot today. Almost done."

"Did you send it to me?" I smile. Mom's my number one fan. I have to e-mail every rough-draft chapter to her. She oohs and ahhs and loves every word. Thank God for a mom like her.

Did I actually think that?

My mind and eyes wander to the computer where Blaine and Esmeralda are still waiting. "Not yet," I say to Mom. "I'm wrapping up the chapter now." I hesitate, remembering my incident with Ari, then the boys, and wish I could find a way to confide without it sounding like I'm a big baby. Or, heaven forbid, like I'm soliciting advice.

"All right. When you get it finished, you send it to me. Are you sure nothing is wrong?"

I blow out a frustrated breath, knowing I'm about to spill my guts, and that in all likelihood, I'll regret that decision a second and a half after I finish. Still, that knowledge does nothing to prevent my mouth from spewing forth my discontent. So much for knowledge being power.

I tell her all about her spoiled, ungrateful grandchildren. And then the diatribe escalates and I cover all the bases. I'm lonely, while Rick (who clearly doesn't deserve to be happy) has Darcy. And now, to top it off, Rick just started being an usher at church. *My* church.

Six months ago, Shawn invited them to the Easter program where he played "Angry man in crowd." His awe-inspiring dialogue—"Crucify Him!"—sent chills down my spine. Apparently it did to Rick and Darcy as well because they both bawled their way to the front during the after-play altar call and haven't missed a service since.

I'm so outraged that I raise my voice a little. "Rick never darkened the doorstep of a church until six months ago. Now he's an *usher*?"

"So what?" Mom's tone leads me to believe she just shrugged her bony little shoulders. "Why do you care if he's an usher or not?"

Okay, that is *not* the reaction I was looking for. She sounds sort of distant, anyway, and I'll bet she's reading the closed-captioned words on the screen instead of really listening to me. That's probably why she isn't getting my point. So I decide to give her another chance to respond in a proper manner before I make my excuses, hang up, and go tackle the rest of that pizza.

"Well, I'm just thinking maybe he's not ready to serve in the house of the Lord just yet." Cringe. Even I'm not buying that one. No way will she be able to pass up the opportunity to kick it into "advice" mode.

"Honey, I don't want to hurt your feelings, but maybe your frustration isn't anyone else's fault but your own. Besides, you don't even go to church half the time anymore."

I sniff. Glad you don't want to hurt my feelings. Clearly, it was a *huge* mistake confiding in her. Pepperoni is calling my name. "Well, Mom, I gotta—"

"Oh, don't hang up just because I said something you don't want to hear. I need to tell you something else—about me. I've been trying to call you all day, but you know how you always turn off your phone."

Feeling like a swatted kid, I squirm in my seat. "I only live three doors down, Ma," I remind her. "And my phone hasn't been off *all* the time. What do you need to tell me?"

She takes a deep breath and it sounds a little shaky. I frown and perk up. This doesn't sound good.

"I've been talking to Charley."

Charley's my brother. He moved to Texas a few years ago, and now he has a thick drawl that everyone knows is made up. Charley's younger than me, but his kid count just topped mine. His wife, Marie, recently gave birth to a set of twins to bring his total number of children to five. Funny how Mom only had two kids, but Charley and I have both popped them out like nobody's business.

"So how is that ol' wrangler?" I ask in a really bad Charley-esque drawl.

"Be nice." But I hear the chuckle in her tone. "Actually, he bought a new house."

"Another one?"

Did I forget to mention that my brother is also loaded? Not J. R. Ewing loaded, but he owns three new-and-used car lots, and let's just say that Texans buy a lot of trucks. Okay, I'm happy for him. He has the oh-so-perfect life. But if I have to hear about his new house, I'm going to barf.

"This one has a large basement apartment."

"Wow." I absently tap my keyboard as the screensaver kicks in.

"The basement apartment is for me."

"Good. You'll be more comfortable when you go there to visit." She's always lamenting having to sleep on my nephew's twin-size bed. "This is their Christmas with you, isn't it?"

"Yes, it is. But that's not the reason for the apartment."

It sinks in that she's trying to tell me something. "What are you saying?"

"I'm moving to Texas."

I blink. My feet slide from the desk and plop to the floor as I sit up straight. "What do you mean you're moving to Texas. Like for good?"

"Yes."

"But Mom, what am I supposed to do about the kids when I'm on deadline?" Okay, that sounded so much worse actually coming out of my mouth.

She doesn't respond, and I'm fully aware that I've hurt her deeply.

I swallow hard and try again. "I'm sorry. You're just such a part of our lives that I can't imagine you not being here."

"You'll get used to it."

"Why are you doing this all of a sudden?"

"It's not actually all of a sudden. I told you a year ago I was thinking about it. Charley only just got a place big enough."

Did she? A year ago. I rack my brain. I'm coming up with nothing.

"So, when are we talking? Spring? It'll probably take that long or longer to sell the house."

"Oh, honey. I'm not waiting until the house sells. I'm itching to get my hands on those twins. I've already listed the house with a realtor, and you'll be here to oversee things. The movers are coming in three weeks, and I've already bought my plane ticket."

I feel so betrayed. All of this going on in her life and I had no idea. All these plans. "Well, I guess you've pretty much made up your mind then."

"Yes, and you'll be fine. You're stronger than you think."

"Sure I am, Mom." Already, I feel the walls closing in, the pressure in my chest. How am I going to get along without her? My mom has been my rock since Rick hit the road.

Who will help with the kids? Make supper when I am buried to my eyeballs in deadlines? Who will write little notes on pink, heart-shaped sticky tabs and press them to my computer reminding me that Jesus loves me and so does she? I feel tears pushing against the backs of my eyes.

"Claire," she says in a tone I haven't heard her use on me since I was twelve. It's soothing. But doesn't last for long. "It's Charley's turn to have his mom close by. And it's my turn to be with Charley's kids. I'll always treasure the years I was here for you, but it's time for you to face some things, my girl."

"Like what? A rubber room?" I can't do it on my own. I don't want to be a stinker. But Charley doesn't need her. I decide to tell her that. "Charley doesn't need you like I do, Mom. He has Marie."

"Maybe this isn't about what Charley or you need. Maybe it's about what I need at this stage in my life."

Oh, hadn't thought of that.

"I love you, Claire, but you are so self-absorbed that you can't see anyone's needs but your own." My mother is pulling out all the stops now that she's about to wrangle some steers deep in the heart of Texas! "For the past five years I've watched you become a hermit, comforting your-self with food and completely losing touch with your children."

Now I'm really miffed. Why did I ever want her to stay? "Okay, Mom." I speak through clenched teeth, trying to remain polite and respectful. "Thank you for your advice. I will call you tomorrow."

"Don't hang up. I'm not finished."

Oh, goodie.

"You can either sink into deeper bitterness against all the struggles you've had, or you can take the bull by the horns and do something to make yourself happy."

I can't believe she just said "take the bull by the horns." What? Has she been taking a course on quippy Texas lingo?

"Is that all?" I ask, tight-lipped.

"No. The main reason you're so miserable is that you

have lost touch with God and fellow believers. We're not meant to be Lone Ranger Christians. We need each other."

I give a hefty sigh, zeroing in on the part where she said I comfort myself with food. Now my mom's calling me fat? I need to get off the phone pronto. Seriously. So I do the best thing I can think of. I agree with her about something. "I know you're right about church. I plan on going this Sunday."

"I'm glad to hear it. I'll ride with you. That church bus is too rowdy with all those kids."

"Fine. I better go now and finish this scene, Mom. Blaine's going to kiss Esmeralda."

"Don't tell me. I want to be surprised when I read it!"

I laugh. Mom laughs. But I'm not laughing on the inside. And I have a feeling she isn't either.

3

The week after Mom drops her little bomb on my already explosive life, I'm sitting in Dr. Grace's exam room, staring at the balding surgeon like an idiot, and trying to wrap my mind around his wretched news.

Judging from the V furrowed in his brow, I assume my expression gives the appearance of a woman who's not quite rolling on all four wheels. And to be honest, I think I must be hearing things. Because this can*not* be happening.

"What do you mean six weeks?" I ask.

He shrugs. I hate it when doctors, lawyers, or IRS auditors shrug like that—nonchalantly, like they're just glad it's me and not them. "I mean just what I said. It's possible that you can heal in four weeks, but not likely, considering your particular career and considering you need surgery on both arms."

Considering my career. That's exactly what I'm doing. Why else would I be here sitting on a cold, hard exam table? (Although I *am* grateful there are no stirrups.) Six weeks is a ridiculous amount of time.

I'm keeping this rant to myself because he doesn't seem the type to put up with a whiny, overweight prima donna. But sheesh, even hysterectomies don't take that long for recovery. This is just a little carpal tunnel syndrome. I know a lady who had carpal tunnel surgery and was typing e-mails in a week. I give him this information and he doesn't seem impressed. So I press on. "Can't you just do a laser thing and get me back to work in a few days?"

The surgeon looks at me over the rim of his half-glasses and scowls. I scowl back because I don't think the question is unreasonable, given modern medicine. I mean, mankind can put artificial hearts into the chests of fifty-year-old men and transplant everything from kidneys to hair (and Dr. Grace might want to look into that one), but this little wrist surgery is going to lay me up six weeks or more? Like I said . . . ridiculous.

"Isn't there any other alternative?"

My file is laid open in his hands, and he makes a little note. Even in my best mental scenario, I can't imagine that it's anything flattering. Looking up at me, his expression softens, and I can tell he's finally connected with my dilemma. "I'm good, but I'm not God. Some things just take time. And healing from the kind of carpal tunnel surgery I recommend for you is one of those things. You'll have to be patient. Now, you wouldn't expect to write a whole book in a couple of weeks would you?"

"Tell that to my editor," I grumble.

A sigh pushes from his lungs, and I know I'm getting on his last nerve. All I have to say is that it's a good thing he's not a pediatrician because he has no patience whatsoever. A horrible bedside manner. But I'm not going to antagonize the man who will soon be holding a sharp blade to my wrist.

Dr. Grace gives me a stern glance and the V returns to his brow. "Wait much longer to get the procedure done and we might have to do something more drastic. And, trust me, the recovery would be much longer in that case."

I grumble to the door and say I'll get back with him when I have a free six weeks on my hands, which, according to my online calendar, is . . . never. I twist the knob and frown. Is it my imagination or is my hand tingling more than usual? The surgery's got to happen before I start my next project or I won't be able to finish it at all, let alone by deadline.

On the way down in the elevator I'm relieved that I'm alone in the mobile cube. Too many people in an enclosed space give me the willies. As if in reaction, my gut tightens as the doors swish open to reveal the busy first floor of the medical building. Unease creeps through me and waves of heat wash my entire body. I'm thinking I might be having a hot flash. Like maybe menopause is going to strike early. That's about my luck lately.

Confusion sifts through my mind as I step out of the elevator, trying to figure out what I'm supposed to be doing and yet somehow knowing where I am. It's very surreal. I'm certifiable, that's all there is to it. I stop walking, frozen.

I think how this whole picture is an analogy for my life. Standing still in the middle of the floor while people whiz by me, not noticing that I'm here. I am invisible. My heart starts pounding and sweat is beading on my brow. Panic is rising. I have to get out of here before I blow a gasket and end up drooling applesauce down my chin in some psych ward.

I'm gasping for breath and my head is woozy. My eyes squeeze shut, and I'm still unable to budge from the middle of the first-floor hallway where dozens of people are maneuvering around me—like this is the Indy 500 and I'm the car that just blew a tire. I gather breath and reopen my eyes, determined to put one foot in front of the other and walk to the end of the hall where I see sunlight beaming in through the double doors. The proverbial (and literal) light at the end of the tunnel.

Oh, God. I think I'm having a heart attack. Please, please get me home. I promise I'll take better care of myself. Cut back on pizza, exercise, stuff like that.

My breathing is coming in short bursts and I have no confidence in my feeble attempt at prayer/negotiating with the One who holds my life in His hands.

Seriously, I'm not going to make it, God. I need help.

"Claire? You okay?"

Oh my, there must have been power in that prayer, after all. I've never had one answered so quickly.

I look up at the sound of the masculine voice. Familiar, dark, Andy Garcia eyes are looking down at me beneath a brow furrowed in concern.

Hello, Gorgeous, I think in my best Streisand voice.

Someone blows past me on the other side, and I feel my body start to tremble.

"You okay?" he asks again.

Somehow I know this man (and being a Christian, I am fully aware that there's no chance it was in a former life), but my mind is numb and coherency is a thing of the past. I can't place him. "Get me out of here!" I gasp.

Warmth floods the small of my back as he wordlessly presses his palm there and guides me to the end of the hall. I keep my eyes focused. Finally we are outside the building. Relief washes over me. I try to breathe deeply, except that two men in white doctor coats are lighting up and the smoke makes me cough.

Coming down the walkway, an elderly woman steps halt-

ingly next to an equally elderly man who is maneuvering
an electric wheelchair in our direction. Andy Garcia Eyes
opens the door for them. With a pointed glance at her husband's oxygen tank, the woman scowls at the smoking docs,
who both look away lickety-split.

The cowards. I have to shake my head at the paradox.
The dangers of smoking should definitely be addressed in
medical school. But I let it go as my hero grips my elbow
and leads me away from the secondhand smoke.

Clarity is beginning to replace my earlier confusion and
my heart rate is returning to normal, despite the downright
chivalry (not to mention close proximity) of this six-foot
two-inch gentleman with movie-star good looks.

He stops at the crosswalk and pushes the button to halt
traffic so we can cross. I know the silence needs to be broken, so I say the first gracious thing that pops into my head.
"Thanks for the rescue." I intentionally refrain from sentence structure that would require me to address him by
name or title. He seems to know me well and this puts me
at a distinct disadvantage.

"Panic attacks, huh?"

"What?"

"You were having a panic attack, right?"

"No. Well, I don't think so." I think I just freaked out for
a few minutes. And from where I'm standing, I'm sorta glad
I did. It's not every day a girl gets herself rescued by a really
cute guy.

A confused crinkle appears above his nose. "Then maybe
you were having a seizure or something. Should I take you
in to see a doctor?"

"I was *not* having a seizure!" At least I don't think I was. Now I'm worrying. "What makes you think it was a panic attack?"

"Tell me how you felt when you were standing there." Traffic stops and we walk across to the parking lot.

"I don't know. Dizzy, my chest was tight. I just felt . . ." Hmm . . .

"Panic?"

"I guess so. I've never experienced anything like it. I couldn't breathe."

"Too much stress. My mom gets panic attacks. Especially when it's her turn to play piano for me on Wednesday nights." He gives me a pointed look and his eyes crinkle in an amusement I don't really get. He leans in for emphasis. "I lead worship on Wednesday nights at your church."

Ding, ding, ding. Now I know who he is. Greg Lewis has two places of interest in my life. One, like he said, he leads praise and worship for the Wednesday-night service at church. Two, he's Shawn's teacher. Only Rick took the kids to open house this year so I didn't get to meet Mr. Lewis up close and personal. I'm definitely regretting that.

"So, what are you doing out of school?" I ask.

"Finally put two and two together did you?" His grin sends a wave of embarrassment over me, and I feel my cheeks heat up.

"Sorry, I didn't recognize you."

"Oh, it's no problem. You haven't been to church that much since I started leading. That's probably why you didn't recognize me right away."

"I have deadlines," I mumble. "And four kids. Wednesdays are nearly impossible to make."

"I understand." He smiles down at me.

I tense, looking for condemnation, judgment, that all-knowing look I get sometimes from the regular attendees. But that look isn't there with him.

"You didn't answer my other question." I'm just glad there's another path to go down in this little encounter.

At first he frowns like he isn't sure what I mean, then he nods and I know he gets it. "Why am I not in school?" He holds up a bandaged finger. "Got it smashed in the door."

"Yowch." I shudder. I don't do injuries and blood very well.

He grins. "Tell me about it."

"Broken?"

"'Fraid so."

By now, we've been standing next to my minivan for a couple of minutes. An awkward silence tenses the air between us. A sure sign it's time to tear myself away and head for home. Clearing my throat, I press the automatic unlock button on my keychain. "Well, thanks again for coming to my rescue."

"My pleasure." He reaches around me and opens my car door with his uninjured hand. My heart sort of picks up and for a second I think maybe I'm panicking again. Then I vaguely recognize the feeling. The first sign of attraction. Increased pulse—something I haven't experienced over a man in a really long time. Now I'm nervous. I've steered *way* clear of men since my ex-husband's defection from our marriage. And really, I see no reason to give in to these high-schoolish butterflies wiggling around in my stomach.

He closes the door after me, and then hesitates while I roll down the window. Casually, he rests his elbow on the window frame, his face so close I can almost feel his breath when he speaks. "I'll be sending home parent/teacher conference notes next week. Make sure you fill in a time to come see me about Shawn."

"Sure." Obviously, he's feeling the same irresistible pull to me that I feel toward him, the magnetic attraction that causes man and woman to fall in love. But of course he can't just blurt out a proposal. And I respect that. First we must meet over what is sure to be an exemplary academic file—after all, this is my Shawny we're talking about. Perhaps he will suggest we meet for coffee afterward.

I flash him a lovely smile (I know it's lovely because as soon as he walks away I check it out in the rearview mirror). He smiles back and says good-bye.

I pull the minivan from the parking lot and into full-blown traffic. My heart rate is returning to normal and so is my common sense. I mentally begin to berate myself for my naïveté. First of all, a man like that would never fall for a chunky mother of four who is going to be forty (in three years). And second of all . . . well, I guess there really isn't a second of all. The first reason is enough to bring me back to reality.

I admit it. I'm jaded where men are concerned. The only heroes in my life, besides Jesus, are the ones I create. Even though Greg rescued me today (and I really credit that to God; after all, I had just prayed when Greg showed up), he's not a heroic fictional character.

Anyway, I'm not comfortable playing Maiden in Distress. I've been taking care of myself quite well for the past five years. And how many people are actually living their dream? I really should thank Rick, the kids' father. In a way, his complete lack of respect for the sanctity of marriage is the sole reason I pushed so hard to become an author.

I couldn't afford to sit around and whine. As a matter of fact, I divided child support four ways and banked it every month for our kids. I worked two jobs waiting tables from 5:00 a.m. to 9:00 p.m. five days a week, with a two-hour split between jobs when I ran home and fed my kids. While the rest of the world slept, I learned to be a writer, pecking away for at least one hour every night. The first six months I turned out two completely ridiculous (although at the time I thought brilliant) and unsellable novels.

I got the hang of writing by my third manuscript and— happy day—sold it to a tiny publisher with a tight budget. Not much in the way of revenue, but I was a published author. Finally. The day my first check arrived in the mail, I spent the whole thing by taking the kids out to McDonald's, buying them each a pair of Nikes, and paying the electric bill mere minutes before they shut it off. The next day I went to work on a new book between shifts. In due time, that one also sold.

A year later, I quit my second job as more titles were added to my résumé. I finally caught the attention of a hotshot agent who took a liking to my "way with words," and wouldn't you know it? The publishers started lining up. When I was finally able to make a livable wage, I gave two weeks notice and said *sayonara* to my handsy, cheapskate boss, who I swear wiped away a tear as I floated through the door. There were no tears on my face, though. As a matter of fact, I might have clicked my heels together midair as I left that greasy spoon.

My memories fade as I pull into my drive. With the kids

in school and the manuscript sent off to my editor (yes, Blaine and Esmeralda finally sealed the deal with an earth-moving kiss), I have no plans for the rest of the day. I go into the kitchen and pop a couple of ibuprofen to help with pain and inflammation in my arms (and try not to think about what the medicine is most likely doing to my internal organs).

I head upstairs. My desk is a disaster area. I figure I might as well clean it up between answering e-mails and adding my two cents worth to the latest discussion on my writer's loop.

I think about Mom leaving right now and tears burn the backs of my eyes. At first I blink them away, then I realize, who's there to see them anyway? So I let them go, grabbing a tissue from the box on my desk and swiping at my nose.

I answer an e-mail from my editor. She got *Esmeralda's Heart* and will read it ASAP. After that, I shut off my computer—a rarity—and sit back in my chair, my mind mulling over the conversation with Mom, carpal tunnel, the panic attack (if that's what it was). Then it dawns on me that maybe God is orchestrating Mom's departure around my surgery. Like maybe she's right about all those things she said.

Would You do that to me, God?

Instinctively, I realize that like any good parent trying to teach a lesson, God most definitely *would* do that to me. I'm feeling the strongest sense of betrayal when I think I hear Him say something deep in my heart. I'm still. There's silence. So I decide to nudge Him.

Why, God?

And then I sense His voice again. In the deep places of

my heart where only He can go. I suddenly know exactly how my kids feel from time to time when I give them an answer and they expect more.

Because I said so.

I know I'm facing a choice. I'm about to have all this time on my hands (no pun intended). Perhaps it's time to learn to live in the world again. To reconnect with the kids, face my fear of crowds, go back to church.

My gut clenches at the thought of the mountains ahead of me. Mountains I have to climb alone. I don't know if I'm up for such a task. I know I need a plan. So I snatch a pen and look around for paper. Nothing. Not even a sheet of printer paper. I grab a Wal-Mart receipt from the middle drawer of my desk and start to make a list on the back. Lucky for me it's a long receipt.

During the next three months I will:

1. Go to church more. (This includes daily prayer time and maybe a Beth Moore Bible study.)

2. Clean my house. (Or probably hire someone. My wrists, you know.)

3. Reconnect with my children. (Will have to plan further for this one.)

4. Exercise—maybe. (But then again, I will be recovering from surgery. Wouldn't want to hurt myself. Could probably walk on the treadmill. We'll play this one by ear.)

5. Figure out why my only socialization revolves around my computer. I mean, I love the writing groups, but does lunch with the girls always have to involve trying to negotiate a turkey sandwich while instant messaging one-handed?

6. *In response to #5—Join ladies' group at church. Perhaps read the book* How to Make Friends and Influence People. *Or maybe one of Dr. Phil's.*

I glance back over the list and add one more thing:

7. *List to be amended as necessary.*

4

Theory: *a plausible or scientifically acceptable general principle or body of principles offered to explain phenomena*

Opinion: *belief stronger than impression and less strong than positive knowledge*

Okay, here's my theory about morning people—and in reference to Merriam Webster's online dictionary, this is more than mere *opinion*, because I'm convinced that someone in Roswell has evidence to prove me right.

First, imagine a big green pod. I'm talking a really, really big one with bunches of sunshiny flowers sprouting from it like a multicolored Chia Pet.

Got that mental picture?

My theory is that morning people emerge from these. They are not human, born of two loving parents like you and I were. Beneath synthetic skin and bone beat alien hearts with no regard for those of us who are night people.

I know this, because every time I'm presented with the chance to sleep in, some wide-eyed morning person breaks free from his or her pod and rings my doorbell at the crack of dawn (and just for the record, anything before 9:00 a.m. qualifies as said crack). Or calls me on the phone, lets it ring fourteen times, then hangs up just when I finally answer. Either that, or they *stay* on the line and then say something ignorant like, "Gee, I'm sorry. Did I wake you up?" Like, duh!

Today is no different and I am *so* not happy. The kids have gone camping with their dad for the weekend, it's Saturday morning, and the doorbell must be stuck or something because no one has the guts to just keep pushing it like that.

I'm not sure how I got from my bedroom, down the steps, and to the front door but here I stand, fury igniting my rapidly beating heart. I fling the door open. My pod theory is definitely one for further consideration. Darcy's on the porch. Her finger is poised above the doorbell, about to push it again.

"Don't!" I command.

She jumps, curls her finger back, and lowers her arm to her side. Her bright grin fades to an uncertain (and maybe a little fearful) quiver of a smile.

She's wearing a pair of snug-fitting Tommy Girl jeans and a St. Louis Rams sweatshirt. Being a Kansas City Chiefs fan, I find myself annoyed. I take a really deep breath. "Why aren't you camping?" I ask.

Her eyes scan over me, and I can only imagine what she's taking in. But you know what? I didn't ask her to wake me up. So there.

"I'm sorry. I obviously woke you."

Obviously. And pretty much beside the point now.

"Did you and Rick decide not to go to Bear Park?"

"Rick took the kids." She looks uncomfortable. "I—don't like bugs and stuff."

"Well, who does?" I say, of course being facetious, but she smiles like I'm defending her sissy reason for staying behind.

She places a warm hand on mine. "I'd hoped you'd understand."

I'd like to slug her in the arm for not getting the fact that I don't make nice in the morning—especially at the pod girl responsible for my awake state of being. One look at her hopeful eyes and smiling (perfectly shaped and colorful) lips, and I know she's clueless to my true feelings. Now I feel like a jerk. She's Melanie, I'm Scarlett—only there's no Rhett in my life, and Rick is *not* Ashley Wilkes. And, well, I'm not beautiful. The analogy is flawed. Shoot. I really wanted to be Scarlett.

Darcy is just standing there, on the step, looking all Darcy-ish and perfect. I know she's waiting for an invitation to come in, but I have no desire to do the polite thing.

"Did you need something?" Yikes. I can hear Mom's voice in my head telling me to play nice.

Her cheeks color and she looks away. "No. I'm, uh . . . Go back to bed. I'll call you later or something. Maybe we can have dinner."

If I were alone I'd growl my frustration into the air. But I practically never growl when anyone is present. "I was just getting up anyway," I say, and her face relaxes. I want to add, I had to get up to answer the door. But I know I'd better not. God is watching.

"The kids told me about your hands," she says softly. "Is there anything I can do around the house to help you out?"

Man! Why does she have to be such a Pollyanna? Does that make me Aunt Polly? I really need to get off this analogy merry-go-round. Every scenario puts me in a bad light. We won't even think about the Wizard of Oz.

"I think I have it under control." I give her a tight smile. "Thanks, though."

She glances over my shoulder. I really think it's instinctive, but still . . . a little nervy if you ask me. I clear my throat. Now I'm the one who's embarrassed because my house is a bit cluttered (and "a bit cluttered" is my way of saying "pigsty"). The kids' schoolbags and yesterday's socks are slung across the living room. Not to mention books, papers, and all four remotes—one for the satellite, one for the DVD player, one for the VCR, and one for the TV. I've never figured out how to program one remote to run all of our home entertainment devices, so we just make do with a little clutter. You should see the mad scramble when one of them is missing.

Next to the couch is a laundry basket of towels I started folding while watching The WB last night. Only I fell asleep with the job half done. I really was planning to get the place shining today. Like maybe around noonish—definitely *not* at the crack of dawn.

Darcy backs up. "Well, I guess if you don't need me, I'll go home. I have stuff I could do. Sorry I woke you."

I'm starting to lose that morning fog, and I credit that for the fact that I'm warming up to Darcy. "Hey," I say, and she turns around. "Do you want some coffee?" I resent that I had to do it, but I know guilt would have eaten away at me all day. I probably would have ended up calling her later to see if she wanted to go see a movie. This is better. Get it over with early, then I'm free to do whatever I want the rest of the day and evening.

She brightens, which makes me feel a little better. I hope God is marking this down on my God credit account because He knows that I always read my e-mail over my first pot of coffee.

Little Darcy has perked right up, oblivious to my sacrifice. She practically bounces into the house like a toy poodle. I don't know why she cares, but she always seems to be trying just a little too hard to get me to like her. Whatever her reasons, I'm feeling more like a good human being now that I've made this concession. I figure I can handle an hour or so.

I catch a whiff of some flowery scent as she breezes by. Yep, just like I thought, fresh out of a flowery Chia Pet pod.

We walk through the living room toward the kitchen and I watch her like a hawk. To her credit, she keeps her gaze averted from the clutter, and once we make it to the kitchen I relax. Can't mess up a kitchen when you order out, like I did last night. At least I did throw the Chinese cartons away.

"Have a seat," I say graciously, and motion toward the table. I head to the counter and put on a pot of vanilla-flavored coffee. I figure we can have two cups each, then I will hint around about needing to shower and maybe she'll bounce on out of here and leave me to my e-mail.

I sit across from her, eyeing the brewing pot. Is it my imagination, or is it dripping much slower than usual? Time for a new pot, perhaps?

Darcy's voice distracts me from the vanilla-scented brew. "When is your surgery?"

"Three weeks. That's the earliest they could fit me in." I

glance at the coffeepot. I think I can, I think I can. Gurgle, gurgle.

"How long will you be off work?"

"Huh? Oh, at least two months, they say, since I'm having one arm done at a time. I don't think it'll take that long, though. One of my friends had carpal tunnel surgery, and she was back to writing e-mail in a couple of weeks. So I'm hoping for that." I'm distracted by the gurgling from the counter, and I can hear in my own voice that I'm not exactly into the conversation. How long before the caffeine withdrawal starts? It's been at least fifteen hours since I had any. And being nice to Darcy this early in the morning is stretching my limits.

"You really need your morning coffee, don't you?" Darcy's expression is one of amused fondness. "Rick is the same way."

Okay, then. I shove up to my feet. Finished or not, I have to have caffeine *now*. And, for the record, that Rick comparison just slashed her two cups of coffee to one.

"It must be a difficult time for you with your mother moving away."

I'd like to explain to Darcy that I don't discuss personal issues with current wives of ex-husbands, but there's no denying the warmth in Darcy's voice. My sense of justice won't allow for me to hold it against her that I'm in a tough situation. No matter how much I resent the fact that she loves the man who cheated on me, then left me with four kids to raise.

"I'd love to help out any way I can."

I give her an airy smile and set our cups with half-brewed

coffee on the table. "Just pray for a quick recovery." Holy cow, could I be more fake?

Her eyes sort of cloud over, and I know she finally gets it that I'm brushing her off. I do feel a twinge of sympathy for her, but good grief. Why would I want help from my ex-husband's wife? It's just a little too weird, if you ask me.

Truthfully, I don't have much against Darcy. Other than the obvious resentment that she's beautiful, ten years younger than I am, and a lot thinner. In my world that makes her a viable enemy. But I'd resent anyone in that position. So I don't discriminate. It's just that I don't want to be her best friend. It's not normal.

Besides, sometimes I get the feeling she wants to take me on as her project. She invites me places, sends me "just thinking of you" cards. Things like that. Makes sure I have plans when the kids are with their father so that I'm not all alone. She's thoughtful. And it's nice, if misguided. But I've been surrounded by children for the past fifteen years. A full day to myself definitely doesn't push me into anything remotely resembling loneliness.

A small pang of guilt pinches me, and I remember my list of resolutions. Do I really have to consider Darcy as part of that? Because if that's what God is trying to accomplish with this whole twinge of guilt, I'm going to have to rethink it a little.

I veer off into discussing what Rick and Darcy are hoping to buy each of the kids for Christmas. Darcy is Little Miss Christmas Sunshine, and she takes to the subject like a catfish to a worm.

We laugh and compare lists for the next few minutes and

relief warms me as Darcy stands to leave without having to be nudged along by a subtle but well-targeted hint.

I walk her back through the cluttered room; again I watch, again she averts, and at the door she pauses.

"I finished *Tobey's Choice* last night." She's not looking at me, and I am almost positive I see a glimmer in her eyes. I frown and look closer; my movement causes her to meet my gaze. Just as I suspected. Tears.

My stomach clenches, unease nips at me like an undisciplined Chihuahua. I don't want to do this.

"Claire . . ."

"I didn't realize you enjoy reading Christian fiction. I'd be happy to recommend some other authors." I rattle off some, hoping that in the meantime she'll give up this desire to delve deep into a chasm she has no business penetrating. It's not her place. I'm starting to panic. Where is my handsome knight, Sir Greg? I'm feeling in desperate need of a little rescuing.

She places her hand on my arm, and I clamp my mouth shut. *All right. Let's get this over with.*

"I know this book was hard for you to write," she says, her voice trembling with emotion. "I—I just want you to know how much I respect you for having the guts to tackle such an enormously personal subject."

I never know what to say in these situations. Again, I'm caught at a crossroads. I want to say I have fully forgiven Rick. That the book was cathartic. Truthfully, it was supposed to be. But I realize I'm still raw from the rejection of being tossed aside and replaced with a better model. Literally. The woman he left me for modeled underwear at the so-called high-class lingerie shop in the mall. Of course six months later, she left *him* for a fat, balding dentist. I figure she was picturing free veneers. Vindication, but not enough to take away the bitterness.

Darcy pauses a second. She gathers a breath and I see her brace herself for what she's going to say. I brace myself, too, and wish a meteor would land in my yard to distract her. Or perhaps she could suddenly be hailed by the mother ship.

No such luck.

"It's hard for me to imagine Rick as the man who cheated on you."

"I would never have thought it of him either."

Now why did I have to go and say that? It was catty and sort of sounded like I was warning her. I see by the wariness flickering across her eyes that she's not sure what to make of my remark. I know I have to undo what I said. "Look, Darcy, Rick's not the same guy he was five years ago when we divorced." There. That's my concession and that's all she's getting.

It seems to be enough for her because she smiles.

All right, then. She likes the book. Respects me for writing it. Anything else? Please say no. Please say no.

"Just one more thing . . ."

Shoot.

"I get the feeling sometimes that . . ."

I frown, sensing this is not easy for her to say. And fully supporting her need to just drop it. But she's not feeling my support, or something, because she forges ahead, heedless of my "Let it go, babe" vibes. "I get the feeling that you don't differentiate between the woman Rick cheated with and me."

My jaw goes slack. I can't move. Can't breathe. That's the most ridiculous . . .

Darcy takes one step down and pauses again. "And, Claire. I would never be the other woman. I wouldn't have before I was a Christian, and certainly wouldn't now." She draws a short breath and looks me squarely in the eye. "I didn't take Rick away from you. And I would really like to be your friend."

Is it my imagination, or did the whole earth stop spinning?

5

A mid-thirties-ish, overweight woman without make-up isn't a pretty sight to behold. Especially when she's frowning into my bathroom mirror like I am and every wrinkle (which are really war wounds as far as I'm concerned) reminds me that I'm not getting any younger. Or nicer, apparently.

I stare at the woman I've become. The reflection accuses me, mocks me, and worse still, reminds me of all the weight I've gained over the past five years.

Darcy's little parting remark left me speechless. And that doesn't happen often. I'm notorious for the quippy come-back. Now my wings are clipped, the wind has left my sails, and more than anything I wish I could rewind a couple of hours and never answer that doorbell in the first place.

Of course her accusation or observation or whatever that was supposed to be is completely and utterly ridiculous.

She looks nothing whatsoever like Gina, the adulterous model, so how could I mix them up? I feel a twinge inside my gut. And that annoys me. The last thing I want to do is soul-search about this. Darcy is Darcy. Sweet, wholesome, put-together like something out of *Vogue*. Not Gina. But married to Rick.

Luckily, the phone rings, and I have no choice but to stop thinking about this and answer.

Mom.

"Hi, honey. Good news. The realtor just called and says we have a bite on the house."

Great. How about twisting the knife just to add a little something to my day? "That was quick. You sure you priced it high enough?"

"Yes. Anyway. The man is coming to take a look on Monday, and I need to clear out the attic."

I inwardly groan, because I know she didn't call simply to give me an update on the work ahead of *her*. She's just mapped out my day. My first free Saturday in weeks, now that the manuscript is on my editor's desk. The day I was going to clean my house, read a book, relax. Possibly take a bubble bath. I see this vision vanish before me like a puff of smoke.

"I have to get dressed. I'll be over in thirty minutes."

Twenty-nine minutes later I'm standing on the porch, wondering why she locked the door when she knew I was coming. But I can't hold a grudge when I see her bright smile. The one I know so well that always communicates her joy at seeing me. It's nice to have someone in your life you know loves you unconditionally. Sure, I might get aggravated at my mom, but the fact remains I couldn't have made it through the past few years without her.

As I step inside the familiar house, the home where I grew up, a feeling of nostalgia sweeps over me. I want to beg my mom not to leave, but I've come to accept the fact that she needs to do this for her own sake. Even if I personally think living with Charley is going to drive her into early dementia.

"Do you want some coffee?" Mom asks.

"No. I just had some." But I have no intention of telling her about my morning coffee date. "Let's just dive right into the attic."

Being the brave young thing I am, I venture forth ahead of Mom. I duck and beat at cobwebs, feeling like Indiana Jones, minus the bullwhip and sardonic grin. I breathe in the musty smell of forty years' worth of memories. My memories. Charley's. Mom's. Suddenly, I'm missing my dad. A gentle giant with a voice like Sinatra. In the corner sits his fishing gear, tackle boxes, old rods and reels. I laugh and snatch up his pride and joy: a gray fishing hat, decorated around the rim with fishing lures and hooks taken from the lips of the unfortunate "big ones" he caught in his lifetime. I plop the hat on my head and rummage through the tackle box. "Remember when Dad used to take us camping?"

Mom gives a snort, and I'm not feeling the love.

"What's that for?" I ask.

"I hated every second of those outings."

My brow lifts with my utter shock. She might as well have said she never loved my dad. True, Mom never was one to complain, but in my mental slide show, I don't see anything that looks like misery. I have a feeling she's overstating her case. "I always thought you were having a great time like the rest of us."

"It meant so much to your father to take us on these little excursions to the middle of nowhere. And you kids lived for the summer campouts; I couldn't very well disappoint you all."

"I thought camping was fun. Still do. How come you didn't like it, Mom?"

She shuddered. "Bugs. I hated the bugs."

I roll my eyes. "Well, who doesn't?" Okay, I've had this conversation once today.

"Don't get smart with me."

I grin. Mom so gets my sarcasm. No need for unflattering analogies.

"So, what do you want me to do with all this stuff?"

Mom shrugs. "I suppose we'll have to throw it out."

I gasp so hard I take in a lungful of dust and start to cough. Mom pounds me on the back, and I'm thinking this woman is *not* the frail old lady she pretends to be. She could probably take me in a street fight.

When I finally compose myself and convince Mom to stop beating me half to death, I look at her to see if dust has affected her ability to focus. "You really want to throw out Daddy's fishing gear?"

"Well, I can't very well take it with me."

"Charley might want it."

Mom laughs and I see her point. "Your brother doesn't know one end of a hook from the other. Do you suppose Rick might want it?"

"Rick's not my husband anymore, Mother. Remember?" I know I sound huffy. But when will she get it through her head that she doesn't need to be nice to him anymore, and as a matter of fact, I wish she'd be mean?

"Of course I remember. But your father always thought so highly of him. Well, until . . . you know."

"Until he started having a lot more sex than I was?"

"Well, there's no reason to be vulgar. You could have simply said he was stepping out on you with other women, which I know very well that he was." Even in the dim light of the attic I can see her face is glowing red.

"I'm sorry, Mom. Do whatever you want with the fishing gear."

"Would you like to keep the hat?" She nods to my head.

"Yeah, I would. Thanks."

After hours of digging through the attic, deciding what to throw away, what she wants to keep, I plod home covered in dust with cobwebs adorning my hair. I trudge through the door and beeline it for the couch, where I flop. I stretch out fully, thinking about all the boxes lined up on the curb, waiting for the garbageman on Monday morning.

And just for the record, I'm a little heartsick at all the things Mom *doesn't* want to hang on to—I mean, what was the point of saving baby teeth in the first place if all she's going to do is throw them away when I'm almost forty? Did she think I might want to make a necklace of them some-day?

Is that what's going to happen to me? My mind flashes to my own attic, where boxes of my children's baby stuff clutter the floor. What am I going to do with the silky blond strands of hair taped to each baby book under the heading "First Haircut"? Will they want the memories I've collected when they grow up, or will the day come when Ari is help-ing me clean out the attic so I can go live with Tank and his wife, Machine Gun? My lips twitch as humor returns, lift-ing my spirits a little.

First of all, the thought of Ari getting her manicured hands dirty is truly laughable, and Tommy would rather slide headfirst into a vat of boiling oil than have me come live with him. The kid is counting the days until his eigh-teenth birthday as it is.

Still, the question begs to be answered. What good does

it do to build a lifetime of memories if they're only going to be tossed away like yesterday's garbage?

The melancholy is weaving through me, first into my brain, then downward into my heart, then, as I try to ease the pain with three scoops of rocky road ice cream, into my stomach. It doesn't work. I can't help but be swept away on a tide of childhood memories. They're so sweet. Those memories. I feel like Ralphie from *A Christmas Story* and I consider, for a moment, writing my life story. Okay, so maybe the time I had chickenpox and Dad, Mom, and Charley put on the entire *Nutcracker* ballet to ease the pain of missing out on my school's field trip wouldn't mean anything to the rest of the world, but to me, those memories are priceless.

With a sigh, I toss the bowl into the sink and head upstairs to shower off the dust. As the steaming water flows over me, I'm struck with the idea that all I truly have left of my childhood are the sweet memories my parents created for me. My mind goes to my own children. What have I built for them to remind them of me when they grow up? Days and nights at the computer, fast-food meals in the living room while I sit with my laptop, weekend plans gone awry because of an unexpected line edit that has to be attended to in three days. It seems as though the only fun my kids have is when they're with Rick.

This thought weakens my knees. There's no denying that Rick was a sorry excuse for a husband. But guess what? He's the better parent. I think I'm going to be sick. I slide *The Mirror Has Two Faces* into the VCR and crawl into bed with the remote. How did Rick become the fun one? He's the one building camping memories with our kids. Of course, for all I know, that could be his way of compensating for breaking their hearts by leaving me when they were little. Furthermore, it's easy to be the fun one when you only have the kids two and a half days a week.

I listen to the music signaling the opening credits, but my brain is focused on that list I made out earlier in the week. Number three on the list: Reconnect with my children. Excitement begins to build as I realize what this new "me" is going to mean to my precious offspring. I imagine their joy, their utter relief that I've finally seen the light. No more will I be the evasive mother of the past. Oh, no. All of that is behind me. I'm turning over a new leaf. From this moment forward, my number one mission in life is to begin building memories for my children to cherish when they're all grown up.

And yes, part of that reasoning is because I don't want them to look back on Rick with more fondness than me. I'm man enough to admit it. But mostly, I want them to one day look through old memorabilia and cherish the moments those things represent.

I close my eyes and listen to my movie playing in the background. I've watched the beginning at least a hundred times and I've yet to see how it ends. I fall asleep every night at various points. I know I could just start from where I left off the night before and that eventually I'd finish, but I can't do it. I have to watch it all the way through in one sitting or it's ruined for me. I can't help it. That's just the way I'm wired.

So, here it is, less than thirty minutes into the movie, and I feel myself drifting into the shadows of unconsciousness. Then an idea springs to mind, and I'm bolt upright before I fully open my eyes.

Family night! One night a week, we'll have a special dinner, watch a movie, maybe have a nice discussion about the movie if it's one with a particularly good message, like *The Lord of the Rings.* Play a game. Maybe some nights we'll go minigolfing or to Incredible Pizza and play in the arcade.

My excitement builds as the ideas zoom in and out of my brain. I've got enough activities to see us through to Jakey's high school graduation by the time the music from my TV crescendos and words come up at the end of the movie. I stare blankly as Barbra Streisand and Jeff Bridges dance in the street, laughing, hugging, kissing, and I have to wonder, what just happened? I finally made it to the end of the movie wide awake, and I have no idea how it ended.

6

It's Sunday afternoon. The kids and Rick got home just in time to clean up and make the 10:45 service at church. They should have been home at 7:00 a.m., but a thunderstorm blew through, forcing a slow drive. So now the kids and I sit in Pizza Hut in the round booth, waving at half the church as they breeze by headed to their own tables.

Tommy is playing around with the Parmesan cheese shaker. Note to self: check the lid before I use any.

"So, that's my idea," I say, knowing full well that the smile on my face is way too bright for the response I'm getting from the kids. I almost hate to ask the next question, but my penchant for emotional abuse spurs me to ask. "What do you think?"

Ari shrugs. "As long as it doesn't interfere with my social life, I guess we can give it a shot."

Not exactly the enthusiastic response I'd hoped for, but better than it could have been.

"I'm not watching any stupid cartoons," Tommy squeaks, a telltale sign he isn't going to be a child much longer. I inwardly cringe and wonder which one of the kids is going to pounce on that adolescent evidence that his voice is changing.

I don't have to wait long to find out. Shawn laughs. "I'm

not watching any stupid cartoons," he mimics with fake squeaks.

Tommy slugs him in the arm before I can head it off. "You better shut up."

"Mom!" Shawn's big, blue eyes fill with tears.

"Mo-om." Now it's Tommy's turn to mimic.

"Tommy! Don't make me ground you."

People are looking at us. I feel like an utter failure as a mother.

"He started it."

"I did not."

"What, are you crying now, you big baby?"

"Tommy! I mean it. Don't say another word. You're just getting yourself into deeper trouble."

Tommy flops back and folds his arms across his chest. His eyes say what his mouth doesn't dare.

My eyes scan the booth, taking in each of my less-than-enthusiastic children. Time for an executive decision. "All right. Here's the deal. Monday nights will be family night. Tell your friends not to call or drop by. Homework will be done as soon as you get home so that it doesn't interfere."

"Mother!" Ari moans. "Monday nights, Trish and I watch *7th Heaven* together."

By "together" she means she and Trish sit on their respective couches while on the phone together and drool over the little blond-headed boy. I give her a pointed look that says in no uncertain terms, "I'm the boss." "Do you want to make it Friday night?"

"No." She scowls and flops back. Now my two oldest offspring are wearing identical expressions and have the same body language. For once they are unified in purpose. Like-minded. Both look like they'd give a kidney for the pleasure of punching my lights out.

My heart sinks. If we can't get through one meal together without a major fight, how will we ever create our cherished memories?

The next day I'm standing in front of the mirror again. This time carefully, methodically applying makeup like I'm da Vinci and my face is the canvas.

I feel pretty good. Retaining a little water from the pizza yesterday, so my face is puffier than I'd like, but maybe Greg won't notice. And anyway, a puffy face with makeup is still better than a skinny face with none.

Today is our parent/teacher conference. Shawn's been acting a little nervous, but I'm attributing it to the natural effect of any kid realizing his mom is going to talk to his teacher. I certainly can't imagine my perfect child having anything to worry about. I've reassured him at least a hundred times.

I blot my lipstick—plum-colored, from Mary Kay. I bought it six years ago and it's hardly been used at all. Who needs makeup when they work inside all day? I move from the lighted bathroom mirror to the full-length mirror hanging on the inside of the door. I twist a little so I can view my behind. It is larger than life. It mocks me with its enormity. Shoot. Why did I have to look? What did you expect, I chide myself. A model's derriere? Now I won't be able to concentrate on making a good impression on Greg at all. I shrug at myself. At least I'll be sitting.

I step into my bedroom, snatch a light jacket from the bed, and shrug into it as I walk toward the door. With one last glance at myself in the dresser mirror I give a sigh and wish I were fifty pounds lighter. Or at least thirty. Even ten would be an improvement. But that's not going to happen in the next—I glance at my watch—forty minutes.

So maybe I won't get any thinner before the meeting, but I don't look that bad. The tailored suit I bought to wear to the Christian Booksellers Association's mega convention this summer is definitely slimming on me. And unless I miss my guess, a little looser than it was two and a half months ago.

The kids are hanging out in the living room with the TV blasting when I walk through.

Ari takes one look at me and rolls her eyes. "Good Lord."

I stare at my daughter in dumbfounded, jaw-dropping shock. Okay, first of all, I can't believe she has the guts to take the Lord's name in vain just like that, in front of me. That's one of the commandments, and we take the commandments very seriously in this house. Second of all, I have to wonder if I really look so bad that she even has the guts to say it in the first place.

I take a mental inventory. My foundation matches my complexion. No dark jawline. I have on a little blue eye shadow—a color I wouldn't have touched with a ten-foot pole while growing up in the eighties, but times are different now. Blue is back "in," like bell bottoms—which I also wouldn't have worn when I was a teenager.

Besides, Ari's not looking at my eyes. Her gaze is fixed on my feet. I look down to see what she thinks is so terrible. Oh, for crying out loud! I'm wearing my leopard-spotted slippers.

"All you had to do was say so," I mutter and head back to

the steps. "And don't ever let me hear you take the Lord's name in vain again." I toss her an I-mean-it-young-lady look.

"Take the Lord's name in vain?" Her eyes are wide with innocence. So wide that I know I'm about to be lied to, and I will have no way to prove the truth. She sniffs. "I was praying for you."

Sure she was.

I breeze into the elementary school building five minutes late for my appointment with Greg. All the way to school, I've imagined him, leaning against his desk, hands stuffed dejectedly in his pockets. He's watching the clock as the minutes tick away. Poor man. He's afraid I'm not coming. Oh, Greg, I inwardly cry, I'll be there, my love. Wait for me. I'll be there. I'm Deborah Kerr, he's Cary Grant, and ours is *An Affair to Remember*. (*Affair* in the puritanical 1950s definition of the word, of course.)

My heart is racing—a result of more than physical effort—as I fly down the hallway, past the kindergarten, first-, second-, third-, and fourth-grade doors. I recognize Greg's name on a whiteboard outside his classroom. I take a second to gulp in some oxygen. Then, pasting a smile on my plum-colored lips, I reach for the door. It is much lighter than I thought it would be, so by pushing on it, I've actually flung it open. I stumble inside. Greg and a gorgeous woman, who were leaning close over a folder only a split second before, are now practically whiplashed as they jerk around to look at the crazy lady standing, out of breath, in the doorway.

I feel utterly stupid, and a thought winds through my brain: at least I'm wearing regular shoes, and not those leopard-spotted slippers. A ridiculous thought that has no bearing on anything whatsoever. It's just there. I walk to the middle of the room and stop. Because no one (and by no one I, of course, mean Greg—my Greg) has so much as said hello.

The woman next to Greg is frowning at me. At least I think she is; her nose is so high in the air, I can't see much past her nostrils and chin. Greg is staring like a deer caught in headlights.

"Am I late?" I ask, my voice barely audible—a result of my barging-into-the-room embarrassment.

Greg stands and meets me in the center of the room. "I'm sorry, Mrs. Frank," he says, cupping my elbow with his wonderful hand. Only one problem: he's heading the wrong way, leading me back toward the door. "Ms. Clark was here early, and, since you were late, I switched you two. Can you come back in ten minutes?"

I glance over his shoulder at *Ms. Clark*. She raises her perfectly arched brow with smug assurance. I see nary a trace of a ring flashing on her wedding finger. My claws unsheathe like an alley cat about to defend its garbage can. This is war. I return my gaze to Greg. Or Mr. *Lewis*, rather. After all, he gave her the power of smugness by giving her my appointment. Five minutes late is barely late at all. He should have waited.

"Mrs. Frank?" he prods.

"Everett," I correct. "And it's Ms."

This flusters him. I can tell it does by the way he clears his throat and looks down—but not fast enough to hide the quick spread of a blush. I feel vindicated for his defection. I toss my chin and pull my elbow from his two-timing fingers.

"I'll be back," I say and shut the door behind me. I beeline for the girls' bathroom. Since school is not in session, I don't have to wait my turn behind a line of giggling, hairbrushing, lip-gloss-applying tweenagers. While I wash my hands, I stare at the fool in the mirror. I wish I could run out the door and head for the nearest Burger King. But to do so would be an admission of embarrassment. And that will never do. I exit with dignity and with the intention of never letting Greg think I have a crush on him. Whether I do or not. And I'm not saying I do—not after the *Ms. Clark* incident of a few minutes ago.

I'm making my way back to the room when I see her heading toward me, her three-inch heels clicking on the shining, white tiles, and in all likelihood causing tons of black marks that the janitors will have to work to remove. She stares me down as she clicks past. I have to force myself not to look away or divulge the fact that I'm intimidated beyond belief by the curvaceous, tight-dress-wearing woman—especially when she is obviously setting her cap for the handsome teacher.

Something inside me dies a little. Something called hope. No man in his right mind would pass up a woman like her for someone like me. I guess in a way the knowledge eases my tension. There's no reason to worry about whether or not he's going to ask me out, because the answer is all too clear.

I tap on the door, just in case I'm thirty seconds late and Greg has given the next fourteen and a half minutes away to the next appointment on his list. We wouldn't want a repeat of the situation with Ms. Clark, now would we?

I peep through the up-and-down rectangular window on the door and note that Greg is alone, sitting in a youth chair next to a round table. His head is down and he's mulling over an open folder. He hasn't moved, so I assume he didn't hear my tap. I knock harder and open the door a crack just as he looks up. He smiles. "Come in, Claire." He stands like a gentleman.

Oh, it's Claire now, is it?

He must read my mind because he gives me a lopsided grin. "Sorry about earlier, but I can't appear to give preferential treatment to friends." He waves me toward a chair that was clearly built to fit the behinds of fifth graders. Nervously, I sit, hoping the lightness in my heart over the "treatment of friends" remark translates to a few less pounds so I don't bend the legs of some ten-year-old's chair.

Nothing creaks or groans (on me or the chair). So far so good. I let out the breath I've been holding and look up.

Greg slides a white sheet of paper out of the folder and lays it in front of me on the table. "As you can see, Shawn's grades are very good. No complaint there. Straight A's, except for gym."

The C looks completely foreign. I've never seen one on Shawn's report card before. I'm not comfortable with it, but as I get used to the idea, I figure it's not that big a deal. Who cares about gym anyway? It's not like he made a C in English, which I would definitely have to bring attention to.

"Coach Ryan says he refuses to dress out and that's the only reason he's got a C. Otherwise, he keeps up with the rest of the class physically."

I gape. "You mean to tell me, he gets points taken away for not wearing shorts?" My son is chubby. There's no getting around that fact. He came to me the first week of school and confided that other kids make fun of him, so I actually gave him my permission not to "dress out," as they call it. Now I feel like a totally unfit parent. Because of me, my son has gotten his first blemished report card.

"Sorry, but that's about the size of it. The kids are required to dress out once they get to fifth grade."

"I think that's cruel."

He gives a sympathetic nod, but doesn't comment. I suspect he disagrees but doesn't want to further antagonize me.

"So, what else is in the folder?" I ask. I can only imagine. Knowing Shawn, and despite his unfortunate C in gym, there are probably literary works of masterpiece proportions lurking in that folder. Enough to make up for ten C's in gym.

He hesitates. My suspicions shoot to the surface. Why is he hesitating?

Cough it up, choirboy.

He fingers something in the folder, then lifts it out slowly, as though straining against a gravitational pull. He doesn't offer me the page right away, and I'm starting to worry. He clears his throat. "Just remember that all boys are becoming hormone-ravaged perverts at this age."

"Not my boy." I said that out loud, didn't I? "Just hand it over."

I cringe as he chuckles.

I take the sheet of notebook paper and read aloud:

Roses are red,
Violets are blue.

I wish I could see
Ms. Clark nude.

I blink. I stare. The page is even illustrated. I know there is no way my son wrote this filth, and he certainly didn't draw the artistically promising picture.

Only it's signed—and dated. In sharp, bold strokes. The kid wrote this and isn't one stinking bit sorry he did so.

"Well?" Greg's voice is properly sober.

I know my face is flaming, so I keep my gaze on the page and look at it critically.

"I don't know much about art, so I can't really comment on the illustration, except he might have been a little generous in certain areas. But speaking from a purely literary standpoint, I'd have to say it's obviously derivative. 'Roses are red, violets are blue . . .' is way overdone." I point to the writing. "And 'blue' and 'nude' really don't work as a rhyme. Although I guess it's better than 'Roses are red, green is the pear. I'd like to see Ms. Clark bare.'"

Greg snorts.

I send him a sheepish grin. But inwardly I feel like crying. "Clark. The woman who left before me?"

He nods. "She started working in the office this year."

"Did you tell her about the poem?"

"She's the one who gave it to me. Apparently, Shawn hand-delivered it with a wildflower bouquet from the field behind the school. That's actually what she was doing here. I figured I'd have a talk with her first. She thought he was making a peace offering for all the catcalls and whistles in the hall."

That explains the stare-down in the hall. My Shawn? "He whistles at her?"

Greg nods grimly. "And the other boys think it's hilarious. They join in. It can get pretty bad."

"Why hasn't this been brought to my attention before now?"

"It would have been except that we never see him do anything wrong. He's sneaky about it and although we know it's him, he's not confessing and we can't catch him at it. The poem was his escalation to the next level. And of course we can't allow it. But this is his first offense, so we're letting him off with a warning. The principal agrees."

I stand and eye him with determination. "I'll take care of this."

No longer do I care if my behind jiggles as I walk away. No longer am I concerned that Greg hasn't asked me to dinner. But the thought that my precious son is capable of writing such nasty things sends shards of disappointment to slice my heart to ribbons. I am a woman whose last pane has just shattered. With this proof that my Shawn isn't the perfect child I've always believed him to be, I no longer live in a glass house.

7

I am just leaving Greg's classroom when I see Rick and Darcy headed in my direction. My defenses are rising. I want to deal with Shawn my way before I tell Rick what the child's become. "What are you two doing?"

Rick is dressed in his usual office attire—a pair of khaki slacks and a blue polo shirt. Boring, but neat and tidy. Darcy is dressed in a pair of brown slacks, with a cream-colored jacket thrown over a brown ribbed crewneck shirt. Her blonde hair is swept up, showing a milky white throat, with just a few strategically placed tendrils of loose hair brushing her neck.

Why do I even try?

Darcy smiles warmly, if a little tentatively. I guess she's remembering our last conversation. "Parent/teacher conference."

"Oh? I just finished. Why are we wasting Greg's time with two separate conferences?"

Darcy's face goes red. "We . . . thought you—"

"For crying out loud, Claire." Rick frowns at me. "You know darn good and well that the last time we suggested a joint meeting you had a cow, that's why." He looks past me. "Hi Greg, are we late?"

"Only about five minutes."

I turn around and glare at Greg with pointed resentment.

How come five minutes late is a crime when I do it? But suddenly it's okay when Rick does it? My eyes must have relayed that very question, because Greg winks at me. "There's no one else on the schedule until after lunch."

I turn my attention back to my ex-husband. "Call me later so we can discuss your son."

"Oh, boy. If Shawn, of all the kids, is suddenly my son, he must have flunked something."

I refuse to dignify that comment with a reply. "See you around, Darcy. Don't let him forget to call me."

He calls forty-five minutes later, from his cell phone on his way back to the office. I hear a certain amount of outrage in his voice, and I know he's blaming me for the whole situation. "What are we going to do as a punishment?" he asks.

First of all, Shawn has been laying low since I got home. I sent him down the street to help his grandmother pack and informed him I'd get back to him after I discussed his behavior with his father.

I've been thinking over appropriate punishments since I read the offensive note. "I think he should definitely have to write a letter of apology to Ms. Clark."

"To say the least. What else?"

"What do you mean? Don't you think a letter of apology is humiliation enough?"

"Not even close, Claire. The boy wrote a nasty note and drew a nastier picture. He sexually harassed the school secretary."

Okay, he may have a mild point. But good grief, had Rick noticed how the woman was dressed? "Do you have a punishment in mind?"

"Yes. Along with the note of apology, he loses TV privileges for a month."

"Well, what am I supposed to do with him if he can't watch TV?" Oh, I hate that I just blurted that out.

"Make him read a book. Or would you prefer to let him spend the month with Darcy and I?"

"Darcy and me," I mutter.

The grammatical faux pas has apparently escaped the good doctor's notice. "If you don't think you're up to it, I'm willing to let him spend the length of his punishment at my house."

"No. I'll agree to no TV for a month, with the exception of Monday-night movie night."

"Monday-night movie night? What's that?"

"I think it's rather self-explanatory."

He hesitates. "Okay, I'll agree to the Monday-night exception, as long as you promise not to cave in at the first sight of those big blue eyes begging you to let him watch *Fairly Odd Parents*, or some other stupid cartoon."

Fairly Odd Parents is anything but stupid. But I choose not to argue that point with someone who considers the Military Channel to be entertainment.

The part about resisting Shawn's big blue eyes might be harder than I thought. But I know Rick is right. And if he's trying to be a real dad, instead of just the fun dad for a change, who am I to thwart his efforts? "So just to make sure we're on the same page, Shawn has to write a letter of apology to Ms. Clark." I know it was my idea, but the thought of that woman's smug face just makes me want to let the whole thing go. But we're building our son's character, not diminishing mine. "Plus no TV for a month, except for Monday movie night."

"And I think he should do some chores."

"Chores, too?" Sheesh, why doesn't he just send the kid to boot camp? My palms are beginning to sweat, and I'm worrying I might short out the cordless. "What did you have in mind?"

"I think he should clean out the garage and . . ."

I'm staring out at my front lawn through the bay window. "Rake leaves?"

"Okay, sounds good. No TV—"

"Except on Mondays."

"Right. A letter of apology, he cleans the garage—"

"Mine or yours?"

"I was thinking mine. Darcy wants to have a garage sale."

Figures. "Fine. He can clean your garage and rake my leaves."

"Fine. I guess that covers his punishment, then."

Rick hesitates and I wait, expecting him to say good-bye. Instead, he continues, "Another thing we need to discuss is Shawn's C in gym."

"Actually, I don't think that's a problem."

"Well, I do." His voice is that firm, why-haven't-you-been-taking-your-medicine doctor's tone, and my hackles rise, because not only isn't he my husband anymore, he's not even my doctor.

"Then you'll have to get over it."

"Wait a minute. You can't just decide he can take an entirely preventable lower grade, when all he has to do for an A is dress appropriately, Claire."

"As a matter of fact, I can decide and I have. I will not

have him teased and taunted because of his short, chubby legs." Which I happen to think are adorable.

"You mean the way he's been taunting Ms. Clark?"

Okay, that is so not the same thing, and any decent father would know it without having to be told. But apparently Rick isn't thinking with his decent-father brain, so I go ahead and tell him. "Teasing a grown-up, even if she is a school employee, isn't the same thing as being made fun of just because you're different. And if you'd ever been chubby or poor or less than perfect, you'd understand the pain and humiliation associated with being that way."

He gathers a deep breath and I know he's gearing up to argue with me, so I take my only line of defense. I hang up on him.

I stare at the phone, not quite believing I just did it. Shoot, I'd hoped for once we could just come to an agreement without the usual drama.

Walking through the video rental store gives me hives. The covers in the horror section terrify me, and I keep having to watch my boys like a hawk to make sure they're not going anywhere near the adult section. Especially in light of Shawn's new artistic endeavors.

To make matters worse, after thirty minutes of roaming the aisles, no one can agree on a movie. Jake wants to rent a Disney release, Shawn and Tommy are adamantly fighting over whether or not to get Harry Potter or the latest Matrix movie, and too-cool-for-school Ari just flips her hair and asks the teenage boy at the counter what he suggests.

Good grief. What do we need a movie for? Our lives play out a drama in real time.

"All right, everyone over here." I call this little powwow in the video game section and Jakey's in heaven.

"First of all, *Matrix* is rated R, so that's out without discussion."

"That bites." Tommy, of course.

"Watch your mouth."

"Whatever."

I'm in no mood to deal with this, so I let him have this last word. I *let* him, mind you. That's the important point to remember.

"We have *Shark Tales* at home, Jake. You can watch it after school tomorrow."

He shrugs and I see a little spit drip off the side of his mouth as he stares, hypnotized by *Mario Cart*. "Can we rent—"

"No. No video games."

"Darn it!"

"Don't say 'darn it.' It's a euphemism."

"What's a euphemism?"

All too willing to help, Tommy grins. "It's when you say something but really mean something bad."

Jakes eyes go round. "I didn't do that."

"*Darn* means #*$&"

Silence yawns between us as we digest the word my son Tommy has just emitted.

Jake gasps like a girl.

"Mom, did you hear what Tommy just said?" Shawn asks, as though I'm suddenly deaf. Struck with a migraine, yes. Deaf, no.

"I heard," I say, my icy glare fixed on the son I no longer recognize.

His lip curls with cocky assurance. "I didn't say anything. I was just telling Jake what *darn* means."

"That isn't what *darn* means," I say firmly. Although, I know darned well it is.

"You're the one that said it was a euphemism."

"Go to the van, Tommy." I'm tired. I hate Monday movie night. I'd rather be reading e-mail or chatting with my friends on Instant Messenger.

I snatch Harry Potter from Shawn's hand and head for the counter. "Boys, go out to the van with your brother. And don't make any noise or touch anything on the way out."

"I thought we couldn't watch Harry Potter," Ari says.

I'm way past caring what anyone thinks of the magical boy. My head is pounding and I'm in no mood for an argument. Still . . . "Just don't tell anyone at church."

She smirks. "Too late."

With a sense of dread I turn to see the look of utter disapproval on Connie Morton's face. Connie is in charge of the children's church department. Along with her husband, they have transformed the ministry from dull puppets and forty-year-old children's songs like "Deep and Wide" and "Give Me Oil in My Lamp" into a thriving, bright place where kids beg to go. I'm not positive my kids are learning anything (besides the sinfulness of Harry Potter and Santa Claus) but they do want to go to church, so that has to count for something.

I smile. "Hello, Connie. Good to see you." A total lie, but then, what would she expect from someone who would allow her children to watch a Harry Potter film?

Her gaze is fixed on the movie box I'm carrying. I can't

help but wish I patronized a modern video store that's all computerization instead of this mom 'n' pop shop.

She smiles back. "It's nice to see you all, too. Renting a movie?"

Like, duh!

"Yes, you know, Monday movie night." I act like this is a decade-old tradition instead of the first time out of the gate. "Pizza and a movie."

"Oh, what a good idea. Family time is so important."

My heart lifts until she jabs in the knife.

"Of course, how much better might a family bowling night be? Or something that encourages conversation."

This woman obviously doesn't know my family. Talking leads to fighting and fighting leads to migraines. Like the one that's making me sick to my stomach. Her icky sweet perfume isn't helping the nausea at all. "Bowling isn't exactly something my family enjoys," I tell her.

"Oh, nonsense. Children love anything as long as their parents are involved."

Again, this chick needs a taste of reality, because my kids wouldn't be caught dead in a bowling alley. And Miss Movie Police's smug, know-it-all attitude is beginning to grate. So I do what I always do, only to later regret it. I open my big, fat mouth: "Well, this parent is definitely going to be watching Harry Potter with them. I never miss all the 'Double, double, toil and trouble' stuff. And what a terrific message about light and dark, good and evil. Definitely something to talk about when the movie's over. See you at church Wednesday night." I want to say "Ta-ta," but I figure that's over the top.

As it is, I leave her sputtering in the kids' movies section while giving the video counter boy a weak smile. That's when I recognize the pastor's son, Patrick Devine. He winks. "Way to go, Ms. Everett."

Ari tosses her arm across my shoulders. "Didn't I tell you how cool my mom is?"

I feel a cheesy grin coming on. As though a spell has been cast, I'm powerless to stop it, so I allow it to widen my mouth as I pull out the four bucks for Satan's movie.

I should have seen it coming. No teenager has ever winked at me before, and my daughter has definitely never put her arm around me in public, let alone testified to my coolness. But basking in the glow of teen approval and the fact that I've just put someone in her place, I'm totally blindsided by Ari's next words: "So, Patrick wants to know if I can go out with him on Friday."

I practically swallow my tongue. I have nothing against Patrick. After all, he *is* the pastor's kid, but Ari knows the rules. Indignation draws on my cynical nature, and I imme-diately know what must be done. "Sure, Friday sounds good." Amid her smug grin and his returning smile, I slowly pull out my checkbook calendar and start counting the weeks until her sixteenth birthday.

"What are you doing, Ma? You already paid for the movie."

I hold up my wait-a-sec index finger and do a little more counting. "Okay, that should do it."

"What?" Ari is frowning.

But I look at Patrick, whose red face is telltale that he's getting the picture, even if Ari is still putting two and two together. "Ari's birthday is exactly three weeks from tonight.

The Friday after that is October 21. Is seven o'clock good for you?"

His Adam's apple moves up and down in his throat, but the humor in his eyes shows me he can take a joke even if Ari can't. "I'll clear my calendar," he says. "Can she get e-mails and phone calls from me, or should I wait until October 28 to ask for her number?"

I like this kid. I look at Ari, whose eyes are suspiciously moist. I take in a quick breath of air. She must really, really like the preacher's son. I had no idea. Why didn't I?

"Ari's free to talk on the phone or e-mail as long as it's kept clean and appropriate."

He reaches for a register receipt (mine—good thing I didn't want it anyway) and slides it across the counter to my daughter. "Seven digits," he says, pointing to the receipt. "Right there."

She visibly melts at the lame-o line. I can't say that I blame her really; just this morning, I was dreaming of meeting Greg at the top of the Empire State Building.

I head out to the parking lot, Ari following silently, which is just as well. What a day. Talk about getting slammed into by a big yellow taxi on the way to your destiny. Family movie night has got to get easier than this.

"Mom, hurry up!"

I look to the van, where Shawn's panicked face is hanging out the window.

"What's wrong?" I say, picking up my steps.

"Jake just blew chunks all over the backseat." He gives me an oily grin. "And all over Tommy."

I open the van door, ignoring Ari's "Oh, gross. I'm not riding in there."

Tommy isn't moving in the very backseat. I see the evidence of his plight all over his shirt. Jake is huddled against the side of the van, obviously waiting for Tommy to beat the tar out of him. But my eldest son is staring helplessly at me, his own face giving the appearance that he might just follow his little brother's example.

I say the first thing that comes to mind: "Well, son, when you spew forth evil words, even while only explaining a euphemism, you're bound to get spewed upon. Serves you right."

His jaw drops and his eyes go wide as I get into the driver's seat (holding my breath) and start the motor. We'll go to the car wash and clean out the van before we go home. I give a quick glance in my rearview mirror and I catch Tommy's eye.

He gives me a sheepish (if not a little sickish) grin. One that tells me he loves me, knows he blew it, and knows he got his just punishment. I have to fight to keep tears at bay. My wonderful, funny Tommy is back. I don't know how long it will last, but for this second, as our eyes meet, we understand each other. I'll take what I can get.

3. *Reconnect with my children . . .*

It's working. It's really working. One out of seven. Not bad. Not bad at all.

8

I'm sick of off-key renditions of "Leaving on a Jet Plane." Mom's been singing it for two weeks straight. And now as we drive the hour to the Springfield/Branson Regional Airport, I am assaulted by a five-person choir belting it out in time to my throbbing temple. Not one of my kids can carry a tune. They must get that from their father.

Mom's house still hasn't sold, but everything is boxed up. The movers will be coming next week to load 'em up and move 'em out. I'm left to take care of the details. I wouldn't mind, if only I didn't mind her moving so much. But the truth is, the closer we've come to this day, the harder it's been for me. And the tougher to keep from spilling forth my discontent about the whole thing—despite my original and selfless determination not to be selfish about her need to get out of Dodge. *Ugh.* Stop it with the Old West sayings, already.

The airport parking lot isn't too crowded when we arrive, so I'm able to find a spot up close. Considering Mom packed everything but the kitchen sink in her two checked bags, this is a good thing. Tommy follows me to the back and reaches in, snagging the largest and heaviest bag. "You sure you can carry that?" I ask. I get a scowl in return. "Sorry. I forget you're not a little guy anymore."

No one else offers to help, so I'm forced to pull rank.

"Come on, guys, grab a bag." My wrists are killing me. I look toward next week's surgery with a combination of dread and anticipation.

The three remaining children grumble to the back and take bags. Which leaves me with one task—close the trunk. With four kids, the two-carry-on-two-checked-bags rule works out perfectly for me.

Mom walks beside me. I feel her tension. "Everything is going to work out great, Mom," I say, not convinced, but hoping to at least convince her.

"I just feel awful leaving you when you're about to have surgery." She stops, mid-stride, and turns to me, guilt playing the corners of her lips and creasing her brow. "Maybe I ought to wait until the first of the year to move in with Charley."

Now, I can do one of two things: play on that guilt and have my own private cook, housekeeper, and nursemaid for the next few weeks, or do the right thing and send her off to the heart of Texas where she can hold her new grandbabies and enjoy the holidays for once.

I'm thinking . . .

Shoot. Sometimes having that inner, still, small voice really cramps my style. "Mom," I say, nudging my head toward our bellboys and -girl. "Look at the kids. They're not babies anymore. And I'm not having heart surgery. I'll be home in a day and they can help out." I slip an arm about her frail shoulders and head her toward the airport. "I'm already looking into a cleaning service to come in a couple of times a week. And Ari is quite capable of fixing tuna casserole or hot dogs, and there's always takeout. So don't fret."

"This is going to cost you a bundle. Cleaning service, ordering out. I think I'd best stay. Do you have that cell phone of yours handy? Let's call your brother."

"Mom, wait. Look. Next month royalty statements come out. If my calculations are correct, my check will more than cover expenses for the next few months." I send her an exaggerated wink. "I might even be able to afford a nice, expensive Christmas present for you."

She rolls her eyes, which have suddenly brightened, and I suspect she's trying to figure out how to mention the TV/DVR combo she's been hinting about for the last two months. "Don't you dare spend your money on me."

"Trust me, will you?"

She stops walking again as we approach the sliding doors. The curbside assistant stares at us with this accusing I-gotta-make-a-living scowl. I offer an apologetic shrug and point to the kids, who are just about through the door with Mom's bags. He turns to a single woman struggling with two rolling suitcases, hoping to make a few bucks.

Mom looks at the door and back at me. Her eyes show her struggle. I know she's dying to hop the plane and get to Charley's house, where she'll be pampered and treated like royalty. Where Marie's housekeeper will clean up after her, and someone else will cook the meals. I can't let her guilt make the decision for her.

I take her by the arm. "Let's go, Mom. You don't want to miss your flight."

"Are you sure I shouldn't stay?"

"Of course. This'll be a piece of cake. Like a vacation for me."

"A vacation from me?" She sounds hurt.

I laugh. "No, Mother. A vacation from working."

"Oh. Well, good. You need to take some time off." She reaches up and pats my cheeks—something she hasn't done since my wedding day when she told me she was praying I'd be very happy. Probably shouldn't mention that.

Ari's eyes flood with tears when we say good-bye to Mom at security. I know she wants to beg her to stay. The two have a tight bond that started the day Mother looked into Ari's serene baby face and declared her the loveliest infant ever born with the exception of baby Jesus Himself.

I'm sorta struggling with my own helpless feelings of abandonment, but I slip my arm around my daughter. My heart swells inside me as she silently lays her head on my shoulder. "Who am I going to talk to now?" she asks, just before sniffing against my new sweater.

The winds of deflation whoosh through my chest. "There's always the phone and e-mail," I manage weakly.

Jake is beginning to climb on the aisle dividers, and I see annoyance playing on the faces of the passengers waiting in line for security to make total fools of them. They have enough stress and definitely don't need some hyper kid slowing down the process by drawing the security officers away from their tasks.

"Come on, guys. We won't be able to see Granny anymore. We might as well go."

"Can we go to Incredible Pizza?" Shawn asks.

Now, pizza sounds good. The thought perks me up and lifts my spirits. I feel myself heading to my happy place.

Ari groans. "I'm so sick of pizza."

I stare at her. Did this child come from my body? She must have been switched at birth, because no daughter of mine could possibly be sick of pizza.

Luckily the boys outvote her, so we spend the next three hours eating buffet pizza while the boys ride the indoor go-karts and play video arcade games and air hockey. Ari sits in morose silence, reading a book I paid way too much for in the airport gift shop just to appease her. I pull out my notebook (not the electronic $2,000 kind) and a pen and begin sketching a new novel idea I've been mulling over for the last two weeks. This one isn't like the others, so I'm nervous to tell anyone about it. My agent might be skittish at the idea of sending it to an equally skittish publisher who brags about "building" my name in romance—like I had nothing to do with it. But the idea dogs me and it must be penned. And who knows? Maybe my current publisher will allow the switch in genre. The unlikely thought makes me feel better.

So I sit blissfully unaware of my kids roaming about the indoor playland while the characters in my head begin to take shape, introducing themselves and demanding airtime. So much for a vacation. But I have to admit, I feel a spark of renewed interest in writing. And some impatience that I have to go through with this surgery right now. But according to my surgeon's dire warning, putting it off would be a grave mistake. So it looks like I have a week to keep fleshing the characters and building my new plot. Guilt pricks me at this thought and my mind flitters to The List. I made a commitment. I glance at my kids. The boys aren't fighting for once. Ari is reading quietly. I strengthen my resolve once more. I am taking this time off to do what I promised myself I would do. Tomorrow I'm getting The List out and recommitting to it.

•   •   •

The next morning I cook breakfast and drive my kids to school. I get home and sit to read e-mail when my eye catches the Wal-Mart receipt on which my seven-steps-to-a-better-me list stares at me as a stern reminder. The only one that really bothers me is the exercise part. What was I thinking? But I've committed to change. And as much as I hate to admit it, exercise might be part of that. I decide to go for a walk. Four blocks later, I turn around and come back. I'm sweating and my feet are hurting from stiff Nikes I've never actually worn before. I resolve to buy some Band-Aids to help with the hotspots before I try again tomorrow.

Baby steps, Claire. Baby steps.

That night I have a chance to work on number one from The List: *Go to church more.* In reference to number one, I will also pick up a Beth Moore Bible study workbook from the church bookstore after service.

It's Wednesday. I promised the kids we'd go to church—as if they really had to beg. The truth is, I'm dying to see Greg again. It's been a week and two days since our meeting at school. I've seen him twice during that time. Once last Wednesday night, but the polite smile he gave me from the platform just before leading worship didn't exactly have me doing cartwheels. And on Sunday we met between services: he was leaving the first as I entered the building in time for the second. I might have to set my alarm a bit earlier next time . . .

Who am I kidding? No man is worth getting up in time to make it with four kids to a 9:00 a.m. service.

Darcy's face is beaming when I walk in at five minutes

till seven. She waves at me and scoots over, just like that, assuming I will mosey up the middle aisle amid the buzzing crowd of worshipers and just plop myself right down in the second row. I pretend I don't see her. On the second row with my ex-husband and his wife is the last place I want to be. I'm trying to figure out a way to politely sit elsewhere when I come face-to-face with Linda Myers, the woman who was able to forgive her husband's affair after reading *Tobey's Choice.*

She takes my hand, her smile warming me and inducing a smile on my own lips. "It's so wonderful to see you." She waves toward a seat nearly in the back. "I'm alone tonight. Mark had to work. Do you want to sit with me?"

I glance about. The kids have run to their age-appropriate sections of the seating. I shrug and wave to Darcy. "Sounds good," I say to the lovely woman who just rescued me from public speculation. Darcy's face clouds, but she nods and scoots back. That's when I notice Rick isn't with her. I frown. It isn't like him to miss church. The only time I remember him doing so was on Sundays when he had his National Guard drills. Rick's a weekend warrior. But this is only Wednesday. There is no drill during the week.

Now I can't keep my eyes off Darcy, sitting all alone on the second row. It wouldn't bother me to sit by myself, but I know it does her. "Hey, Linda. I need to speak to Darcy Frank. Can we sit together another time?"

Her eyes light with a smile of understanding. "Of course. Hey, you know what? I wouldn't mind a closer seat myself. Mind if I join you?"

Now, relief shoots through me. That's better. Another woman sitting with us will even things out a bit and squelch gossip that might start from having the two Mrs. Franks sitting together.

We sashay up the aisle just as the musicians take the stage. I nudge Darcy. "Scooch down two seats," I whisper. Delight widens her Angelina Jolie lips. "Sure!"

"Where's Rick?"

"Filling in for Craig at the hospital. He's on vacation. Must be a full moon. Between both of their patient lists, ten women have been admitted to labor and delivery tonight. Rick's going to be running his head off."

I refrain from making a snide comment and lift my gaze to the stage, where the band is warming up.

Funny how I never noticed before that Patrick Devine is the drummer. He grins at me when I notice him and gives me a salute with his drumstick. Linda chuckles and leans over. "Looks like Paddy there is trying to get Mom's approval."

I grin. "He's already got it. But don't let on. I don't mind a little flattery and kissing up."

"Trish said Ari's date with him is on the calendar for the Friday after her sweet-sixteen. That was some smart parenting."

I can't help a laugh at my own cleverness and joy that someone approves. "It's hard to believe she's already dating."

"Tell me about it. Trish turned sixteen in August. Is Ari getting her license on her birthday?"

This is when Darcy joins the conversation. She leans over, her sweet fragrance wafting over me. "She has to have her permit for six months before she can get her license.

We're taking her to take the permit test on Friday after school."

This makes my brows go up. "You are?"

Darcy's eyes grow wide. She looks scared. "You didn't know?"

"Nope." My jaw clenches. I refuse to make a scene in the Lord's house.

But Darcy can't leave well enough alone. "Ari asked Rick last time she was at our house. She said you never have time."

Heat sears my neck. The music has begun, and Greg is encouraging the congregation to stand up. That's the way we do the music at our church. Active praise and worship. And the music is upbeat and a little rockish on Wednesday nights. I like it. Usually. Tonight I'm feeling a little blind-sided. My baby is getting her learner's permit in two days, and I had no idea. I feel Linda squeeze my elbow to let me know she understands. I think maybe I've found a friend. This goes along with number five on my list: *Figure out why my only socialization revolves around my computer.* Relief pours through me. Maybe I'm making a little progress.

The music draws me back and I find myself clapping along with Paddy's drumming. As a spirit of worship filters through the sanctuary, I close my eyes and lift my hands toward heaven. I'm able to push aside the permit/license thing and concentrate on God. The pastor's sermon—"It's Not About You"—seems uncomfortably appropriate. Afterward, I head over to the bookstore, a little room off the sanctuary. I browse the study books and locate a Beth Moore workbook that looks especially interesting.

"Oh, we're getting ready to start that in our ladies' meeting on Friday morning." I turn to see Darcy behind me. She must have followed.

"Oh?" I start to put it back. But Darcy's words stop me. "Claire, why don't you join us? You're not working for the next few weeks. It would be the perfect thing to get you out of the house."

Shoot. Suddenly I remember number six on my list. Which includes *Join ladies' group at church*.

I think maybe God is playing a joke on me.

9

Friday night, I walk down the steps wearing a Kansas City Chiefs sweatshirt and a new pair of jeans, slightly snug (but I figure as long as they're not cutting off the blood flow to any vital organs, they can only serve to hold in bulgy areas—of which there are many).

The doorbell rings.

Linda's smiling face greets me as I slip onto the porch. "Ready to go?"

"Yep." The thought of a movie hit me just right. When she called earlier and invited me, I jumped at the chance to get out of the house.

I'm feeling really cool as I slide into Linda's little red Miata, the kind of car you can own if you only have one kid. I'll be driving a minivan for the next ten years at least. Bummer.

She pulls out of the driveway and we zoom down the road, small talk filling our conversation.

How was your day?

Fine.

Isn't this weather gorgeous?

Sure is, so glad the rain held off a few more hours.

The Miata speeds up during a long stretch of straight road. My heart lifts and I feel like a teenager. Until we stop at a red light, that is, and an actual group of teenagers screeches to a halt next to us. The crazy, dangerous, giggling lot of them make me nervous, and I'm glad Ari has a couple of more weeks before she can go anywhere without an adult driver.

"Don't you wish you had their energy?" Linda's amused comment tugs a smile to my lips.

"Their energy and bodies, combined with my wisdom and tax bracket."

Her laughter fills the little car. "Me, too."

"So, Mark had to work again?"

Her laughter fades and she gives a somber nod. "Again. Always. Lately, he's just Mr. Employee of the Month."

My eyebrows go up at her sarcasm. I feel responsible. After all, my book saved her marriage, I can't let anything pull these two apart again.

"Want to talk about it?"

She shrugs. "Nah. There's nothing I can do about it anyway. If he has to work, he has to work, right?"

"Right." I guess.

She whips the Miata into a miraculously close parking space for a Friday night at the movies and kills the motor. "So, did Ari pass the test?"

The topic that is a thorn in my side. I'd like to grunt my answer, but I squash the cavewoman tendency and nod. "With flying colors."

"Good for her!"

"Yeah."

Obviously sensing my need for a different topic, she tosses her keys in her purse and opens the door. "When's your surgery?"

I get out and close the door, slinging my purse over my

shoulder. I sigh as it slides down and lands in the crook of my arm. "Monday."

She looks at me over the top of the car. "That soon?"

"I've been off work for four weeks. I'm ready to get it over with."

"If you need anything, let me know, okay?"

My independent nature rises up. "There's nothing to this. It's practically not even surgery. I'll be fine. Thank heaven for takeout, right?"

She laughs and links her arm with mine. "I guess so. Let's go watch a chick flick."

I smile and move in step with my new friend.

5. *Figure out why my only socialization revolves around my computer* . . . This one is a no-brainer and goes back to the Bible. To have friends, a person has to be friendly. Who knew?

I look at my right hand all wrapped up in bandages and I'm trying really hard not to scream bloody murder. I'm sitting in the passenger side of my van and my daughter is actually driving me home from the hospital, because the pain meds make me loopy. Too bad they don't make me loopy enough to stop the fear of my fifteen-year-old daughter's driving.

I thought I'd be going home yesterday. But the doctor decided to keep me in overnight to watch my vitals. My blood pressure shot up a couple of times. Another sign I need to lose weight before I have a stroke.

"Careful, honey. There's a . . ." I cringe at the bewildered look of a fiftyish man in the passing vehicle we just barely missed sideswiping. "Car."

"I *know*, Mom. I saw it." I know I'm stressing her out with my nervousness. But sheesh, she's stressing me out with her driving. I'm just glad the hospital is only five minutes away from the house. I drove myself over yesterday, and Ari took a cab today. I don't know why I didn't agree to Darcy's offer of a lift.

"I can't believe you're being so stubborn about this," Rick said in his I'm-exasperated-but-I-know-you-won't-budge tone.

I'm a little ashamed to say that I reminded Rick quite firmly that *he's* the one who decided his little wife could take my daughter down to the license bureau and get a learner's permit, so let's let her use it already. Now, I'm regretting my hasty choice. I see a red light and my daughter doesn't appear to be slowing down.

"Ar—"

"Don't make me nervous, Mother. I know the difference between red and green, okay?"

"Then how about acting on that knowledge?"

"I'm slowing down," she spits back just as the light goes green.

Okay, she's doing fine. I can't help but pray the rest of the way home, though.

When we arrive in my blessed semicircle driveway with the slightly askew basketball goal hanging from the garage, I am relieved beyond words. Enough so that I send a "Thank You, Jesus" to heaven and receive a scathing look from Ari.

I step out of the car on wobbly legs—partly from having the surgery, partly from post-traumatic stress disorder due to the ride home. Darcy's SUV is parked along the curb in front. "What's she doing here?" I ask. Irritation rises in me and I fight to remind myself of my blood pressure.

"She came to help. Be nice to her, Mom."

Like I really need my fifteen-year-old telling me to be nice. "I'm always nice," I grumble.

She rolls her eyes. "Sure you are."

You'd think I could get a little more sympathy and fewer character lectures at a time like this. "I could have died on the operating table, you know. Then you'd be sorry for being so snotty."

"There was, what, a million-to-one chance?"

It was a little narrower than that. But she's close.

We ascend the porch steps and Ari actually thinks to open the door for me. "Mom's home!" she yells.

The scintillating smell of a pumpkin-scented candle wafts to my nostrils and I feel myself relaxing. Of course not only does my house smell yummy, it looks fabulous, a direct result of Darcy's presence, no doubt. I can't see Ari with a feather duster, and I know for a fact she'd be lost if I asked her to vacuum.

The boys bound down the steps. Shawn throws his chubby arms around my waist and buries his forehead in my stomach. "What's wrong, honey?" I ask.

He looks up at me. "I just missed you."

I kiss his spiked hair—the angel.

"Can I see your stitches?" Jake asks. He doesn't turn his gaze from the cast, and I can see his little mind trying to fig-ure out how he's going to get it off so he can see the gross stuff underneath. "You bleeding?" His blue eyes widen with hope, and I get the feeling he'd have been in heaven if the surgeon had invited him into the operating room.

"Not anymore," I say drily. "And no, you can't see my stitches."

Darcy appears from the kitchen just as I'm disengaging from my boys and heading to the couch. "Can I get you anything?"

Yeah, my house without a Darcy in it. Shoot. I hate it when I think truth and feel guilt. Darcy can't help that her nature demands she step up to bat for anyone she cares about. Just why she cares about me is beyond my scope, but I will follow Ari's advice and be nice to her. "Coffee would be great."

Darcy's face lights up. "Oh, good. I put on a fresh pot as soon as I got back from dropping Ari at the hospital."

I glance at my daughter and scowl. Cab, huh?

She shrugs. "She offered. Why waste five bucks to go half a mile?"

Oh, gee, because I said so, maybe? But who am I? I'm just the mom around here. In pain. Unappreciated. Disobeyed. Good grief, the medicine must be making me melodramatic. Reminds me of when Rick and I were first married and I was put on birth control pills that were way too strong for me. Talk about whacked-out hormones!

I flop down on my nice, overstuffed cranberry-colored couch and stretch out like it's my leg that just got operated on instead of my arm. Darcy appears carrying a tray with—get this—a mug I presume is holding coffee, a little plate with a sandwich (please, God, don't let it be cucumber), and a tiny vase sprouting a single yellow wildflower, which she most likely picked herself from the little patch of growth next to the fence in the backyard.

She sets it down across my lap. The little legs fit around me, which is a miracle. A pleased smile tips her mouth. "There you go," she practically sings. "I know you must be hungry. Hospital food, ugh." She sticks her finger into her mouth in the classic "Gag me" motion. Lovely.

"What kind is it?" I ask, nodding toward the sandwich.

"Peanut butter and jelly."

Relief washes over me. At least she didn't attempt anything fancy. I couldn't have stomached it. And look, she even removed the crusts. I don't have the heart to tell her I happen to be in that American minority who love bread crusts. Oh, well. "Thanks," I murmur, embarrassed to be waited on this way, but knowing she's doing it out of the kindness of her heart. And really, it does feel sort of cozy. Wonder how long I can milk it? Through dinner? "That was really sweet of you."

"It's my pleasure." She is wearing my apron that says, "On the eighth day Eve made chocolate." Resentment creeps through me. Not that she is wearing it, but because she has to wrap the tie around twice and there's still give in it. I'm not even going to mention whether I have to wrap it around me more than once. The comparison is getting monotonous.

"Well, I'm going to go fold some laundry," Darcy says.

"Okeydokey, Alice," I say, knowing there's no point in arguing.

"Who?"

If she's too young to know who Alice is . . .

"Three words," I say a little snippily. "Nick at Nite." I mean, I watched them all in syndication, too. I'm not *that* old.

She nods as understanding dawns. "Oh, from *The Brady Bunch*?"

Whew!

She giggles. "I'll be back. Just holler if you need something. Boys, how about helping me with the laundry?" I'm about to laugh at the ludicrous suggestion. Like my boys are really going to stop playing Xbox and just—

I watch with jaw-dropping disbelief as the dirty, traitorous rats follow her like she's playing a flute through town. I reach for my crustless peanut butter and jelly sandwich, feeling like a ten-year-old with a cold. As I chew the comfort food, I have to admit Darcy definitely has that mothering instinct. Even my kids respond to her style.

My mind suddenly fills with a thought just as I try to swallow. Peanut butter gets stuck on the way down, and I start to cough. For three minutes, I focus on not dying by peanut butter strangulation, until finally some hot coffee dissolves the goo, oxygen returns to my brain, and the images flood me once again. Darcy's young. She's going to want children. Rick's children. Siblings for my kids.

My stomach hurts. I set the tray aside, maneuvering carefully with my one good hand. For the first time in as long as I can remember, I have no appetite. I lay back, fighting tears, and close my eyes. Exhaustion overcomes me, and I feel myself drifting to the sound of muffled voices coming from the laundry room.

Claire?"

Rick's voice is not the first thing I want to hear when I'm waking up from a dream whereby Greg is serenading me at our wedding. Mine and Greg's—*not* mine and Rick's. That would be a nightmare.

"Ummm," I say and turn over. "Ouch!" I rolled onto my wrist. Not smart.

"Wake up, Claire. I need to ask you something."

"Ask someone else." I'm tired, in pain, and don't feel like getting along.

"I can't."

I slowly open my eyes and try to sit up. Only I can't push myself up with my wrist. And my other arm is awkwardly positioned.

"Here, let me help." I'd rather feed my eyes to hungry vultures. But I have no choice but to accept because he's already gotten hold of me around my waist and is pulling me up. The gesture feels familiar and yet unsettling. It's too close. Besides, my waist is decidedly thicker since the last time hands were anywhere near me.

"I can get it the rest of the way," I say, pushing at him. He backs off and I wiggle from side to side in what I'm sure looks like a floor show. Finally, slightly out of breath, I nod. "What do you want?"

"I thought I'd take the kids for a few days while you recover. Is that okay with you?"

"Darcy's idea?"

His face goes red, but he gives a little smile. "Yes."

"It's really not necessary, Rick. I can get by fine. It's not brain surgery, after all."

He stoops down, eyelevel. "Okay. Here's the thing. If you don't let those kids come home with me, my wife is not going to budge from this house until she's convinced you're not going to overdo."

My lips quirk at the panic setting in on his face. "Might have to fix your own dinner?"

His eyes are serious as he replies. "I need her home. I miss her too much when she isn't there. She *is* home to me."

Okay, this is an awkward moment. And made even more

so by the fact that during the last eight years of our eleven-year marriage, he never wanted to be home with me, and we are both thinking that very thing. Well, at least I assume we are.

"Sure, Rick. They can go."

A smile spreads across his face. I'm surprised to notice the lines around his mouth. I haven't looked at Rick—I mean really looked at him—since he walked out. Then, he was tall, well-muscled, fair, gorgeous, and young—like a Nordic god. But from this close proximity, I really can't help but notice how his features have matured. The gray at his temples. The hair in his nostrils. *Ew.* Well, another sign of age. I can be nice enough not to mention it, for a little while, but in order to keep that resolve, he'll have to get out of my personal space pretty quickly because I'm starting to feel claustrophobic.

"You two having a powwow?" Darcy's voice brings welcome relief to the tension I'm feeling.

"Yeah," I say. "Looks like you're going to have the kids for a few days."

"You know, I was thinking about that." A little frown creases the area just above her nose. When I frown I look like Andy Rooney. Darcy looks like a cute, petulant child. Shirley Temple.

Rick is on his feet now. I avert my gaze as he slides his hand possessively around her tiny waist. "What do you mean, sweetheart?"

"I'm just worried that Claire might need help and no one will be here."

"Oh, please," I say quickly. "It's only one hand. I'll order finger foods for dinner."

"I don't know . . . Oh, wait." She snaps her fingers. "I have it." Her eyes brighten and I feel dread coming on. I am not going to like this suggestion at all. I can tell.

"Claire needs to come and stay in our guest room. That way, I can look after everyone under one roof."

Rick's face blanches. Zero to 60 in a split second. The look of utter shock and horror, combined with the suggestion in the first place, strikes me as funny. And I start to laugh. I can't help it. I know Darcy is feeling stupid about now, but I can't stop. "I'm so-rry, D-d-dar-cy." I'm gasping for air. Why do I find this so hilarious? Maybe it's the painkillers.

"It was just a suggestion," she mutters.

"I know. But come on. Think about how ridiculous it is."

She shrugs and snatches at the string of her apron, lifting the whole thing from her head. "I thought it was a good idea. Still do. But I can't force you. I'll just go tell the kids to get some clothes together."

We watch her leave and Rick turns on me, his eyes dark. "Why do you have to make her feel so stupid?"

"Okay. First of all, get over yourself. We're not married. Second, if that wasn't a dumb-blonde suggestion, I don't know what is. And third, you just stood there looking like you'd been run over by a truck instead of taking care of the situation yourself. One of us had to speak up."

"Darcy is far from a 'dumb blonde,'" he says, totally blowing off the part of my answer where I made reference to his own responsibility in the situation—typical. "And if you had any discernment about people, you'd know that instead of always giving her a hard time."

Okay, now I'm spitting mad. "If I had any discernment

about people, I would never have married a two-timing jerk like you in the first place, let alone wasted eleven years of my life!"

"Oh, gee. Thanks, Mom. Nice to know you think we're all a big mistake."

I turn to find Ari nonchalantly leaning against the kitchen door, totally eavesdropping on her parents. Her expression is a cocky let-me-just-cause-a-little-trouble-for-Mom look.

Rick folds his arms across his chest. He gives a smug lift of his eyebrows.

I shoot up from the couch, then am forced to regroup as dizziness swarms my head. But I refuse to be taken down by my traitorous daughter or her father. "She knows darn well that's not what I meant."

Jake picks that moment to bebop through the room holding his Game Boy and never bothering to look up. "That's a euphemism, Mom." And then, to my utter horror, he proceeds to tell his father, not only the definition of *euphemism*, but the word for which *darn* is one.

Rick scowls at me. "Nice, Claire."

"I didn't teach him that," I defend myself.

"Claire, what are you doing up?" Darcy returns, carrying a suitcase, which I assume is filled with the kids' clothes. "See, this is what I'm afraid of; you're not going to take care of yourself."

Rick steps forward and relieves her of the bag. "Claire can handle herself, Darce." He walks toward the door. "Kids, hug your mother good-bye, and let's go."

"Can I drive?" Ari asks them while giving me her obligatory squeeze.

I have to grin when Darcy looks at Rick with an expression of pure delight. "Of course you can, Ari. I'll take the boys with me, and your father can give you a driving lesson on the way home."

Rick's face turns red. But in helpless surrender he hands over the keys to the excited teenager holding out her palm.

"Have fun, you guys," I say as the boys hug me with a little more enthusiasm than did their sister and follow the exiting group milling about the foyer.

When the door closes behind the kids, I sink down once again. Loneliness washes over me. I close my eyes, but for some reason the image of little Rick and Darcy clones won't leave me be. They'll be their kids, brothers and/or sisters to my kids. But what will that make me? Auntie Claire? My lips tighten into a grim smile. But I'm not feeling the humor. Not one bit. Because I have a dreaded feeling in my gut. And my gut is hardly ever wrong.

My life is getting ready to change once again.

And I really hate change.

10

I'm an hour into *The Mirror Has Two Faces* with high hopes of getting to the end this time when the doorbell rings. It's 6:15. With a sigh, I work around my bandaged arm and shove up from the couch. The wood floor warbles below me, like a time-warp special effect, and for a sec I think I'm about to land in the waves. I close my eyes and the feeling passes just as the doorbell rings again.

I pad across the room, my socked feet slipping along the floor as I walk through the tiled foyer. I look through the peephole, squint to make sure I'm seeing things right, then turn the knob with my good hand.

Linda is smiling and holding what appears to be a casserole dish between two blue potholders. "Hey, I heard you were alone tonight and in pain. Mind if I come in?" Her eyes twinkle in the dusky sunset, and she lifts the dish just a little to draw my attention to it. "I brought dinner."

She's dressed in a pair of loose, yellow exercise pants with a matching yellow jacket, and her long red hair is pulled up in a clip. And to my utter amazement, she's not wearing a spec of makeup. And hey, she doesn't look that great. Yeah! That's more like it. This woman is normal. When Darcy doesn't wear makeup she just looks like she's a gorgeous woman without makeup. When I don't wear makeup in public, little children run terrified to their mamas.

I open the screen for Linda and she catches it with her elbow, pushing enough so that she can get through and step inside my (thankfully clean) house.

Curiosity grumbles up from my empty stomach as I smell the heavenly aroma rising with the steam from that dish. Still, I don't want to appear too anxious. "You really shouldn't have." But I'm thinking how I'd like to grab the dish and run to the kitchen.

To my shock and (I admit) delight, she shrugs and makes like she's going to turn around. "Oh, you don't want it? Okay, I'll just take it home and freeze it for the family."

Her teasing smile is infectious and very much does the trick to lighten me up. "Don't you dare. I'm starving. I was just about to order myself a pizza."

"Oh, girl. This is way better than pizza."

I think my new friend and I have just had our first disagreement. But since she's the one doing the cooking, I am not going to argue the superiority of pizza to any food on the face of the earth. Not until I've eaten anyway.

She looks at me, eyes questioning, head cocked to the side. "Should I take this to the kitchen?"

Oh, duh. For the record, let me just admit I'm a terrible hostess. "It's that way." I jerk my thumb toward the kitchen and she leads the way. As I step into my second-favorite room in the house (the first one being my office), I'm surprised to see the sparkly clean everywhere I turn. My dream kitchen had always been furnished with stainless steel appliances. Then, when I got them I realized they are so much harder to keep looking nice than the other kind. Smudges jump out from them and call, "Hey, slobby housekeeper, you want to grab a towel and wipe me down? I'm way too expensive for a dull shine. Perk me up, already." Apparently, Darcy heeded that call earlier, because my appliances haven't looked this good since the cute Sears guys delivered them two months ago.

So Linda sets the dish on my counter. "Are you hungry now?"

She must see the famished-wolf look in my eyes, because she doesn't wait for an answer, but opens the cabinet just above the dishwasher. She looks at four boxes of cereal and turns to me with a bewildered frown. "Where are your plates?"

A little sheepishly, I point to the cabinet next to the stove.

Okay. I know I have a funny system for organizing (and I use that term loosely) my cabinets, but here's my thinking. We rarely put dishes away anyhow, so bowls are almost always in the dishwasher. We grab a bowl. Set it on the counter, open the cabinet and grab the cereal. See? Using your head a little is a huge timesaver. The same reasoning holds true for the stove cabinet. Finish cooking, grab a plate, fill it, and go sit down. No need to use serving bowls when it's just the kids and me, and the plates are right there handy. I don't know. I think it makes sense.

I don't go into this with her, though. And to her credit, she doesn't pry. She grabs two plates and looks around at the drawers.

No way am I going to have her trying to figure out that system. "I'll get silverware."

She smiles. "I hope you don't mind if I eat with you. Trish is with Ari, and Mark is working late again."

I wonder if I'm detecting a note of worry in her voice. I don't know her well enough to recognize voice patterns, but as the former wife of a man who cheated, I recognize the worry when I see it. Regaining that trust is difficult. It's not my place to pry, and I don't get the feeling she really wants to open up, so I offer her the best thing I know to offer: friendship.

"I'd enjoy the company," I reply truthfully. "With the kids gone, it's pretty quiet around here. I'd get online, but typing one-handed is too frustrating."

She grabs the potholders and the casserole dish and heads for the table. "Do you have something to put down so we don't mess up the wood?"

I slide a forest-green place mat to the center of the table. "That ought to work."

With a melodic burst of laughter, Linda sets the dish down. "You're low-maintenance, aren't you?"

I think that's a compliment. I realize now that she assumed I'd have one of those coaster things you put down on the table, but to me, I figured there was a place mat right there—why not use it? Part of me hates that I take the path of least resistance in any given situation. It means I don't have the spotless home I'd like to have or the most decorated walls. It means I wear short, spikey hair that only takes ten minutes of wash, gel, and go instead of the long, flowy styles that are in fashion. But there's no need to defend myself. Linda's guileless expression confirms that her statement was a compliment, not a criticism.

I nod. "I have to be low-maintenance. Nitty-gritty details make my busy life too stressful."

"That's admirable." She sighs and dishes up a spoonful of the casserole that looks like some kind of chicken cheesy bake.

"Is it?" I walk to the dishwasher to find a couple of glasses, only to see it's empty.

Darcy strikes again.

"Of course it's admirable. You don't get sucked in by the idea that you have to keep up with Mrs. Jones. Perfect house, perfect yard, perfect figure."

Hey, what's wrong with my yard? That thought is eclipsed by the last remark. I don't have to ask what's wrong with my figure. "Yeah, well. Perfect, I'm not. That's for sure."

"I hope you know, I just mean that you are yourself and don't pretend to be anyone else. You don't change to suit other people's ideals."

"Sure, I knew what you meant." All too well.

I open the cabinet next to the refrigerator and take out two glasses, maneuvering pretty well one-handed, if I do say so myself. I open the fridge and take inventory.

"Okay, Linda. I have milk, Pepsi, Diet Pepsi, Coke, Diet Coke—don't ask, but there seems to be a vast difference of opinion over cola taste tests in this house—and if I know Darcy, there's a pitcher of freshly squeezed OJ." I lift out a glass pitcher filled with pulpless orange liquid. "See what I mean?"

Linda laughs. "That woman is amazing."

Whatever. "So what'll it be?"

She chooses one of the diets, and I choose the other. Got to save those calories where we can, don't we?

"Thanks for letting me stay. I haven't had a girls' night in ages."

"Me neither." I don't do girls' nights out. No girlfriends. I'm not even sure what to do. I mean, sure, I've seen my share of *Sex in the City* episodes, but nothing is coming to mind. But then, a movie is always a safe bet, isn't it? "Hey, do you like Barbra Streisand?"

She washes down a bite with a gulp of her diet soda. "Are you kidding? Who doesn't?"

My sentiments exactly. "Ever seen *The Mirror Has Two Faces*?"

She shakes her head. "I'm married to a man's man. The only movies I get to watch must include blood, violence, and lots of gunfire. Barbra Streisand is definitely not on the list of acceptable choices when it's time to pick out a movie."

I have an opinion about that disclosure, but somehow I don't think God wants me to toss it out there and give the devil any ammo against this marriage. And guess what? I still feel a little bit responsible to watch over it after my book was a catalyst for their reunion.

Still, why is it that a man won't watch a chick flick, but he always wants his wife to watch a guy flick? Trying to explain the word *compromise* to a testosterone-overloaded male is like trying to teach a dog not to sniff. There's just no training them in that area. If you try to talk them into watching a chick movie, they decide they need to build a doghouse or something.

Okay, my man-hating hormone is kicking in, so I turn to food to calm me down.

"This looks great. What is it, anyway?"

She grins. "Cheesy chicken casserole. What's that got to do with a Barbra Streisand movie?"

"Not a thing. Except maybe we can eat in the living room and watch the movie. You got time?"

"All the time in the world. Trish is spending the night and going to school with Ari tomorrow." Her face clouds. "And there's no telling when Mark's going to be home. So why should I hang around and wait for him to remember he has a wife?"

Let it go, Claire. Let it go.

"Looks like my lucky night, then." Okay, I'm over the hump. Once I change the subject, I almost never go back and say what I was changing the subject to avoid saying in the first place.

"Thank you. I've been wanting to see that movie for years."

She's not the only one.

I stand and take my plate in my good hand. She takes her plate and somehow maneuvers the glasses so that she can carry both in one hand. "You've waited tables, I can tell." I grin at her.

"Is this a past we share?"

"How do you think I got through the first few years after Rick left?"

She's leading the way into the living room, but I hear her sigh. Now that's a cry for help if I've ever heard one. Anyone who actually sighs aloud is just asking for a little advice.

I sit on the couch and Linda deposits my drink on the coffee table, then takes her seat in my tan-and-cranberry recliner. "So, is everything okay with you and Mark?"

"I don't know." Her voice has dropped to such a low volume that I can barely hear her.

"You know, working late doesn't necessarily mean anything."

She nods and turns to me. "It's just that . . . last time . . ."

"It started with him working late?"

"So he said. Of course he wasn't really working. He was with his mistress."

"And you think he's cheating now?" I wish I would have just stayed out of it. But once I opened that can of worms by asking her if everything was okay, I pretty much committed myself to seeing the conversation through to a natural conclusion.

"I can't know for sure. And I can't ask him."

"Why the heck can't you?" I just don't get it. I'm not built to avoid confrontation. It just bursts out of me. I should talk. I mean, good grief. Rick had been having affairs for years before I had the courage to face it. I finally pinned him down one night after he came home late and just demanded the truth. Of course there's no way I can tell Linda that. Besides, I really just want to let it go. It's bringing back a lot of painful memories. And I'm recovering from surgery. I shouldn't have to think about my strong need for inner healing at a time like this.

Tears have begun to slip down her cheeks, and I know there's no way I'm going to get out of having this talk. "Because if I ask him, he'll think I don't trust him. And we've been through so much."

"But—"

"I know. If I don't trust him, I should either confront him or leave him."

"Living in misery every time he leaves the house isn't healthy. Not for you or Mark and probably not for Trish, who most likely feels the tension in you."

She swipes a tissue from a box on the table next to her chair. I don't remember putting them there. As a matter of fact, I usually grab toilet paper when I need to wipe my nose. Darcy must have thought I needed some in the living room. I silently bless the dear June Cleaver wannabe, because I would have died if I'd had to offer Linda a square of Charmin for her little nose.

"I know Trish is worried. She remembers all the arguing. Many nights she'd hear me crying in my room and come crawl into bed beside me."

My heart turns over at the mental picture. I know Ari remembers similar things. In my mind's eye I see my ten-year-old, eyes wide and worried. "Mommy, is Daddy coming home?"

Heartbreaking. My eyes dare to well up with tears. I blink away the hateful reminders of my still-aching heart as fast as they come. It's not that I still love Rick. Not that I'd ever, in a zillion years, want him back. But the memories of that time bring the pain of that time. I suppose if I could just forgive and forget, the hurt would fade. So far, that's not happening. That's what makes Linda's next question one of the hardest I've ever had to answer.

"How did you do it?"

"Do what?" I'm not admitting to anything just like that.

"In *Tobey's Choice*, the pain was too real to be imagined.

I assumed that's the reason you and Rick broke up. Infidelity?"

Well, then, Little Miss Deductive Reasoning has it all figured out except for one thing: I haven't forgiven Rick. God knows I've tried. Prayed, fasted (well, okay, only one meal and that was breakfast, so it probably didn't count since I don't eat breakfast anyway, but there was effort in the thought of fasting), confessed it over and over, "I forgive Rick for being a toad-sucking cheater. I forgive Rick for being a toad-sucking cheater." And nothing. No beam of forgiveness light landed on my head and created a magic cure. I don't know. Maybe this is something I'm going to have to repent of every day for the rest of my life. My Rick-hating sin. I kid you not, it's a daily battle. I constantly find myself asking forgiveness for wishing he'd get poison oak between his toes or that he'd be at Wal-Mart picking up something for Darcy and someone would key his Mercedes—a really deep key damage all along the driver's-side door—or something equally annoying but not life-threatening. And I'm really not proud of it. Really. I pray to forgive. But the prayers just aren't working in this case.

"I'm sorry," Linda is saying. "I don't mean to pry."

"No, you're really not. And you are right. Rick's tendency to look outside our marriage for sex is definitely what killed it. But I have to say, neither of us was a Christian back then. Rick is a changed man, and I honestly believe he is and will remain faithful to Darcy."

Actually, that is true. I honestly believe it, like I said. I also honestly believe I might have to excuse myself and hurl from the necessity of giving that little spiel in defense of Rick's newfound fidelity.

Linda's phone goes off before she has a chance to respond. I have one of those awkward moments where I'm trying not to eavesdrop, but (a) I'm curious as to who is calling her. And (b) I mean, she's just sitting there. What am I supposed to do? Stick my fingers in my ears and start humming the "Star-Spangled Banner" so that I don't hear a word she's saying?

So I listen. I don't have a choice.

"I brought dinner to Claire Everett's house. She had surgery today. We're about to watch a movie." She pauses. I see her brow go up in surprise and I can't help but listen closer. "I can't believe it. I'll be home in a few minutes." She hangs up and tosses me a look of apology.

"Mark, I take it?"

She nods happily. "He came home early to surprise me. Even brought Chinese food and everything. Apparently he worked it out with Trish ahead of time so that we can be alone, and that's why she begged to go spend the night with Ari."

I'm thinking Mark is giving her a guilt dinner. I wouldn't be surprised if there are rose petals leading to the bed. Diversionary tactic.

Linda is already on her feet. "Do you mind if I take a rain check on the movie?"

"Of course not. Go. Be with your husband."

Just don't believe a word he says.

Sorry, Lord. At least I didn't say it out loud.

Despite my insistence that it's not necessary, Linda waits while I eat, then refuses to leave the dirty dishes.

"Pray for me, Claire," she says, squeezing my good hand. "I want to believe him. I want to trust that he loves me. This is so hard."

I say goodnight, turn off the porch light, lock the door. I think about starting the movie over, but there's no point. The thought of watching a budding romance leaves me cold.

11

I'm all alone, so is it any wonder I'd like to sleep in? It's reasonable, and any reasonable person would understand this. So why is my phone ringing at 8:00 a.m., a most ungodly hour? I've got to get a caller ID phone up here. The only explanation I can come up with is that a telemarketer must have weaseled through the do-not-call list.

A growl rumbles in my sleep-husky throat and I'm tempted—yes, I am, I'm sorry to say—to use my pervert whistle on the caller. I reach for the whistle then reconsider. I've been studying Beth Moore, my new role model for godly womanhood, and I'm almost positive she's not going to bite someone's head off over an early call, even a telemarketer. So I count to ten before answering the ringing demon.

"Hello?"

"Claire?" No telemarketer, here. It's Pod Girl. Flowery, morning-person, pod-girl Darcy, and her voice sounds like she's not sure she dialed the right number. "Is that you?"

"It's me. Everything okay, Darcy?" I ask, almost pleasantly. I'm so proud of me.

She's not buying it. "Oh, good grief. I woke you up again, didn't I?"

I'm gonna have to say yes to that one. "It's okay. What's up?"

"Nothing." Her voice is small. "Just wanted to check on you. I'm sorry, Claire, I waited as long as I could. I couldn't stand it anymore."

A smile tugs at my mouth. "Well, I appreciate your restraint up 'til now."

I'm almost positive I hear a sigh of relief. "So how was your night?"

"Okay. I took a Vicodin. Slept like a baby."

"You know people get hooked on those things." I can almost hear the *tsk-tsk* combined with concern in her voice.

"I don't have an addictive personality." Unless you count my addiction to caffeine, e-mail, pizza, Lifetime movies, *Days of Our Lives* . . . "I'll take ibuprofen if I need anything to take the edge off today."

"Good. Since you're awake, I'll be over in a few minutes to fix breakfast and straighten up for you."

Is she kidding me? I'm desperately trying to come up with a good reason why that's a really bad idea, but I'm almost sure I'm not contagious. And if I know Darcy, any other excuse would be brushed under the rug.

"Do you want to do the Beth Moore daily lesson together today? I haven't done mine yet."

"Sure." Defeated by kindness, I give up. After I tell Darcy good-bye, I push back the covers and haul my behind out of bed a full two hours before I wanted to.

Oh well.

Too bad Darcy has such bad taste in men. Given different circumstances, we might have been great friends.

Trying to write left-handed has got to be the hardest thing I've ever done. Well, besides childbirth and maybe finding out Rick was cheating. Still, it's definitely frustrating. But I've decided if I'm going to have time on my hands—er, hand—for a few days, I'm going to keep working on my new character sketches and plot. I am so excited by the new story that I lose all track of time. Still, when the phone rings just after five o'clock, instinctively I know it's Mom. Caller ID confirms my suspicion. Showoff Charley had a phone line strung downstairs in Mom's basement apartment just for her. So the caller ID actually has her name on it. Edith Everett.

"Hi, Mom."

"How'd you know . . . Oh." Newfangled inventions like caller ID still trip Mom up every so often. Affection surges through me and brings a smile to my lips.

"How's Texas?"

"Too dadgum hot."

Dadgum? The only times I've ever heard Mom use that word are when she returns from Charley's after vacations. I suppose she's going to be cussing with the best of them from now on.

Mom's still complaining. "I miss my fall weather."

I knew she would. "Well, it's barely October. It's still in the sixties here."

"Are the leaves turning yet?" I hear longing in her voice. My heart aches a little. I miss her. I wish she were here just to share a cup of coffee with on her deck. Or mine. I miss running down the street to borrow a couple of eggs or flour or whatever. I hate that my life has changed so in such a short amount of time.

"Not the evergreens."

She chuckles. "Hardy-har-har."

I hesitate. I don't want to be the one to bring up my pain, but doesn't she remember about my surgery?

"Any calls about my house?"

"Not this week, Mom."

"Well, maybe I'll just move back."

She's fishing. No doubt prompted by missing the gorgeous Missouri autumn weather, my children, her friends at the center. It wouldn't take much for me to drop a few hints and *whoosh*—the sound of Mom rushing to the airport after only a week in Texas.

"You ought to give Texas a little longer to prove itself to you, Mom. You've always loved your visits."

Her sigh reaches me and I feel her indecision. Only one thing to do in this situation. Talk about me to get her mind off it. I'll make the sacrifice.

"My surgery went well yesterday."

"Oh my goodness! I plumb forgot."

Plumb?

"How are you feeling, Claire?"

"Other than the throbbing pain in my right hand, I guess I'm feeling okay."

"It's bad, huh?"

"Only when I'm awake." I admit it. I'm milking this for sympathy. But sheesh, if a girl can't beg for sympathy from her own mom, who will feel sorry for her?

"Do you have plenty of help? Is Ari taking care of the boys for you?"

Yeah, right. What world is she living in? The only "taking care of" Ari is bound to do for her brothers is knock the tar out of them if they look at her funny.

That's why a laugh escapes my throat. I can't help it.

Mom is completely out of touch where Ari is concerned. "Well, she did drive me home from the hospital yesterday. Although whether that was help or not is yet to be determined." I leave out the part about my daughter nearly side-swiping a poor grandfather innocently driving down the street or the red light she almost didn't see.

"Ari . . . is . . . driving?" She ekes out the words, her voice suddenly dropping in volume. I picture her slightly arthritic fingers pressed to her throat, a telltale sign of her worry. "When did this happen?"

"Ask her father," I say with a sniff.

She sniffs right back. "Her father isn't part of the family anymore, remember?"

Inwardly, I groan. I'm being taken by my own words.

"Well, Rick okayed Ari getting her learner's permit, so he's teaching her to drive."

She hesitates, and I think she's about to give me an earful about the dangers of inexperience behind the wheel. "I guess she isn't a little girl anymore, is she? How's she doing, then?"

Okay, not the response I expected but probably the healthiest for her blood pressure. "I made it home alive, but I think I might need to take a Valium any time I get in the car with her."

"Well, she can't be any worse than you were." Mom's laughter sprinkles through the line, a sound I've longed to hear during the past week. "I gained a new appreciation for on-the-spot prayer when you were learning to drive."

I laugh with her. "I think my driver's ed teacher is still in therapy from the months she had me in her class. To this day, I have to remind myself to pay attention to the road."

"So you never answered. Are you taking it easy?"

"Rick and Darcy are keeping the kids for a few days so I can rest."

"That's good. But who is taking care of you, Claire? You can't cook and dress all one-handed." I hear disapproval in her voice and it washes over me like a spring rain. There's something about having someone care about you. Being concerned on an adult level.

"I can dress just fine, and a friend dropped by with dinner last night. There's plenty left over for me to heat up later." I don't want to try to explain my bizarre relationship with Darcy, so I refrain from mentioning my breakfast casserole, freshly squeezed OJ, and whole wheat toast, lightly buttered. That Darcy. What a Martha Stewart. Well, Martha Stewart meets Miss America.

"What friend?"

I tell her about Linda. But I steer clear of last night's conversation. From experience, I am fully aware that my new friend wouldn't want me to reveal her painful suspicions. Not even to one neutral bystander.

"It's so nice that you're making friends, honey." She says this in a tone that she might have used my first day of grade school. "I can fly home for a few days if you need me."

Hope shoots through me, and I know all I have to do is say the word and Mom will be hopping a plane to come and take care of everything. The thought of it sends me such a feeling of relief that I am this close to saying, "Oh, yes, Mommy, please come take care of me." But her words flash through my mind: *Maybe this is something I need to do for myself.*

Truth slams me like a line drive to the gut. I can't let her come running back to take care of me. It's not easy to get around one-handed, but it's doable and there's no point in her making the sacrifice. Besides, I sort of get the feeling she'll give up her new life if she comes home this soon. If she decides to move home for the fall weather and snow in the winter, that's one thing. But to do it because she doesn't think I can get along without her isn't right.

"Mom, I appreciate the offer, but I'm almost forty years old. I can manage."

"Oh!" Her voice rings with startled deflation.

"It's not that I don't want you," I quickly explain. "You know I'd love to see you. But I have it all worked out, so there's no need for you to leave Charley's twins. Tell me about them, anyway. Do you know I've only gotten one measly picture of my nephews and that was when Marie was in the hospital?"

"They're a couple of doozies, Claire. You should just see the little dolls. I keep them downstairs with me while Marie home schools the older children. I'm simply having the time of my life."

Wow. I wonder sometimes how she can be so satisfied being the mom—the one who is there for everyone. I decide to ask her point-blank. "Is keeping them really something you enjoy, Mom? Or do you feel obligated to babysit?"

"Claire, let me tell you something, honey. I might get tired sometimes, but I know better than anyone how short this life can be. When my grandbabies grow up, I want them to remember their granny. I don't want to sit in some apartment somewhere all alone, wishing I'd taken less time for my own desires and more time building relationships with my family."

"So there are things you would like to do, then?"

She gives me that well-if-you're-going-to-force-the-issue huff. "Oh, I don't know. I suppose I'd like to tour France someday."

"You're kidding. I didn't know that."

"Now you do. Only, to tell you the truth, honey, I'd rather be changing these diapers in a basement apartment in Texas than see any French villas."

I know she means it. But something inside me still wonders if she's where she's happiest. I don't want to pry. I wonder why it took her going off to essentially play the same role with Charley that she's played with me for the past five years, for me to realize that Mom has no life outside her children and grandchildren.

We exchange a bit more small talk, then say good-bye. After all, according to Mom, six in the evening is still a daytime call. I smile when I press the receiver. She also doesn't get the concept of free minutes.

I sit in my living room glancing about at the emptiness. The bright, low sun beams through a crack in my curtain and I watch it, fascinated with the colors of light.

Oh man, I need to get out of the house. The doctor said I could walk as long as I didn't get too tired. So I change into a pair of sweatpants and a T-shirt and grab my shoes. Then my heart sinks. I can get in and out of clothes, awkwardly, with one hand, but there's no way I can tie my shoes.

But I'm committed to the effort of continuing my very first walking program (number four on my list), so I head up to Ari's closet, grab a pair of her running shoes, which are slightly tighter than mine, tuck in the laces, and head for the door.

The smell of freshly cut grass in the cool autumn air invades my senses. I am filled with a sensation of goodness. Of newness. Of excitement that something good is about to happen to me. And just last night I was dreading the inevitable changes that will someday make their way into my life when Darcy turns up pregnant. Tonight, all that is behind me, for a while anyway. I breathe in the freshness as I head down my steps and to the sidewalk. Out of habit, I turn toward Mom's house. The leaves on the maple tree in her front yard are already turning a gorgeous reddish gold. I think of how she gathers the leaves when the branches turn them loose and they glide to the ground, and makes fall decorations for her house.

I am forced to blink away tears of loneliness. But I snap out of it fast as I see a truck driving by, slowly, from the corner of my eye. My pulse quickens. The sun is sinking lower in the western sky, but the pink and orange beauty eludes me as I start to wonder if I'm being stalked. The truck is barely inching along the street. None of my neighbors are out in their yards this time of day. I didn't think to bring my cell phone. I am totally regretting my hasty "new me" sort of feeling that tricked me into putting on running shoes and leaving my house only to become a six o'clock news statistic.

I pick up my pace, fear shooting like fire through my veins. I'm too spooked to turn my head because I know deductively that this guy is stalking me. I am about to shoot through the Barkers' yard and pound on their door when the truck pulls up alongside the curb and stops.

Fight or flight kicks in and I pick the latter. I make a sharp left and realize my legs are about to get a shock. I'm about to break into a run.

"Claire, wait!"

Claire? I don't know any stalkers.

"It's me. Greg Lewis."

I jerk to a sudden stop and whisk around. Relief floods through me at the sight of Tall, Dark, and Handsome. But for once, I'm not impressed enough with his looks to keep my irritation from sprouting from me like a spring flower. "You scared the crud out of me, buddy. What's the big idea making like you're a dadgum stalker?" (Oh boy, I'm as bad as Mom.) "You're lucky I didn't have my phone with me. I would have dialed 911."

Greg opens the door of his black-and-gray Avalanche. "Sorry, I wasn't stalking you. I was looking at that house back there. The one with the FOR SALE sign. Then I thought I recognized you." He frowns and looks at my hand. "What happened?"

"Carpal tunnel. Are you looking for a house to buy?"

He nodded. "Does it hurt?"

His question strikes me as odd. "Mom's house?"

"Huh?"

"Oh, you mean does my arm hurt?"

He tosses out a throaty laugh. I grin. The whole conversation is crazy. Just like my crazy life.

"That's your mom's house for sale back there?"

"Yes. She moved to Texas. I can give you a quick walkthrough, but you'll have to call the realtor for the official tour if you're really interested."

"Sure, I'd like that. Would right now be too much trouble?"

Is he kidding?

I shoot him a smile. "Anything to get out of exercise."

"Glad I can help." His lopsided grin makes me want to run my fingers through his hair. Good thing half of them are out of commission.

"My house is a few doors down. I need to go get the key. Do you want to walk with me or wait on Mom's porch?"

"We'd be neighbors?"

Do I detect a note of pleasure? I nod. "Looks that way."

He winks. "I'll wait here for you. Otherwise, people might talk."

I feel warmth rush to my cheeks. But I roll my eyes, my way of covering up. "Sure they would. Like anyone really cares what their neighbors are doing anymore." I speak from experience. We tried a neighborhood watch system once, but when the group's leader was arrested for breaking and entering a house three blocks south, we gave it up.

I practically rush home and grab Mom's key from the key holder hanging above the light switch in the kitchen. I stop off at the bathroom to check myself out in the mirror. Oh, crud, is that what he saw? My short hair isn't spiked, but it's definitely sticking out in every direction. I turn on the water and quickly wet down the mess. I still don't feel great about how I look, but there's no way I'm going to slap on makeup. That'd be way too obvious.

He's leaning against the porch railing when I get back. Mom's house. A white two-story dwelling with a green door and green shutters. My mother's dream home. I was ten when we moved in. The tree house Dad built for Charley and me is still wedged in the massive oak that stands in the middle of the backyard.

"This is a home for a family," I muse as I slide the key into the familiar lock. "My mom lived here for twenty-seven years."

"This is where you were raised, then?"

I nod. "Mostly. Dad was military. But he retired when I was ten. My parents saved every extra penny to buy this house."

We step inside. Greg's hard-soled shoes echo off the walls as he walks across the hardwood floors. He looks from one side of the spacious living room to the other. "This is beautiful," he says. "Your mother took great care of it."

"This house was her pride and joy. She worked on it all the time." And so did Charley and I. I smile as memories slip through my mind. "I hated the last Saturday of the month, though."

"Why's that?"

I stand in the middle of the living room and suddenly I see my family. "On the last Saturday of every month— without fail—Dad and Charley (once he was old enough) would move all the furniture out, then Mom and I would clean all the windows, wash the curtains, and wax the floor."

"Sounds like a tough day."

"It was. The only good part about it was that afterward, Dad took us all out to dinner."

"Good memories." His voice is gentle, as though he recognizes how difficult the thought of someone else occupying my childhood home is.

"I envisioned a family living here."

He cocks his head to the side a little and frowns. "That's the second time you've mentioned a family."

"I'm sorry. I guess it just didn't occur to me that a bachelor would be interested in a four-bedroom two-story home."

"Widower."

I feel the blood drain from my face at the obvious pain in his eyes. "You're a widower?"

"I assumed you knew. My wife died two years ago. It's just been me and Sadie ever since."

"Sadie?"

"My daughter."

"Well, for the love of Pete. I had no idea you were raising a child. Greg, I'm truly sorry."

He gives me a sad smile. "It's not your fault. You didn't know."

The silence hangs, heavy, intense. Awkward. "Do you— uh—want to see the upstairs?"

He shakes his head, as I'd expect him to. "I've seen enough to know I'm interested in seeing the rest. But I'll call the realtor and do the rest through them."

"All right." I shut off the lights and follow him out to the porch. By now, the blinding sunset has given way to twi- light. I turn the key in the dead bolt and let the storm door swing shut. Greg is standing on the porch. Waiting. "Well," I say, not sure what to say. "I—um—guess I'll see you at church tomorrow night, right?"

His mouth twists in a wry grin. "I wouldn't be much of a gentleman if I didn't walk you home."

Walk me home? I shiver in anticipation at the thought of gorgeous Greg strolling along next to me, our shoulders brushing lightly in the dusky night. But a girl can't seem overly anxious. Or desperate. My Tough Chick persona comes to the surface. I like Tough Chick. She's cool. "Don't worry about it. I've been taking care of myself for a long time. I can walk a few blocks."

This brings out a chuckle. "Sure. You were about to bolt like a thoroughbred stallion just because I parked my truck alongside the street."

"No. I was about to bolt because you were stalking me."

I raise my chin in the air and brush past him. Greg falls into step beside me. Clearly he is undaunted by Tough Chick's obvious ability to control her own life. I find it sort of endearing. But I take care not to allow our shoulders to brush.

"How's Shawn doing since he got in trouble?" I ask.

"I'm not encouraging him to write poetry, that's for sure."

I'm glad the evening hides my embarrassment. "Well, you should know he's being severely punished for that little stunt."

"Severely? You're not locking him in the woodshed without supper every night, are you?"

"Of course not."

He nudges me and Tough Chick gets the joke.

"Oh. Well, he's cleaning his dad's garage and he did a superb job of raking my leaves." Unfortunately, as I say this, we arrive in my yard and crunch dried leaves all the way to the porch. Two large lawn-and-garden plastic bags are sitting half filled in the center of the yard. "Well, he's working on it."

He hesitates at the door and I don't invite him in. I know he'd just say no and then I'd be embarrassed. Instead, I hold out my hand like we just landed a business deal. His mouth quirks in another lopsided grin and he takes my hand between both of his. "Thank you for showing me the house. And I'm sorry I scared you."

The warmth of two large, male hands cradling mine has totally melted Tough Chick to Giggle Girl. But I can take her, so I contain the giggle to a mere smile in return. "That's okay. I didn't walk far enough to get my heart rate up, so that scare was probably the only aerobic activity I've had lately."

He laughs out loud.

"Thanks for walking me home, even though it wasn't necessary."

"You're welcome, Claire. I'll see you tomorrow night at church. And by the way, it's good that you've been coming more lately."

A cheesy smile lifts my lips as I walk inside.

12

For three days I wander aimlessly about the house. I can read the posts coming through on my writer's loop and peck one-handed, pitifully short answers. But I'm having serious withdrawal all the same and Instant Messenger is out of the question.

I'm unaccustomed to not having work coming out my ears. I've been pushing one deadline after another for the last few years and, quite frankly, at the moment I'm at loose ends. I've been working on my new idea steadily and I really think I'm on to something. Enough so that I'm dying to put a proposal together to send for my agent's opinion, but I need the computer to do that. And I need both hands.

At night, I wake up with panic zooming through every inch of my body, until I realize, "Hey, it's okay. There's nothing for you to do. Go back to sleep."

I blame my stir-crazy state of being on the fact that I let Darcy talk me into attending ladies' Bible study this morning. And though I insisted I could drive one-handed, she insisted better than I did. That's why I sit in her SUV, listening to her tell me how great the kids have been and how they should stay a few more days until I'm fully recovered.

"Did Shawn clean the garage?"

Her face clouds over. "We're still working on it. He

doesn't seem to worry too much about punishment, does he?"

He's never been punished all that much. I admit it. He's always sort of been my baby, and I've overlooked things I could probably have addressed a little more forcefully—his lack of enthusiasm over doing chores, for instance. Okay, so the kid's a bit lazy. A character flaw, but not a crime.

"Rick is just going to have to insist about the garage," she says. My defenses rise.

"Maybe someone should help him clean it up." I hear the tension in my own voice and fully expect her to apologize.

Instead, she turns and looks me squarely in the eyes. "No one helped him come up with a humiliating poem about poor Ms. Clark, did they? Honestly. How will he ever learn if no one holds him accountable for his actions?"

"He is being held responsible. He's raking leaves and cleaning the garage, plus he's grounded from TV for a month. What do you want me to do, lock him in the wood-shed without supper every night after school?" So what if Greg's outlandish statement was the first thing that came to mind?

"I just think it's one thing to dole out punishment when you're angry. Another to stay committed to it. And clearly, he's being let off the hook. My garage still isn't even halfway clean, and I saw your yard, Claire. Leaves everywhere, bags lying about like they've been filled and dumped back out. And as far as TV goes, he still gets to watch TV on Monday nights and you let him play video games." She shakes her head as we pull into the church parking lot. "I just don't see how you can call that his punishment."

Well, when you look at it that way . . .

Our conversation comes to an abrupt halt. Partly because I'm going to slug her if we don't stop talking about my boy. Partly because we've arrived at the church. I feel Darcy's tension. I know she's leading Bible study today, and I have a little sense of glee that she's so nervous. Okay, it's not nice. But it isn't nice of her to talk about my son. So there. Our relationship has definitely regressed in the last few minutes.

Suddenly she turns to me and grabs my hand. She's shaking. "Claire, pray for me."

I gulp a huge amount of air and feel it come back in a burp. "Excuse me," I whisper. Her wedding ring set is gouging into my palm. Sheesh, she should get those sized so the rock doesn't turn around. The pain brings me to clarity and I realize that to deny her my prayers would prove my jealousy, my resentment, my eternal anger that she has a wonderful marriage to Rick, the toad-sucking cheat.

I gather myself and bow my head to murmur a mostly heartfelt prayer. When we look up, her eyes are filled with tears. "Thank you. I can do this."

"Of course you can." I squeeze her hand. "God wouldn't have put you in this position if He weren't going to equip you to succeed."

Words are true. Attitude stinks. Darcy sees truth minus attitude and reaches out. Her embrace lasts only a second. My shame just won't quit.

Lord, when am I going to get over it?

Ten minutes till one. I've been home all of one hour since ladies' Bible study, which was a rousing success for Darcy and ended in her being named to plan the Christmas luncheon. (Wouldn't you know it? Look what my prayer accomplished.) My morning was uncomfortable. Darcy's success is great, but leaves me feeling like a failure for some reason. I have no time to analyze because I just happen to notice the blinking light on my answering machine. I push the button and keep my attention focused on the device like it's going to be offended if I look away while its talking.

"Claire, this is Greg. There's—uh—another situation with Shawn. Can you come in?"

Groan!

What could it possibly be this time? I leave the house without even bothering to check my makeup. The child is going to land me in an early grave. I try to understand how on earth he could be my angel boy—sensitive, loving, Mommy's little lamb—at home and this . . . this . . . troublemaker at school. It doesn't make a bit of sense to me, but I have every intention of getting to the bottom of it.

Class is in session when I arrive. I tap and open Greg's door. He smiles at me and gets up. After saying something to his TA, he heads toward me. "Class, read for a few minutes. Mitch is in charge until I get back."

I look around, but there is no sign of my boy. My heart plummets. "Where's Shawn?"

Greg takes my elbow and ushers me into the hallway.

"He's in the principal's office."

"Is it that bad? What did he do?"

We start down the hall toward the office. "More poetry about Ms. Clark."

"Oh, no. What is it going to take to get through to that kid? Do you think someone is forcing him to write that stuff?"

Greg stops mid-step. He stares down at me from his

more than six feet height. His eyes are filled with disbelief. "You're kidding, right?"

"I wouldn't kid about a thing like this."

"Sorry, but I thought you must be. Look, no one forces Shawn to do anything. He's one of the toughest kids in my class."

Well, wouldn't Tommy like to hear that? There'd be no more teasing Shawn about being a sissy! I can't help the sense of satisfaction I feel at the news. Still . . . "I just don't feel like we're talking about the same kid."

"Then he should be in showbiz, because he can obviously act."

I'm not dignifying that little comment with a reply. Instead, I stalk off down the hall toward the office. Greg is on my heels. I can hear his shoes on the waxed tile. "Don't go in there with an attitude, Claire. That's not going to do anyone a bit of good. Ms. Clark is livid and demanding his suspension."

My jaw drops as I whip around. I come face-to-chest with him. He grips my arms to steady me, then steps back. I lift my chin so that I look him in the eye. "Suspension?"

A shrug lifts his well-muscled shoulders. "This is his second offense."

"Offense. Isn't that a bit strong? What, is he a criminal now?"

"Don't discount what he's done just because you love him. Ms. Clark is the one who has been wronged. She's humiliated."

I don't want to admit how ticked off I am. Greg is quickly losing his appeal to me. So he just better watch it.

Shawn is sitting on a blue-plastic chair when I walk into the office. He looks up and tries on a smile as our eyes connect. But I'm having none of that charm. Apparently my expression conveys my fury, because his face blanches. I glare at him and he ducks his chin.

"Oh, Ms. Everett. You're here." The sixty-year-old substitute secretary scrambles to her feet. "I'll let Mr. Cross know."

"Thank you."

She comes back a second later. "He says go on in."

My heart rate starts to go up as I walk toward *the office*. Yikes. What is it about the principal that's so scary? I was such a nerd in school, the only time I ever went to the principal was to deliver something from one of my teachers. So it's not like I have bad memories to draw upon that justify my fear. It's crazy.

I'm aware that Greg is still following. I guess he's the witness for the prosecution. Or the prosecutor.

Mr. Cross greets me from across his desk. He doesn't even have the decency to stand. Chivalry is dead indeed.

Well, maybe not. Greg holds my chair as I sit. I have to concentrate to stay mad at him when he sends me a supportive smile.

"So . . ." Mr. Cross is staring at a white sheet of notebook paper. I dread the thought of what he's reading.

He clears his throat and without another word, slides it across the sleek wood finish. With trembling fingers I retrieve my son's incriminating evidence. I look down, swallow hard, and start to read silently.

> *Dad's garage is clean*
> *Mom's leaves are ra-ked*

This broken word gives me a dreaded premonition.

> *I still wish I could see*
> *Ms. Clark naked.*

It's not funny anymore. The first one could have been a fluke. A boyish prank. This one he had to really think about: ra-ked, naked. That's clever. Too disgustingly clever. I'm so humiliated!

"I don't know what to say." I look up from the poem and meet the principal's eyes. They are smiling, despite his straight-lined mouth. The guy is actually thinking this is funny.

He must see my shock, because he wipes the amusement from his face lickety-split. "Mrs. Frank."

"Ms. Everett." How many times do I have to correct these people?

"I beg your pardon?"

"My ex-husband's wife is Mrs. Frank. I took my last name back."

"Oh. Sorry. Ms. Everett, then." He leans back in his chair and folds his arms across his chest. Totally closed off. "It seems as though Shawn didn't get the picture the first time he wrote such a note. Last time he missed a couple of weeks of recess. This time his punishment will have to fit the crime."

"'Crime' is a little strong . . . ," I begin.

Greg sits forward. "Mr. Cross. I'd like to suggest in-school suspension for him. Shawn has never gotten in trouble be-fore in school. Not even once since he started kindergarten. That's pretty good for a sixth grader."

"I don't know . . . Ms. Clark was pretty adamant."

"Since when do you allow the school secretary to dole out punishments to students?" I can't help it. Anger shoots through me at the thought of that haughty woman deciding my son's fate.

"She's the one who was wronged."

"All the more reason for you not to let her decide. Good grief. How objective can she be? And for the record, how appropriate is it for an elementary school secretary to be wearing skintight clothing? Every time I've seen the woman she's wearing a plunging neckline. Does she really think little boys aren't going to notice?"

"Sexual harassment isn't acceptable in any case," the principal replies. "Regardless of a woman's attire."

"Really?" This man is just annoying me. "Well, what would you do if one of the eighth-grade girls showed as much cleavage as that secretary?"

He smirks and so does Greg.

"Well, okay, but if she wore revealing clothing? My kids have all gone to this school since kindergarten. I know there is a dress code of sorts spelled out in the handbook. If girls aren't allowed to wear anything revealing, then I fail to see the reasoning behind allowing the secretary to do so." I've worked myself up into full-blown indignation. "Unless you like a little eye candy strutting around the office."

Greg's hand presses against mine. He's telling me to leave well enough alone. But it's not his kid who is being mistreated here. I wonder how silent he would be given the same circumstances. I frown and jerk my hand away. I'm about to give the principal what for, but Greg beats me to the punch.

"Mr. Cross. In-school suspension is appropriate for a sec-

ond offense. Shawn didn't harm anyone. He didn't verbally
assault anyone. He wrote a poem and read it on the playground."

My jaw drops. "He read it on the playground?" I picture
him standing in the center of the merry-go-round, his stage,
shouting his indecent poetry all across the playground. Just
wait until I get that kid home.

The principal sits forward and clasps his hands together
on the desktop. "All right. In-school suspension. Two weeks.
But one more incident like these two, and I'm suspending
him for ten days." His sea-green eyes focus on mine and I
know he means it.

"Thank you," I say grudgingly. I stand, and both men follow my example.

The principal walks me to the door. At this close proximity, his Polo cologne is so strong I'm afraid I might get a
nosebleed. "Take him home for the rest of the day. The
school day is almost over anyway. Tomorrow he'll begin the
day in the counselor's office. And that's where he'll do his
work until he's off ISS."

Greg and I leave Mr. Cross's office together. Shawn is still
perched on the same chair. I motion for him to come on.
"Go get your schoolbag and get to the van."

Subdued, he obeys. I turn to Greg. "I guess I owe you a
thank-you for keeping Shawn in school."

"You're welcome."

"I just don't get it, Greg. Shawn isn't like this."

He opens the door for me. We step out of the school office and straight into the cafeteria.

"Would you permit me to give you my opinion?"

I shrug. It can't hurt. "Sure. What's your theory for my son's about-face?"

"I think Shawn is starving for attention."

Is he kidding? Shawny is the only one of my children who does get my attention. He's the only one who wants anything to do with me. "I spend a lot of time with him."

He doesn't have a chance to answer as Shawn has returned, his backpack slung over his right shoulder.

"Thanks again for going to bat for us, Greg. I really appreciate it." Even if he is wrong about the cause of Shawny's sudden splurge of perverted poetry.

I am so angry with my son that we don't speak until we reach the van. We get in, buckle up, and I start the engine. Then I look at him and say the first thing that comes to mind.

"For your information, the garage is *not* clean and the leaves are *not* ra-ked."

13

My arm is throbbing when we walk through the door. My head isn't far behind in the pain department. I recognize my state of mind as that place just between "I need a candy bar" and "Give me a whole case of chocolate; I'm about to blow a gasket."

I need to take a little time to calm down, and then call Rick before I decide what to do with Shawn this time.

"Are you going to beat me, Mom?" His enormous blue eyes are liquid pools and my heart wrenches.

"Of course I'm not going to beat you." Good grief. When have I ever laid a hand on that kid? And could that possibly be the problem? "I can't speak for your dad, though. He might spank you this time." Over my charred, dead body. Still, a little fear might help his behavior the rest of the afternoon.

Shawn plunges his head into my midsection, momentarily cutting off my breath. "Do we have to tell him about it?"

I pull away and cup his round little face in my left hand. I lift his chin so I can look him in the eye. "You know we do."

I'm a little taken aback by the quick anger that shoots to his eyes. "I don't see why. He doesn't even live here. He's not like a real dad." He jerks out of my arms and slings his backpack across the room. I watch horrified as the Thomas

Kinkade print hanging on my wall, just underneath a leafy swag, begins to sway. My breath catches in my throat, and for a millisecond I think the frame will right itself.

Crash!

As if in slow motion, I turn my gaze on my hooligan of a son. His eyes go wide and as I stand there waiting for remorse, he buzzes by me before I can snatch him back. He pounds up the stairs. In shock, I stand looking at the broken glass, the backpack. Roaring begins in my ears. I snatch up the phone and dial Rick's office. The secretary starts to put me off. But I'm having none of that. I don't care if he's performing a lobotomy (which gynecologists rarely do), I'm going to speak to him.

"Look, Angela. You know dadgum well who this is. I have to speak with my hus—" Good grief! "—Dr. Frank immediately. This concerns his son."

"Yes, Ms. Everett," the long-suffering, barely out of high school receptionist says with a sigh. "I'll see what I can do." Click. Now I'm on hold.

I listen to eighties tunes for five minutes until Rick's voice finally interrupts Phil Collins singing "A Groovy Kind of Love."

"Claire? What's going on? I have a loaded schedule this afternoon."

"We need to talk about Shawn again. He wrote another poem."

A groan escapes his throat and makes its way through the line.

"What now?"

I give him the *Reader's Digest* version. "I think we need to get him into counseling, Rick."

Another groan. "Do you realize that means family counseling? We'll all have to go."

Ew.

Still, if it will address these issues he's obviously facing.

"Okay, look. I don't like that thought either, but he's obviously dealing with some things. Now is the time to get him help, before he ends up in jail."

"Jail?" Rick gives an exasperated huff. "Isn't that overreacting a little?"

"I'm sure every parent of a kid in jail wishes they'd gotten their child help when he first started showing signs of trouble."

Hesitation from him. "Okay, that might be a valid point. Do you want to look for a counselor, or should I?"

"Well, you're the one with all the doctor friends. Just make sure you get someone who is certified in family counseling, specializes in dealing with children, and I definitely want a Christian."

"In other words, you want me to look for someone, but make sure he meets your standards?" His sarcasm isn't lost on me. But I don't have the energy to go there.

"Yes. Get a referral from one of your friends if you want, but I don't think it's a good idea for us to actually take him to a friend. Shawn won't feel as though he can open up freely."

"All right. Look, Claire. I'll see what I can do. But I have to get back to work now. My patients are getting . . . impatient."

He sniggers, I groan. The guy never has been any good at discerning the dorky jokes from the good ones.

We hang up. Exhaustion overwhelms me and my arm hurts like crazy. My heart aches even more. My Shawny in need of counseling. This is *not* the way I envisioned my time off. By now, we should be bonding as a family. We should be the Cleavers, darn it. Not the Conners from *Roseanne*. I head to the medicine cabinet and reach for the ibuprofen. After swallowing three, I grab a trash bag and drag myself back to the living room.

One-handed, I labor to clean up the glass. When pain jabs my fingers, I pull back quickly, tears filling my eyes. Not from the sting of a pricked finger, not from the sight of my own blood trickling out. From frustration, fear, a little—okay, a lot—of anger. I just wanted to do things right. And I'm failing miserably.

My Shawny. The one child I thought I could count on not to give me any trouble. We are a dysfunctional family. And I'm smart enough to know that dysfunctional families are not grown overnight. My family is falling apart, and I'm solely to blame. Well, and Rick.

The doctor, who looks suspiciously like an older version of Greg, stares at me over a pair of half-glasses. "I'm ready to diagnose your son."

He gives no indication as to whether or not this is good news or bad news, so I sit still, my hands clasped demurely in my lap. For some reason, I am wearing a miniskirt and orange panty hose. I don't know why I'm wearing those things. Weirder still, Mom is sitting on top of the doctor's desk, playing with the pencils in his pencil holder. She's swinging her legs and her four-inch heels thump against the desk with each swing. I want to ask her to please come down from the desk, but the doctor is about to speak.

"Mrs. Frank."

"Ms. Everett," Darcy and I say at the same time. Darcy? When did she get here? I look at her and she sticks out her tongue at me.

My jaw drops, but she just grins and looks away as though I'm not important enough to even bother with.

She's sitting in Rick's lap, in a tight-fitting shirt that needs to be buttoned up at least three more buttons, but she's suddenly looking very Anna Nicole Smithish in the button area, and I realize there's no way such a feat is possible.

Hmmm. Something's wrong here.

"So anyway," Doctor Greg is saying, "As I was saying, I have discovered your son's entire problem, and it can be solved today with a simple action."

Relief shoots through me like lightning down a TV antenna. "We'll do anything, Doctor. Just tell us, what can we do for our son?" Speaking of TV, why do I sound like a really bad actress on *Days of Our Lives*?

He ignores me and stares at Rick, who has his nose buried in Darcy's very blonde, very big hair.

With an exasperated huff I reach out and slug him. "Pay attention."

Tossing me a glare, he settles his hand on Darcy's hip and looks up at the doctor. "Yeah?" he says, like he might have when we were nineteen.

What is going on?

"I'm afraid the boy's entire problem is his mother."

I gasp.

"I knew it!" Darcy hops to her feet—which are bare, by the way—and gets in my face. "It's all your fault," she sings in a taunting melody, and suddenly I realize her belly is bulging with pregnancy. "All your fault."

Ooh, if she wasn't barefoot and pregnant, I'd . . .

Rick looks seriously at the doctor. "I've known for some time Claire is a terrible influence on the boy. But what can a father do? The courts have spoken."

Doctor Greg steeples his fingers across his desk. "Give me a moment to think about your solution." He sighs in ecstasy as Mom rubs his *temples*.

Mom! For crying out loud.

"Doctor?" Rick prods. "What should I do? My son means everything to me."

"Sure he does, you snake," I explode. "That's why you walked out on him to be with Bimbette, here."

"Do you see what we have to put up with? Day and night. It's always the same." Darcy makes mouth motions with her thumb and fingers. "Yak-yak-yakity-yak."

The doctor nods in sympathy. "I see no other alternative."

"What?" I say, feeling suspiciously like I'm not going to like the forthcoming solution.

"You'll have to kill her."

Mom looks up and finally speaks. "Yes, I suppose that's for the best. I mean, look, I had to travel all the way across the country to get away from her."

Across the country. Right. All two states.

Shawn comes forward. I hold out my arms to him, tears flowing down my cheeks at the betrayal in this room. "Come here, baby," I say. "I'm finding you a different doctor."

"Want to hear my new poem, Mom?"

"Okay." I'm dubious. A little fearful even and not entirely convinced this doctor was a good choice.

Violets are blue
Roses are red
I'll be all better
Once Mommy is dead.

Kill her
Kill her
Kill her

I feel a scream tighten my throat, but no sound comes out.

"M-om, are you dead?"

"What?"

Ari's standing over me. "Are you okay?"

Thank God. I'm not dead.

"You scared me half to death," she says, anger edging her voice. "What are you doing down there?"

The fuzz is clearing from my brain and I take stock of my surroundings. "I was cleaning up the glass from the picture."

I remember more. Overwhelmed, I'd known I needed to pray, so I got on my knees in front of the recliner. "I guess I fell asleep."

That dream must have been punishment for not hanging in there for the entire prayer. I never planned on falling asleep. I was only going to pray until time to pick the kids up from . . .

The kids! I forgot to pick them up. Wait a minute. "Hey, how'd you get home?"

"Mr. Lewis saw us waiting," Ari said. "Thanks a lot, by the way."

"Greg brought you?"

"I hope you don't mind."

Dread slides through me at the sound of his masculine voice. I turn ever so slightly and look up from my lowly position.

"I appreciate it."

He reaches down. "Let me help you up from there."

How about taking me away from all this, Sir Greg? But then, he wants me dead!

Leery, I take his hand.

Did he just grunt when he lifted me up? Ugh. Why didn't I just use the ottoman for support and get up without his help?

"Thanks." I can't quite meet his gaze. "And thanks for driving the kids."

"No problem. I was headed this way, anyway."

Oh? Was he coming to see me? Hope shoots through me like a quiver full of Cupid's arrows.

The phone rings and Ari dashes past me to the kitchen. "It's for me," she hollers, even though I'm standing right there. "I'll get it in the kitchen."

I toss Greg an apologetic look for my daughter's rudeness. "You were saying you had to come this way anyway?" To ask me out?

"I'm meeting the realtor at your mom's house." Bummer. Or not. Greg just down the block. That could work.

"Do you want something to drink? I haven't seen her go by yet."

Oh, groan. Stupid thing to say. So obvious.

He gives me that lopsided grin.

I feel a blush steal across my cheeks.

Thankfully, Jake saves me. He trots into the room, pushes a beanbag chair from the corner to right in front of the entertainment center, grabs the game controller, and switches on the TV. Then he flops down on his stomach across the beanbag chair. He's ready to go.

"Hey, wait a sec, sport."

"What?" He doesn't bother to look away from the little video figures winding their way through a dark forest.

"Did you do your homework?"

"No."

"Do you have any?"

"Yes." Still he doesn't look up.

"Turn off the TV and go do it, then."

"Can I wait until I die?"

I roll my eyes and look up at Greg, whose face is masked in amusement. "I bet no one from our mothers' generation ever had to hear those words."

"Maybe the Dark Ages," he comes back.

I laugh. Then straighten up at the thought of some poor child with the plague. I scowl. "Not funny."

He chuckles that wonderful, deep chuckle.

Still reveling in the joy of shared amusement with a guy I have a crush on, I have a little trouble working up a stern voice. "Jake, turn it off. You can die later."

Tommy barrels through the door as Jakey throws the controller and pushes himself up.

"Watch your attitude, young man," I call after my stomping-off son.

"I didn't do anything," Tommy says in a tone that makes me wonder what he's been up to.

"I was talking to Jakey."

"Oh. Why is there a car parked in Granny's driveway? Is she moving back?"

Not if I can help it. I've suddenly lost that overwhelming sense of loneliness. This new development with Greg has me believing in destiny all over again. And we don't want Mom to miss hers.

"That's my cue." Greg sends me a wink.

I walk him to the door. "Sorry things are so chaotic around here."

"Kids and chaos go together."

That reminds me. "Hey, how come I've never seen your daughter?" In need of an answer to this sudden probing thought, I walk him to the porch.

He leans toward me and gives me a wry grin. "I have her locked away in a tower until some young man worthy of her comes along."

The guy is just too cute. But seriously. I go to church with him. Have never seen her. He teaches at my kids' school. Never seen her.

A knowing look flickers in his eyes. He gives a short laugh. "Don't worry. I do have a daughter, and no she isn't locked in a tower somewhere. We're living with my mom while I look for a house."

Disappointment kicks me in the gut. He lives with his mother? Figures.

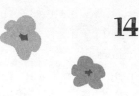

14

I step inside, trying not to think about the mama's boy who left his truck in my driveway and walked down the block. Does this mean he plans to stop in and say good-bye before he goes home? Oops. I guess I *am* thinking about him.

Pondering this last, I'm taken by surprise at the sight that greets me when I enter the living room. I stop mid-stride. "What are you doing, Toms?"

Tommy turns around from his place by the wall. "The picture fell. I was putting it back up." He gives me a "Duh, what does it look like I'm doing?" look and finishes straightening the glassless print. "What happened to it anyway?"

"An accident."

"Looks like someone threw a ball or something."

If anyone should be able to read the signs of destruction, it's him. Since he learned to walk I've had to clean up more broken windows, knickknacks, and picture frames than breakage from all of the other kids combined.

"Anyway, thanks for putting the picture back up for me."

He's been acting so much better since Jakey barfed on him.

A shrug lifts his shoulders, and I notice that he's beginning to fill out. His muscles becoming more defined. I should have seen this coming, but still it takes me by surprise. Plus it makes me a little sad to think of him growing up. I don't feel like I've had enough time with him. As though his childhood just slipped by me.

"What?" he squeaks, then colors.

I snap out of my reverie before I grab him and kiss his whole face. "What, what?" I ask. The picture of innocence.

"Why are you staring at me?" His face is clouded in suspicion.

I stick out my tongue. "Who's staring?"

"Whatever, dude." He shakes his head and walks toward the kitchen.

"Don't call me dude," I call after him.

"Whatever."

This is going well. I follow him into the kitchen. I mean, I have nothing better to do, right? And the goal is to bond with my kids. Can't really do that if the kids aren't around.

Ugh. I wish I'd just stayed in the living room and minded my own business. Tommy has the fridge open and is drinking from the milk carton. "Ew, Tommy. Get a glass."

He pops the lid back on the container and sets it on the shelf. Wiping away the milk mustache with the back of his hand, he kicks the fridge closed. "Don't need one."

"Don't do that again. It's nasty." Note to self: buy a new gallon of milk.

"Whatever."

I'm sorry, but that's the last straw. He's said that word to me three times in three minutes. Enough already. "Is that the only word you know?"

"Maybe."

Hey, guess what? That was a bad answer. "You're

grounded from using that word." Did I really just ground him from a word?

"What word?"

"'*Whatever*.'" I mean it. I put my hand on my hip and dare him to defy me.

Undaunted, he does just that. "You can't ground someone from a word."

"I'm your mother. I can ground you from whatever I want."

"You just said 'whatever.'" His lips are tugged into a smirk and I have to fight to keep from smirking right back. Discipline is so not my strong suit.

"I didn't say it like that. And I mean it. You're grounded from that word."

"But it doesn't make sense."

"I don't care what makes sense. You can't use *whatever* for a week. It's time to break that habit."

"And what if I still use it?" The challenge in his eyes raises my hackles.

"Then I'm taking away your skateboard."

His eyes grow wide for a split second, then he composes himself. The epitome of cool dudeness. "Wha—" He shrugs as the wheels of his mind come to a screeching halt on the edge of that word. "Fine," he bites out. "One week."

Score one for Mom. I'm starting to feel a little like my old self. Saucy. I like it.

"Speaking of my skateboard." He grabs his schoolbag off the table and rifles through it for a sec. "I need this signed," he says, shoving a sheet of paper at me. Prickles of panic needle through me. Notes from school that need my signature usually indicate something I'm going to be really ticked about. "What now?"

"It's just a permission slip. Don't flip."

"I never flip," I snap. "And watch your attitude."

"Wh— Yeah, okay."

This is going to be fun.

I read over the form. It isn't from the school. "What is it?"

"Skateboarding contest. I need to take it back by tomorrow to get on the list."

"Whoa, boy. Not so fast. Where'd you get it?"

"Dan's mom owns The Board. They're sponsoring a contest next week."

"Are you kidding me? There is a thirty-dollar entrance fee! What are they sponsoring?"

"Mrs. Ireland is providing all the food and drinks. All we have to do is bring our board and the permission slip."

"And thirty big ones. Not a chance."

"Please, Mom. If I pay my own way?"

"With what, your dimples?"

He blushes at the reference to those gorgeous valleys in his cheeks he'd rather forget exist. "I have all that money in the bank."

Oh, no, he didn't just suggest using his college money for a stupid skateboarding entrance fee.

Wordlessly, I walk to the sink and turn on the faucet, let the water run for a few seconds, then turn it off.

I turn to my son, who is frowning like I've totally lost my mind.

"Hear that?" I ask as the water gurgles through the pipes.

"Yeah."

"What is it?"

"Uh, water draining from the sink, maybe?" His sarcasm isn't helping his plight any.

"Wrong. It's the sound thirty dollars makes when you spend it to enter a skateboarding contest."

"It's not money down the drain." Ah, the boy gets it at least. "First prize is a Zero skateboard."

"And this is supposed to impress me?"

An exasperated sigh pushes through his lungs. "A professional skateboard. It costs over a hundred dollars retail."

Hmm . . . maybe thirty bucks isn't way overpriced. And since when is my son using words like *retail*? "What's second prize?"

"Skateboard shoes. Vans."

Okay, I've shelled out seventy dollars for those, so I do know what Vans are. Not bad.

"Third?"

"Three-month membership to The Board."

"What does a membership consist of?"

"Unlimited skateboarding for a year."

"How much is a membership? I didn't even know they offered them."

"Fifteen dollars a month or two dollars every time you go."

I do some mental number crunching. Every time he asks to go, I give him two dollars. And that's at least three times a week. That's twenty-four dollars a month! I hear the sound of nine bucks a month swishing down the drain. Six dollars a week for five weeks would cover that entrance fee.

"Get my purse out of the living room. It's on the coffee table."

"Yes! Thanks, Mom." I brace myself for a hug. But it

doesn't come. I'm a little disappointed, but I'm happy also, because he's so happy.

He stands beaming as I fish through my purse for a pen and thirty dollars. Gurgle, gurgle, gurgle.

Left-handed, I sign as neatly as possible, fold the paper, and hand it back to him.

"Think you can win something?"

"I know I can. Want me to show you some moves?"

The kid's actually offering me a bit of his life. No way am I turning that down. "Sure."

"We have to go outside."

We head through the living room and out the front door. He scowls when we reach the porch. "Lewis's truck is in the way."

"Mr. Lewis."

"What's his truck doing in the way?"

"He's looking to buy Granny's house."

"I wish she didn't move."

This sudden admission takes me by surprise. The kid isn't exactly forthcoming with his feelings. But he's gotten close to Granny lately. Helps her take out garbage, carries in wood for her fireplace.

"You know what I'm really going to miss most?" he says, turning to look in that direction as though by doing so will bring her back.

"What?" I swallow hard.

"Hot chocolate and cinnamon toast."

"You can have those things at home. I'll fix them for you when it gets cold out."

He shrugs. "Wh— Okay. I'm going in."

"What about showing me your moves?"

"I can't until Lewis moves his truck."

"*Mister* Lewis."

"Yeah. Mr. Lewis."

He slams back into the house. I'm about to follow, but I'm caught by a gentle autumn breeze. I sit on the porch swing and gather in the smells of burning leaves somewhere in the neighborhood combined with the distinct fragrance of coming rain. I love autumn rains. They come to wash away the dust and heat of summer and to get the earth ready for the beauty of winter ice and snow.

Aren't I just the optimist tonight? Ice and snow are treacherous. Or they can be. Just as treacherous as they are beautiful. But I need a good perspective tonight. I glance down the block and see Greg walking back. I wave. A smile stretches his lips as he waves back. "Hey, looks like we're going to be neighbors if everything works out on the business end."

"Mom's going to be glad to hear that." And oh, baby, am I ever glad! Oh, Lord, I'm a desperate housewife.

He stops in front of the house and I walk down the steps to join him. We are standing on the sidewalk. Two people just shooting the breeze. Nothing to get excited about. But I can't quite convince my heart of that, and it insists upon doubling in beats per minute. We are standing fairly close and he looks down at me, his dark eyes gentle and soft.

"I have a favor to ask of you."

Anything, Romeo. Ask and it's yours.

"Do you think I could borrow your mom's key so I can show Sadie around?"

"No problem. Do you want to come for supper?" Oh shoot. I didn't thaw anything out.

"Another time. I'm sure Mom will already have something cooking."

Whew. Dodged that bullet, and note to self: Don't invite gorgeous neighbor for supper unless you know you have something decent to serve him. Especially if you ever plan to snag him into a date. And did he really say, "Another time"?

"Okay, no problem."

"I'll be back around seven to get the key, if that's okay with you."

"Sounds fine."

He climbs into the Avalanche and cranks the engine. A smile and a wave follow before he backs out of the drive. I stand there like a lovesick puppy, watching him drive away into the sunset.

The door swings open and shut behind me. "'Bout time," Tommy grouses. "You ready for me to show you some of my moves?"

"Yep."

"Okay, but don't flip out when you see all the jumping and dangerous stuff."

"Dangerous?"

"I said don't flip out."

"I never flip out."

"Yeah . . ."

I say it for him, "Whatever."

I watch him, impressed, for about an hour, with only a slight time-out when the pizza delivery guy comes, and I think the kid just might win that board. He has a great chance anyway. And he's actually smiled at me five times if my count is on. Four, if the last one was a grimace of pain when he missed the board and fell on his backside.

"Hey, Mom. Come learn how to do a kickflip."

"Are you kidding me?"

"No. You can do it. Dan's mom boards all the time."

"Well, goodie for her. I'm not getting on that thing. I'll kill myself."

"Oh, well, that's a good thing to say."

"Hey, speaking a positive confession is one thing. Stating the facts is another. And if I get on that board, I'm going to die. Or hurt myself at least."

"What are you, chicken?"

Okay, now that was uncalled for.

"Bwark, bwark, bwark."

Oh, he is so grounded.

"All right, smart guy. Show me that kickflip. But if I hurt my hand . . ."

"You're not going to be skateboarding with your hands."

"Well, you weren't supposed to be skateboarding with your behind but it didn't keep you from falling on it, now did it?"

He doesn't dignify my comment with a reply. "The first thing you have to learn is how to stand on the board without falling off."

I'm amazed at how hard it is to balance, and a new appreciation for my son's talents emerges. I never land a kickflip, and I fall off the board at least ten times. Still, by the time Greg's truck pulls down the street, I'm sweating like a marathon runner. My son slings his gangly, sweaty arm around me and gives me a one-armed hug. "You did good, Mom."

He snatches up his board and heads back toward the steps.

Ari is standing on the porch, watching. "Cool," she says, then turns and follows her brother inside.

"Taken aback" is about the mildest phrase I can think of to describe the shock I'm feeling. On another level, I'm inundated with pride, joy, a sense of peace, and oh, yeah, maybe I'm not such a bad mom after all.

15

Okay, I'm definitely a poor excuse for a mother. At least according to Rick's mom. When you marry a man, you marry his whole family, so how come when you divorce a man, you still have a nosy mother-in-law who thinks she can call and tell you how to raise her grandkids? Blech.

My keeping-up-with-the-Joneses, member of the DAR, president of the garden club, and member-in-good-standing of the country club (naturally) former mother-in-law is not happy with the choice we have made to enter into family counseling. And, rightfully so, she holds me 100 percent responsible for the suggestion. Rick must have wimped out and put the heat on me. Like he's always done.

"I just don't see why normal, productive citizens have to get *therapy*." She says *therapy* like it's a bad word. I'm not sure what she's saying next because my ear itches and I move the phone to the other one.

". . . would think if they knew their doctor had to go see a psychiatrist."

Okay, I can figure that one out. "Trust me, Rosette." (No, I'm not kidding. Her parents actually named her that.) "Rick's not going to lose any patients over this. And we aren't seeing a psychiatrist. We're seeing a family counselor."

"Well, I don't see the necessity of airing your dirty laundry to a perfect stranger in the first place. In my day, we dealt with our own matters and left other people to theirs."

With a great amount of difficulty, I refrain from suggesting that perhaps if her little family had considered counseling after the first, second, or tenth time Rick Sr. cheated on Rosette, perhaps their son's marriage wouldn't have fallen apart in the first place. But I manage a large amount of self-control and keep my mouth shut. Time for a switcheroo in topic.

"So, did Rick tell you Ari is driving now?"

A gasp loud enough to break my eardrum shudders through the speaker in my ear, and for a second I wish I'd eased her into the new topic.

"When did this happen?" And the ever-silent, but nonetheless understood, *"And why was I not consulted beforehand?"*

"A couple of weeks ago. As a matter of fact, Ari drove me home after my surgery." Oh, I'm so mean, I can't stop myself. I have to say it. "And we only got into two near-accidents. But Rick says she's doing much better. Although she backed into the trash can at his house and dented his fender."

"On the Benz?" Her voice sounds like she swallowed an orange.

Oh, yeah. The sleek, brand-new, black-as-night Mercedes Benz. Once perfect, now with a dented fender. Life is good.

"Really, Claire, you should teach the girl to drive in your van. One more scratch on that old thing won't hurt. But the Mercedes! That's going to cost a fortune to fix."

"Well, he could always turn it in to the insurance company." Snicker, snicker. I'm sure she hears amusement in my voice.

"There's no need to enjoy Rick's misfortune so much. And you claim to be a Christian. I thought Christians were supposed to be loving."

My former mother-in-law doesn't even pretend to be a Christian, but boy does she grab every opportunity to use her limited knowledge against me when I don't behave in her best interest. Hey, guess what else Christians aren't supposed to do? Picture themselves with their fingers around their ex-monster-in-law's throat choking the life . . . Okay, that was overboard. But, good grief. The woman would make a preacher seriously consider emitting a four-letter word. I glance at the clock. It's getting close to seven. "Excuse me, Rosette," I say, interrupting whatever she's saying, which, no doubt, isn't flattering to me. "I'm expecting company in a few minutes so I need to go."

Okay, "company" is perhaps a bit of a stretch. But I find it painful to simply think of Greg as a man who wants a key. I prefer to think of him as the man who made an excuse to pick up a key so he can see me again, if ever-so-briefly. Smile.

"Oh? Is one of your girlfriends coming over?"

Smooth, Rosette. Real smooth.

"No."

"Well, I know it can't be a man." That smug assurance in her voice jabs my pride like a sword.

"As a matter of fact, yes, it is."

"You're dating?"

"Hard to believe I could, isn't it?"

"Hey, Mom," Tommy calls. "Lewis just pulled in."

"Sorry, Rosette. I have to go. He's here."

I hang up with only a slight feeling that sending a wrong

impression might be considered the sin of lying. I offer a hasty prayer of repentance just in case. And fluff my hair on the way into the living room.

When I get there, Greg's presence sucks the breath from my lungs. His long legs fill out a pair of snug-fitting faded Levi's, and a gray-and-red Chief's hoodie shows me the guy can pick his teams. Destiny (the sovereign, Jeremiah 29:11 kind) presents a marketable plan to me and I fall for it hook, line, and sinker. I want this man to notice me. To think of me as "date" material. "Wife" material is further reaching than even I want to allow destiny to offer. But a cozy sit-down dinner with a little music in the background would be nice.

He smiles when he sees me. "See, I told you I actually have a daughter."

"Huh?" Oh. Gravy. I didn't even see the kid standing next to him. The beautiful raven-haired child might have been Snow White. Enormous dark eyes and flawless skin. "Oh, Sadie. Of course I've seen you at church. I just can't believe I never connected you to your dad. You look just like him!"

She gives me a gap-toothed grin and I'm hooked. "Everyone says that."

"And they're right."

I reach into my pocket and produce Mom's key. "Here you go."

Rick takes it and in true romantic fashion, his hand brushes mine. I fight to keep from reacting. "We were hoping you'd give us a tour," he says.

Is he serious? I glance up at him through the squinted eyes of skepticism.

"That is," he says haltingly, "if you're not too busy."

Never too busy for you, babe. "Just let me tell the kids." I jog up the stairs, trying to make it appear as effortless as possible just in case he's watching. Once I've turned the corner, out of his sight, I stop and gulp for air, pausing long enough to catch my breath before I walk down the hall. I tap on Ari's door then open it. I don't knock for permission, but rather to let her know I'm there. I mean, I know some people think kids need their "privacy." But I remember being a kid, and personally, I think the only privacy they're entitled to is bathroom times and when they're getting dressed. Other than that, their time is my time. Period.

Ari is at her computer desk. "Hey, Ma. Can you read this over for me? It's a short story for English."

Pride shoots through me. My daughter is a wonderful writer. Much better than I was at her age. So the possibilities for her are endless if she wants to be a writer like her mother. "I'd love to, after I get back from giving Greg a tour of Granny's house."

"I thought you did that the other day."

"This time he wants to show Sadie around."

"Ugh. I hope he doesn't buy it. That kid is such a brat. I'd hate to have her living in Granny's house."

Sadie the angel? "She seems so sweet."

"Ha! The halo is a cover-up for the horns. Trust me."

Worry niggles through me. What if she's right?

"Anyway, run Jake a bath, will you? I shouldn't be very long."

"Why can't Jake run his own bath?"

"Because he forgets about it and the water overflows and floods the bathroom. That's why. Besides, I said so."

She heaves a great sigh and tosses her wireless mouse onto the desk.

"All right. JAKE! BATHTIME."

I cringe. Does she have to yell? What must Greg think? He'll never ask me out if he thinks my kids are unruly . . . The irony of that hits me like a line drive to the gut. He already knows about Shawn. No wonder he's not asking me out!

I give Shawn and Jakey's door a tap. Shawn is lying on his bed, hands behind his head and staring at the ceiling. Exactly the place he's been since he ran upstairs this afternoon. "I'm going to show Mr. Lewis and Sadie Granny's house. I'll be back. Did you do your homework?"

He ignores me.

"Answer me, young man."

He turns his head. "No."

"Then do it. And it had best be done when I get back."

"I don't have any."

"Oh. Well, then. Take a bath after Jakey and then get into your jammies. When I get back we'll read our chapter of *Purpose-Driven Life*. It's your turn to read."

He dismisses me with a nod.

That kid. You'd think someone in the kind of trouble he's in would show a little remorse—or, at the very least, fear.

Last stop, Tommy's room. I tap and enter. Tommy scrambles. My suspicious nature comes to the foreground. "Whatcha doing, Toms?"

"Geez, Mom. Can't you knock?"

"Sure I could." If I wanted to.

He gets my drift and scowls.

"So what were you doing that you don't want me to know about?"

"None of . . . nothing."

Oh, he is so lucky he changed his direction of wording.

"You were obviously doing something. What was it?"

"I'm writing a note."

"A note?" I'm seeing a forged note from his dad or me, excusing him from school without our knowledge. "What kind of a note?"

"To a girl, okay? I like someone."

"Oh, how sweet." I clamp my hand over my mouth. He didn't want to hear that. No wonder he hides his crushes from me. I can't be trusted not to gush over him. I clear my throat. "Sorry."

"She doesn't like me anyway."

The little tease! "What do you mean she doesn't like you? Of course she does." Unless she has mental problems.

"She hates the skateboarder look."

Ah, smart girl. Please, God, let this crush be strong enough to get him over this phase in his life. No more wanting to wear eyeliner or lip rings. No more talk of name changes. I'd be so grateful if You could work that out for me.

"Well, maybe she'll change her mind." I pause. "Unless you'd like to reconsider the long hair and black clothes."

"Nice try." He grins and my heart melts. The boy is still the same on the inside. I don't care what he looks like. Well, I care. But it's not the most important thing.

"I'm going to show Mr. Lewis Granny's house."

"How many times does he have to go through it?"

"This time he's showing Sadie."

"Keep that kid away from me. She drives me crazy."

Two-fer. No wonder Greg can show sympathy to Shawn. He's got a handful himself.

"Finish up your homework if you have any. When I get back we'll do our next chapter in *Purpose-Driven Life*."

He heaves a great sigh. Some things a teenager just can't get excited about, I suppose. But I'm determined to be consistent with this. This is our third night. Third chapter. I'm discovering purpose. They're mostly grumbling.

I head back to the stairs. Greg looks up at me like he's a senior high school boy and I'm his prom date as I descend the steps. He smiles, and he's leaning on the banister in Rhett Butler fashion. My heart plummets as his eyes travel the length of me and back to my face. I look away before I can see the disappointment or disgust in his eyes.

Better just face reality, I tell myself in no uncertain terms. Andy Garcia Eyes can have anyone he wants. And believe me, girlfriend, he doesn't want you.

"All set?" At the sound of Greg's voice I force my eyes back to his. Oddly, there's only kindness—affection even—shining back. I'd love to stay in this eyes-melting-into-each-other moment, but I'm aware of his daughter waiting by the door.

Curious about my kids' attitude about Sadie, I focus my attention on the little girl. Her eyes are widely innocent. Too innocent? I wonder. But when she smiles, I have trouble picturing her as the demoness my children have made her out to be. I find myself drawn to reciprocate the smile. "Ready to see the house? I bet you can't guess what's in the backyard."

"What is it?"

I send her a wink and she grins. I'm charmed. "You'll have to wait until we get there. It's a surprise."

"A surprise?"

"Mmm-hmm. Do you like surprises?"

"Yes!" Her hair bounces and shines with her enthusiastic nod.

We walk to the door and Greg steps back to allow me to precede him onto the porch. What a guy.

He walks beside me, shoulder to shoulder, as his little girl skips ahead of us on the sidewalk. I'm thinking I could get used to seeing his truck in my driveway when he leans in close and keeps his voice quiet. "So what's the surprise?"

Sadie is already making a beeline to the back. "Come on. I'll show you," I say, picking up the pace.

When we catch up to her, Sadie is standing in the middle of the yard. She turns to me. I catch my breath at the disappointment and anger in her eyes. "Where's my surprise?" Her lip is pushed out a bit and her little hands rest impatiently upon teeny, tiny hips.

Oh, boy. I've found the first questionable thing about Greg: Sadie. The kids are right. She's a total brat.

To his credit, Greg hops to it. "Sadie, is that anyway to speak to Ms. Everett?"

Slowly, she shakes her head and drops her gaze.

"You know what to say," he prods.

"Sorry." Or at least that's what I think she said. Her chin is pretty much pressed against her chest.

Greg turns an apologetic gaze on me. "She's gotten a little out of hand since her mother died. My mom hasn't got the heart to discipline her."

"It's okay," I say, somewhat convincingly. *How* long has it been since her mother died?

I've lost all desire to share my tree house with this demanding and somewhat belligerent child. But I can't help but think of how Tommy has changed, and Shawn, too (as I'm discovering), since the divorce. And they still get to see their dad. There's no telling how their personalities might have changed if they had to deal with permanent separation from one parent or the other.

I gather a breath and smile at Sadie, whose eyes still hold a demanding question. At least her body language has calmed down.

"Look up into the big tree in the middle of the yard."

Her little chin rises as she tilts her neck. A gratifying (to me) gasp shoots from her lips. "A tree house! Daddy, look! I have my very own tree house!" She runs for the ladder.

"Sadie, wait!" Greg calls. "It might not be safe."

Figures. She's not stopping. By the time he catches up to her, she's on the second rung. Half expecting her little rump to catch a swat, I'm surprised when Greg catches her close, snuggling her against his chest.

I watch in bemused silence. Methinks the child's grandma isn't the only spoiler in this family.

"Sadie, honey. You can't climb into the tree house by yourself. You could fall and get hurt. And I don't know what I'd do without you."

A daddy and his little girl. What a sight. My heart melts a little more for this man. I'm afraid if I am forced to witness much more of his perfection, I might just lose my heart altogether. A perfectly delicious, if somewhat terrifying, thought.

●　　●　　●

I hear one of the kids splashing around in the tub when I get home forty-five minutes later. Ari's door is closed, as are the boys'. Just as well. I need a few minutes to sort out my thoughts about Greg's spoiled daughter, not to mention the butterflies in my stomach at the memory of Greg's smile.

I'm definitely losing it where this guy's concerned. And so far he's been nothing but friendly. No kisses or hugs, not even a handshake that lasts a bit too long. I think maybe he's just not that in to me. Hmm. Don't they have a book about that? I make a mental note to check it out on Amazon.com next chance I get.

That gives me an idea. I clench and unclench my fingers a few times to test the waters of my wrist pain. Not bad. A slight twinge, but I bet I could check my e-mail. I find myself drawn to my computer like a crazy moth to a flame. E-mail! I need it. I'm dying for some interaction with like-minded individuals.

I tiptoe to my office, fully aware that every person in my life would have a cow if they knew of my intention. But no one intercepts me as I sink into my lovely, black, ergonomically crafted desk chair. I feel the pleasant familiarity of butt-in-chair syndrome as I reach toward my computer. Only guess what? Some smarty has taped the Wal-Mart receipt with my List to my monitor. I can only guess it was Ari. She knows me very well. I snatch it away from the screen and scan the lofty goals I impulsively penned a month ago.

During the next three months I will:
1. Go to church more. (This includes daily prayer time and maybe a Beth Moore Bible study.)

Okay, so far so good. Church attendance is up. And, for the most part, it has nothing whatsoever to do with Greg. Okay, maybe a little. But the Beth Moore Bible study part has nothing to do with him.

2. Clean my house. (Or probably hire someone. My wrists, you know.)

I don't want to talk about it. The cleaning service went bankrupt just before I signed an agreement. No need to point out that perhaps they just weren't that good.

3. Reconnect with my children. (Will have to plan further for this one.)

Monday-night movie night hasn't been wildly successful so far. But I keep hoping. At least my relationship with Tommy is looking up.

4. Exercise—maybe. (But then again, I will be recovering from surgery. Wouldn't want to hurt myself. Could probably walk on the treadmill. We'll play this one by ear.)

Well, okay, I did try this one a few times, but nothing steady yet. I'm still working on the motivation factor. Maybe tomorrow.

5. Figure out why my only socialization revolves around my computer. I mean, I love the writing groups, but does lunch with the girls always have to involve trying to negotiate a turkey sandwich while instant-messaging one-handed?

Of necessity I have not been in contact with my instant-message pals, over the Internet, that is. Made initial friendship with Linda. Although I haven't done much more than say a friendly hello lately. I'll call her later for sure. Darcy . . . Her friendship would be hard to resist if only . . .

    6. *In response to #5—Join ladies' group at church. Perhaps read the book* How to Make Friends and Influence People. *Or maybe one of Dr. Phil's.*

I have, in fact, joined the ladies' Bible study. We are going through a Beth Moore Bible study workbook, and I'm growing spiritually. This makes me happy. I have *not* read *How to Make Friends and Influence People* or any of Dr. Phil's—although that's still not out of the question.

With a great sigh, I look back over the list. Talk about your slow starters.

The pounding bass of some Christian rock band is vibrating my walls, signaling the completion of Ari's homework. I tape my list back to my monitor and head across the room. With one last, longing look at my computer, I switch off the light and go to Ari's room, surprised to find that I'd much rather read my daughter's short story than e-mail anyway.

Maybe I'm making progress after all.

16

8:05 a.m.: Just got back from taking the kids to school. Will walk outside for one hour. I lace up my shoes and head for the door, determination pumping through me like I'm in training for the physical event of a lifetime. I'm ready for this. Time to get serious. No more fooling around with the exercise commitment. Today is the first day of the rest of my life. I will become a lean, mean walking machine.

8:10 a.m.: I am Tough Chick, emerging from the house and walking down the steps to the sidewalk, arms swinging like a power walker. I am Rocky Balboa. *Na-na-naaaaaaaaah . . . Na-na-naaaaaaaaaaaaah . . . Na-na-na-Na-na! . . . Na-na-Na-na-Na-na-na-na-na-Naaaaaaaaaaaaaaah . . . Na-na-NA!*

I go along for a while. I am full of optimism. Walking is not hard, after all. Babies walk.

But my legs are beginning to quiver. Whew. I need to slow down. I'm starting to breathe heavily. Okay, I wonder how long I've been walking. I glance at my watch. Hmmm. Tap it. It seems to be running right. I look again. No kidding? Three minutes. Wow. An hour is a much longer amount of time than one might actually think.

Was that a raindrop? I don't want to get my wristband

wet. Maybe I should just . . . I stare hopefully into a brilliant autumn sun.

Okay, no excuses. I will do this. When the going gets tough, the tough get going. I *will* lose thirty-five pounds and be the me I always knew I could be.

This commercialesque pep talk fills me with renewed determination and spurs me onward. I am invincible. One foot in front of the other. Heel-toe. Heel-toe.

Huffing and puffing, I feel myself running out of steam. Oh, man. How many minutes? I bring my arm up and view the time. What *is wrong* with this stupid watch? I think it's actually going backward.

The cell phone at my waist vibrates. I take the opportunity to stop, lean against an oak bereft of leaves, and answer.

"Are you okay?" the voice on the other end of the line asks.

"Who is this?" I pant in reply.

"It's your mother. Are you okay?"

"I'm fine."

"Why are you breathing so heavy?"

"Exercise."

"Oh!" Why does she sound so surprised? "Well, then I'll let you go so you can finish."

"No!" Oh, please, no. "I'm about done anyway." I check my watch.

8:25 a.m.

Fifteen minutes is a nice start to my goal of walking one hour a day. I will not allow my overachieving alter ego to make me feel like a failure. I got out, I walked, now I'm stopping. So Tough Chick can take her competitive nature and stuff it. Period. Tomorrow I will do better. Today I will sit on the ground surrounded by red and gold leaves, with my back against this mighty oak, and I will enjoy a chat with my mother.

I share with her my heartbreak over Shawn's weird new obsession with the trampy secretary Ms. Clark and consequently the necessity of family counseling.

"Sounds like he wants to get caught, if you ask me," Mom says in her straightforward, in-a-nutshell fashion. "He read his poem on the playground?"

"Yeah."

She starts to laugh.

"Mom! Not funny."

"Sorry, I'm just picturing him standing in the center of the merry-go-round reading his poem."

I wince. I see her point. "Does sound like a cry for help, doesn't it?"

"A little bit."

"I guess the counseling is a good idea."

"When are you starting that?"

"Tomorrow, as a matter of fact."

"I'll pray, honey."

"Thanks, Mom."

So, Rick, Darcy, and I are sitting in the waiting room while family counselor Andy Goldberg, PhD, speaks to our son. Andy is a short but handsome fortyish man with Jewish ancestry and Christian beliefs. He is amazingly kind and was referred to us by our pastor after two of Rick's suggestions turned out to be duds.

The three of us have been silent for fifty-three agonizing minutes, them on one side of the room and me on the other.

So far we have avoided eye contact, but movement from their side gets my attention and like a trained seal I look up. Darcy is staring at me. I feel frumpy, as usual, dressed in brown slacks that are just a little snug. But not as snug as the Lycra hose. I moved like a contortionist as I struggled into these instruments of Satan just to hide the bulges below my behind and on my thighs. The hose are snug on my stomach and cutting into my waist. In short, I'm miserable for more reasons than one, and I'm not positive the torture hose are even working. I'm still feeling a little bulgy.

Darcy, on the other hand, is wearing a very smart navy-blue suit. The hem comes just to the knee, and even sitting down she looks put together. I detect not one wrinkle in her outfit.

"So, what sorts of things do you think he's telling Dr. Goldberg?" Darcy seems nervous, a condition that raises my suspicions. The pain in the lower half of my body, combined with the unbearable wait, has made me cranky. This must be why I spew forth the first thing that pops into my head as I stare into her oh-so-perfectly-made-up China doll face.

"Why? Are you worried?" Why do I do that? I immediately regret my hasty words. I *like* Darcy. I really do. It's her toad-sucking husband that I despise. Problem is, Darcy and Rick go together.

She tenses. Rick's hand slides to her bony knee. He gives her a comforting little squeeze. "Claire, there's no reason to be hateful."

Oh yeah, bud? Are you wearing control-top panty hose? That's all the reason I need. I feel Tough Chick coming on, making it impossible for me to back down and apologize to

Darcy for snapping at her. Pride is an ugly, ugly thing. The thing is, I recognize it for what it is. And still, I can't seem to let it go. I shrug. "I wasn't being hateful, *Rick*," I shoot back, "I was just asking Darcy if perhaps she'd like to tell us anything that might be helpful in trying to figure out this sudden change in our son."

He scowls. "Darcy isn't the problem here."

"Oh, so I guess you're saying it's my fault Shawn is writing soft porn?"

"He didn't say that, Claire." See, this is why I can't be friends with Darcy. She's always on his side.

"Oh, didn't he?" I shoot back with enough venom to silence a mountain lion. She clamps her lips together and sits back, obviously not about to go there with me. I hate the fact that Darcy is taking the high road.

Rick, however, is obviously willing to go down whatever road I'm speeding on because he sits forward and gives me an icy glare. "You really need to deal with your issues."

"And what issues are those, Doctor?"

"You know."

"Oh, you mean the ones inevitably caused by an unfaithful husband's abandonment?"

"For the love of . . ."

The door opens and by unspoken agreement, we straighten up, lest the doctor think we're all nuts.

He stands tall behind our son, a hand resting easily on Shawn's shoulder. "Why don't you have a seat there, bud? Let me have a word with your parents."

I stiffen as Rick and Darcy both stand. But Darcy apparently realizes I'm in no mood to share my parental status with her. She sits.

Rick and I follow the doctor into his office. I glance around. Hmm. No couch. There are, however, a couple of overstuffed chairs and a love seat in one section of the room. On the other side is his desk, a deep cherry with a slate top. He waves us to the two semi-comfortable chairs on one side of his desk while he occupies a brown-leather chair.

"So. What did he say?" I ask.

Dr. Goldberg gives me a smile. His eyes crinkle, and I immediately like him. He has a gentle face that would be easy to trust. "I can only repeat what we discuss if he gives me permission. Or if he tells me his intention to commit a crime or is going to do something that is harmful to him. Otherwise, our conversations are confidential."

Slack-jawed, I have to wonder what good it does to bring the kid to counseling if I am not going to be privy to any information that might help me figure out how to deal with him. I decide to relay this concern.

After listening without interruption, he gives me a patient nod. "I understand how you must be feeling, Ms. Everett." At least he got the name right. Finally, someone who really does listen. "But please realize this isn't about you learning how to change your son's behavior. It's about getting to the bottom of his reasons for such actions in the first place.

"Without being able to share specifics, I can tell you from the little time I've spent with him that he loves both of his parents very much. He is angry at his father and feels the need to protect his mother above all else."

Rick scrubs his fingers across his jaw. "She's bitter. Of course the boy is angry at me."

Feeling the indignation that comes from being falsely accused, I hear the rise in my voice. But I address the doctor, *not* the toad-sucking cheater. "He's right. I *am* angry. And with good reason, but I do not speak bad things about my children's father when they're around." I stop and no one speaks. You could cut the skepticism in the room with a knife. "Well, okay. At least they're not around as far as I know," I admit.

"Maybe not intentionally," Rick shoots back. "But even if they don't hear your resentment toward me in actual words, they can feel it every time you say something sarcastic to me or Darcy."

"Darcy is your wife, right?" the doctor interjects. "Shawn mentioned her."

Shawn has been talking about Darcy? My suspicions rise again.

A nearly imperceptible nod moves Rick's head.

Dr. Goldberg scratches a few notes onto his pad. Rick and I both clam up.

The doctor draws a breath and looks up from his notes. He glances first at me, then Rick. "We're here about your son," he says gently. "It's obvious that you two have things to work out between you, and I suggest you do your best to deal with those issues. But we have to concentrate on getting to the bottom of what's eating Shawn and causing him to act up. Do you both agree?"

Another jerky nod from Rick.

"I agree," I say grudgingly. And I do. Oh, God. Why is this so hard? Tears jump to my eyes, catching me off guard with their sting. I blink them back lickety-split and pray no one but me knows they ever existed.

"I'd like to see Shawn alone, once a week. And I'd like to see the whole family once a week also, on a different day."

I cringe and I feel Rick recoil. I mean, we knew it was coming, but somehow the reality of family counseling is even more repulsive than before, now that it's staring us in the face with its mocking truth: our system of silent resentment and surface politeness has worked quite well for us both thus far, but apparently it's tearing Shawn, our sensitive child, to pieces. Am I ready to deal with all of the things that are inevitably about to come out?

I feel Rick's hand on my arm. Slowly, I am drawn to his gaze. Those incredible dark-blue eyes. Eyes I once thought reflected the color of the ocean, eyes that used to sparkle with his love for me.

Now they are filled with questions. Do we want to do this? Is our son worth the pain of learning to forgive?

I'm sitting at Churchill's, my favorite coffee/sandwich shop, drinking a skinny latte, and avoiding the chocolate cheesecake I would normally order. Excitement dances in Linda's eyes as I take in the information she's just dropped on me.

"You're kidding me!"

Linda shakes her head and giggles like a schoolgirl.

"When?"

"Mid-December. We'll renew our vows on the seventeenth, and the next morning we'll fly out for almost a week of sunny beaches and romantic nights . . ."

"Spare me the nights."

She giggles again. "We'll be back on the twenty-third so we can spend Christmas Eve with his parents and Christmas Day at home with Trish. Can you imagine trying to plan a wedding and Christmas plus a honeymoon in the Bahamas all at the same time?"

I shake my head. It brings my blood pressure up just thinking of it. "So this is why he's been working late so much?" I'm amazed and a little surprised, I have to admit. I really thought the guy was at it again. Once a cheater, always a cheater. In this instance, I'm so glad I'm wrong.

Linda's eyes shine with love and excitement. "I can't believe it. We never had a honeymoon the first time around."

She reaches across the table and takes my hand. "I want you to be my matron of honor."

I feel the horror spring to my eyes as I picture myself in a tight satin fuchsia gown, holding pink roses and trying not to trip, thereby landing on my face in the aisle, with my dress around my neck as I moon the guests.

My reaction sifts the joy from her face.

"It's all right, Claire. It was nervy of me to even ask." She pulls her hand back to her side of the table and sucks a gulp of Diet Coke with trembling lips. "It's just that Mark and I both know without you we wouldn't be where we are. Our marriage healed, us headed for the altar again to recommit to each other."

"Linda, I had nothing to do with it, really." The book is fiction, woman. Get a grip. But I feel a prick from that "still, small voice." The one I recognize as the God of all creation. The One who placed the writing bug in my heart. The One who gave me the idea for *Tobey's Choice*.

As I write every day, I ask God to give me the words that will draw my readers closer to Him. I ask Him to speak as He sees fit into every heart. He used Tobey's unfaithful husband and his ultimate repentance to speak into Linda's life.

To cause Mark to confess his sin and to seek forgiveness and restoration.

Why is fiction so much easier than real life when you're the author?

Shoot. I'm going to have to be this woman's matron of honor.

My cheeks puff with my next breath. "What color am I wearing?"

17

During the past few weeks, I've come to love my alone time with God more than ever before. Not to sound like a cliché, but I feel as though my spirit has walked out of a shadow into a soft, gentle light. One that illuminates and warms but doesn't blind or burn.

I'm not sure when my daily Bible reading became obligatory, rather than fellowship with the Lover of my soul. But somehow, between the stress of deadlines, wasted time online, and life in general, I became complacent in my relationship with Him. No wonder it was so easy to hide away from my church family.

I stretch out, snuggling under my goose-down comforter, prop myself up with three fluffy pillows (my little guilty pleasure—new pillows every three months), and take out my devotional workbook (the Beth Moore Bible study) and do my lesson for the day.

I know many people find mornings to be their best time for prayer, Bible reading, devotions, whatever. But, night owl that I am, I prefer bedtime. After the kids are down for the count and the world sleeps in the silent darkness outside my four walls. I feel like I truly am alone with God during these hours. Somehow, I'm able to set aside my worry about the kids and my roller-coaster emotions concerning Darcy. I'm able to simply put Rick out of my mind.

Tonight, I find myself approaching the King's table with a bit of trepidation. His sweet conviction has pricked my heart since the counseling session, and I know I blew it with Darcy and Rick. I gave in to my I-hate-you-ness at Rick and took it out on Darcy. Definitely projected my loathing of him onto her. (See? One session with a doctor of psychology and I'm ready to spout politically correct mumbo jumbo like "projected onto her." I'm so easily led.)

The Bible study is just what I need, a walk through the ark of the covenant as it relates to personal relationship and worship. I end up on my knees, in awe of a holy God— though why He would want my time eludes me. Especially after my attitude today.

The clock downstairs bongs eleven just as I get up off the floor and close the workbook. I feel cleansed, whole, completely at peace as I gather a deep breath of accomplishment. Following my nightly ritual, I exit my bedroom to check in on the kids one last time before I pop in my movie (yes, the same one) and turn in.

I open Shawn and Jakey's door, walk inside. I stop at Shawn's bed first. He's curled into a little ball and sleeping like the angel I know him to be. A tuft of hair is lying in an unruly wave across his forehead. I reach out and push it away with my fingertips. Bending forward, I press a kiss to his cheek. He moves, moans, then settles back into peace.

Jakey's covers are flung carelessly from him and he's sprawled in his racecar jammies, one leg hanging off the edge of his bed. He begged for bunk beds, but knowing his restlessness, I didn't dare chance it. He'd fall off for sure. And really, do we need broken bones in this family? We have enough problems as it is.

I cover him back up, knowing it will do no good and that in all likelihood, thirty seconds after I leave the room, he'll have them flung off again. I press a kiss to his cheek also, but sleep-like-the-dead boy doesn't budge. Smile.

As I head down the hall to Tommy's room, I tap and enter. Lord, he snores like his dad. I walk in (maneuvering around clothes, shoes, a skateboard, and textbooks that I'm almost positive he never opens), do a once-over. He's all covered up, snoring happily. I barely contain a sudden burst of joy. Things have improved so much since I started having family movie night. He's like the boy he once was. Oh, his hair is still long and unruly, he still wears his jeans way too big and low, and he still says annoying things like "What up, Dogg?" But I can handle this phase he's going through as long as the attitude doesn't go south again. Following God's example, I will look past the outward appearance and look at what I know to be in his heart.

Softly, I close his door. One more stop to make before I try to finish my movie—ever the optimist.

Low tones are coming from Ari's room and for a second my heart nearly stops. Does Ari have someone in there? I stand outside and listen for a second. "I'm telling you, Granny, she's flipped her lid."

Granny? The phone didn't ring, so Ari must have called Mom. She knows better than to do that so late at night. And by the way, *who* exactly has flipped her lid?

"It's like she's not the same mom anymore."

Hello, wasn't that the point? I mean, really.

"I'm not kidding, the other day she was outside on Tommy's skateboard. Trying to learn a kickflip."

What a little Benedict Arnold! If she is so sure I flipped

my lid, then why did she give me a "cool" nod after the skateboard episode? I'm really close to flinging open that door and confronting her, but her next words stop me in my tracks. "I know she has time off with this whole surgery, but she's turning our lives upside down with all these changes. I mean, Monday movie night? Please."

If that's the way she feels about it, she can just forget about any movies wherein the main actor is good-looking or teenage.

"Yes. I see your point," she says grudgingly, and I can only guess what my mom has advised. "But how can she possibly think that paying attention to us for three months while she's forced to stay off the computer is going to make up for the last few years? Besides, we all know that as soon as she's well, we won't be reading a chapter a night in *Purpose-Driven Life* or having Monday movie night. It'll be back to the way it was before."

Leaning with my back against the wall next to her slightly open door, I feel like banging my head. In a million years, I never would have guessed Ari was so skeptical about the whole new life we're making as a family. My disappointment hits me on a couple of different levels. First, I honestly believed that she was with me on this. Talk about seeing what you want to see. And second, she thinks my reason for doing the family stuff is because I have nothing better to do.

"Do you think you might come back, Granny?"

I hold my breath, listening to Ari sniffling. "I know. I do understand. It's just that the cheerleader carnival is next week, and all the other mothers are bringing baked stuff or something. I'll be the only girl on the squad who doesn't bring anything to sell."

She blows her nose. "Huh? I don't know if she would. Does Mom know how to bake stuff?"

My cheeks warm. Okay, so homemade baked goods aren't my strong suit. I admit that. But she has to admit I'm darned good at regular food.

But she has a point. Mom always made the cupcakes for school parties, served as "room mother," or volunteered in the classrooms in various capacities. Good grief. In many ways, my mom is also Ari's mom. My heart sinks to my toes. How do you regain lost years with your child who is close to becoming a young woman?

It's too late for cupcakes. She's too old for grade school stuff. But the cheerleader bake sale sounds like a good place to start. How hard can it be to buy a brownie mix and follow the recipe, right? I'll make my daughter proud of me. I tap on the door and she jumps as I step inside. "I gotta go," she says and essentially hangs up on Mom.

"Time for lights-out, Ari."

"Okay. 'Night."

I watch her slide her bare toes under the quilt and then follow with the rest of her body.

"Everything okay?" A slight frown mars her forehead.

"Everything is fine, sweetheart." I stride to her bed and grasp the quilt. Her eyes are wide like she's not sure whether she should holler for help or not.

"Ma, what are you doing?"

I snatch at the corners of her quilt and pull it up to her neck. Next I tuck her in properly. "There." I smile. "I haven't tucked you in for ages."

"You heard my conversation with Granny, didn't you?"

My eyes go wide in feigned innocence. But seeing her dubious scowl, I know there's no point in denying it. "Yes, I overheard."

"Man, we really gotta talk about some privacy issues."

"You *were* talking about me, you know. I had a perfect right to eavesdrop."

"It was still a private conversation," she shoots back, apparently not in the mood to apologize for telling my mother I've flipped my lid.

"You really want Granny to come back that badly, huh?"

"Don't you?"

I shrug. "I miss her." And her brownies, right?

I almost blurt out my intention, but instead I think Ari might need a nice little surprise, so I decide to leave my contribution to the cheerleading bake sale completely under wraps. She'll see the depth of my love for her. Maybe I can't make up for lost time, but the least I can do is bake a pan of brownies.

Well, personally, I think that's a terrible idea!"

My heart goes out to Darcy a little as she stands in front of the dowagers on the Christmas decorating committee. I understand why she hesitates to stand up for herself and her ideas (which are pretty good). Her main opposition is coming from Pastor's aunt. How do you disagree with someone like that?

"We've always used the nativity to decorate," Mrs. Devine expels, glancing around for support. She receives just enough nods to encourage her to continue her dissenting opinion. "My goodness. I can't even imagine the outrage Jesus must feel for all the churches decorating with

Christmas trees. Why, it's like setting up golden calves right on the platform with twinkling lights and ornaments."

I clear my throat as Darcy appears to shrink smaller and smaller. I'm afraid she will be carpet fuzz if this woman is allowed to continue. "Now, wait a second," I say. Darcy perks up, her eyes alight with shock and maybe a little hesitant hope.

"Darcy isn't suggesting that we discount the nativity. As a matter of fact, I heard her mention setting it up as always. She is merely suggesting adding to that particular decoration to beautify the Fellowship Hall. She isn't asking to put it in the sanctuary or even the main building.

"And besides. Didn't baby Jesus and one of the wise men get broken last year when the youth group was taking it all down?" (And for the record, after Pastor caught the teenage boys playing football with baby Jesus, it was unanimously agreed upon that the youth group *not* be asked to undecorate from now on. Personally, I think they did it on purpose to get out of the extra work.) "As far as I know those haven't been replaced, and it's a little late to go ordering new stuff."

Mrs. Devine's face goes a fascinating, if not frightening, shade of red. Clearly this woman is not used to being refuted. But hey, she can get over it. Why ask a peacock like Darcy to do a luncheon, complete with decorations, and then expect her to use twenty-year-old decorations that are no reflection of her style and taste? Peacocks are beautiful and meant to strut their stuff. And so is Darcy.

"Well, I will not attend if you decide to go with pagan decorations."

Tears shine in Darcy's eyes. The woman's bullying has just gotten on my last nerve. I start to stand up, but a short woman with gorgeous white hair and dark eyes and complexion speaks up. Greg's mom. Possibly my future mother-in-law. "Excuse me for butting in, but I think Darcy's idea is wonderful. I love poinsettias and Christmas lights. I don't see how it could hurt as long as we don't use things that might be offensive to some, such as Santa or reindeer or elves. There shouldn't be a problem. Perhaps, we should ask Pastor's opinion?"

The room trickles into silence. Bring Pastor into a decorating dispute? I can tell Joan isn't about to chance it. Everyone knows that Pastor's as giddy as a four-year-old during the Christmas holiday. It would be a pretty safe bet to assume he'd side with Darcy, familial ties notwithstanding.

Only one or two of Mrs. Devine's disciples remain silent as the other women begin to nod and voice their agreement.

I send Darcy a wink. But she isn't smiling. I see her staring after Mrs. Devine as the woman jerks to her feet and leaves the room. As though she feels my attention, she turns to me. I see pain in her eyes. There is no triumph that the women's group has sided with her rather than the unspoken leader for over twenty years. How can this woman be for real?

"Shall we pray and dismiss?" she asks in a somber voice.

Normally, I would take off without talking to anyone (which, by the way, hardly helps out with number five on my list), but I feel like I need to speak with Darcy. We haven't really conversed this week, since the appointment with Dr. Goldberg. I've seen her at church, but she's been subdued. Not her usual smiling self. This morning, she presented the idea for the decorations with very little zeal.

I wait while the women milling around her thin out. When only Greg's mom, Darcy, and I remain in the room, I step forward. Darcy sees me and bursts into tears, flinging herself into my arms. "Oh, Claire, I've caused division. All I do is cause division."

I let her cry a minute, then I hold her out at arm's length. "Darcy, are you kidding me? Shaking things up a bit is a great thing. Look how many of the women are happy about the change in decorations. And good grief, they're decorations. You're not introducing a new doctrine."

"That's right!" the other woman pipes in. "You stick to your guns, sweetheart. It won't hurt Joan one bit to eat a little crow."

"Thank you, Mrs. Lewis." Darcy squeezes the older woman's hand. "I'll do my best."

The back door of the church opens just as Darcy wipes her eyes and nose. My heart does a little loop-de-loop at the unexpected sight of Greg in the doorway. He looks like a creature from Greek mythology surrounded by the glow of the autumn sun beating down on his position.

Before his own mother has a chance to greet him, I blurt the first thing that comes to mind. "Shouldn't you be in school?"

He chuckles and strides into the room. "I took the afternoon off. I signed the papers today." He winks at me and I feel my cheeks warm.

"On your new house?" his mother asks as he bends down and presses a kiss to her smooth cheek. "It's amazing how quickly the sale of a house can go when all the parties are in agreement."

"I couldn't agree more." Greg smiles his amazing smile. His eyes soften when he looks at his mom. "I came to see if I can take you out to lunch to celebrate."

"I think you can." Her eyes twinkle and she smiles with pleasure. Watching the two of them, I am completely taken in by the easy camaraderie. It's not difficult to see where Greg gets his charm.

"Well," Darcy says, "I think we'll go grab some lunch, too. You game, Claire?"

I'd rather eat my eyebrows than have lunch with Darcy and have to discuss the menu for her Christmas luncheon (a menu sure to cause more vocal displeasure from Pastor's aunt), but how do I get out of it gracefully? Just as I'm in the throes of this dilemma, Mrs. Lewis speaks up. "Why don't you two join us? We're going to the Chinese buffet."

Okay, have I ever mentioned that next to pizza, Chinese food is my all-time favorite?

"That's a great idea. Don't you think so, Claire? We love Chinese."

I happen to know that Darcy is anti-carbs. And if there's one low-carb item on the Chinese buffet, I think it's broccoli, and she doesn't need to spend $8.99 (drink included, free refills) for a plate of broccoli.

I send her a "What's going on?" look, to which she responds with a wink. A knowing wink. A sly, knowing wink. A sly, knowing wink that expresses that she knows I have a . . . Oh, my gosh! Darcy knows I have a crush on Greg! How? It must be that pod-girl thing. It's a well-known fact that aliens read minds.

I'm aghast. There's only one thing to do when I'm in such a state. Let the babbling commence.

"Oh, no, I better go . . ."

Darcy gives an airy laugh. "Go where? Your cleaning lady will be at the house all afternoon." (In keeping with number two on my list. Still, I am definitely going to get muzzles for the kids. Who said they could go blabbing about my new housekeeper, who I'm almost sure drinks the Diet Coke, not to mention the fact that she never vacuums behind any of the furniture?)

"That settles it." Greg's mom is totally staring me down, daring me to refuse one more time. She was so sweet and supportive only ten minutes ago. Where did this warrior princess come from? "Let's stop standing around talking about it and go have lunch. My treat."

"Oh, no," Greg pipes in. "My treat."

"Oh, no" right back at him. There's no way he's buying my lunch when we're not even on a date.

"Really," I say in my going-along-but-only-so-far voice. "I'll buy lunch."

Darcy shrugs and gives a playful grin. "Looks like our waitress is getting a good tip."

18

I wake up on Saturday morning knowing there's something going on today, but for the life of me I can't figure out what it is I'm supposed to be remembering. The kids are at Rick's for the weekend, so I'm pretty sure it's nothing to do with them. We will start fittings for the matron of honor gown next week, so I know for sure it's not that.

No counseling sessions on the weekend.

Racking my brain here! Nothing. Shoot. Still can't shake the feeling that I'm missing something. Oh, I hate that!

I push back the snuggly comforter. No point in trying for that five more minutes today. Sleep will inevitably elude me like the five pounds I seem to be missing. There's a happy thought. I've stayed on the wagon these past couple of weeks, with one small exception for the whole Chinese lunch thing. And given that I was sitting across from Greg, who could really do justice to a buffet? I mean, really. I ate like a bird.

My doctor will be pleasantly surprised, I'm sure, when I go in for round two of my surgery in three weeks. Maybe I could even lose another five or ten pounds by then.

Okay, now I'm all motivated to go walk. Amazing how easy it is to get out there now that I feel a little improvement. I can't really see those five pounds yet, but there is strength in my legs that wasn't there before. I'm able to walk for twenty minutes now without feeling like I'd fight the Saint Bernard down the street for his water bowl and a nice rest inside his shady doghouse.

I slip into my gray-and-black exercise pants, a long-sleeved T-shirt to ward off the slight chill of an October morning in Missouri, and pull on the Nikes. Like Pavlov's dog, my body senses the coming activity and my muscles come alive. I'm anxious to hit the pavement, to watch the minutes (all twenty of them) rack up as I put one foot in front of the other.

I stop by the kitchen for a glass of water before heading outside. I grab my watch and keys from the counter, and I'm off.

Na-na-naaaaaaaaaah . . .

Oh, yeah. I'm getting there. I am so high on life and the desire to take my fitness to the next level, I think I might actually be ready to—Okay, I'm speeding up, walking faster. All it would take for this brisk walk to become a jog is a little bounce. Should I or shouldn't I?

This line of thinking takes me by surprise. I've never had aspirations to go that extra mile, make it harder on me than absolutely necessary, but I see myself running. I'm really skinny. In a good, healthy kind of way. Can I really be a runner?

I'm walking really fast, so I give a sort of jump. Okay! I'm jogging. I can't express my happiness that I, Claire Everett, geek in school, overweight in adulthood, am becoming athletic. Oh, but jogging hurts. And I can't catch my breath. Have I really only gone half a block? Enough already. I hate jogging. If I had Tommy's skateboard, I'd ride it home rather than have to walk on my cramping calves.

Tommy's skateboard!! The competition!

I whip around and head back toward the house. It was supposed to start at nine this morning with the first elimination round.

Knowing I'm late, I do the unthinkable. Something I swore only seconds ago I'd never do again. I break into a jog.

I'm out of breath and my lower body hurts when I slide my key into the door, but I have to admit, just knowing that I can jog that far makes me want to try again.

Someday.

I shower, dress, and make a beeline for my minivan. Against all that is right and proper, I apply makeup on the go and narrowly miss sideswiping a VW. The teenage driver flips me the bird. I can't believe how intolerant people are. I head downtown to The Board, find a parking spot with difficulty, and end up having to walk a block. Skateboarding kids are taking over the world. The streets are filled with black-clad, makeup-wearing, I-know-you're-hiding-an-Uzi, scary teenagers. My heart starts to pound as three such boys walk toward me, side by side. Then I realize, hey, Tommy would look just like them if I'd let him.

"Hey, Ms. Everett." The kids halt in front of me. The one who spoke is grinning like I'm one of his peeps or something. I square my shoulders and reach into my bag like I have a gun, just in case these kids aren't as sweet and harmless as my kid. I totally don't, of course, but I do have breath spray, and I'll squirt it right in their eyes if I have to.

The grinning talker looks sorta familiar. I squint, trying to remember if I've actually seen him before or if they all just look alike. The young man has a scraggly tuft of hair growing (or possibly taped) to his chin, equally scraggly dirty-blond hair, a nose ring, and a lip ring. No one I know has such an appearance, so I surmise this person has been rifling through my garbage seeking a victim for identity theft.

This chick will not be said victim.

I screw up my courage and give him the deepest, darkest frown known to womankind. The kind of look that says, "Don't mess with me, I know karate."

I see something flicker in his eyes. "Everything okay, Ms. Everett?"

Okay, I'm getting really creeped out now. "Look, bud."

"Lance Avery." He laughs. "You don't recognize me."

The older brother of Tommy's best friend since first grade.

"Oh my gosh, I haven't seen you in ages. I'm so sorry, Lance."

"It's okay. I get that a lot. Just never from my old Sunday school teachers."

I feel a blush spread across my face. "So, how have you been?"

He swings his head forward and back. You couldn't really call it a nod, because the neck follows the head. "All right" (which comes out sounding like "Aw-ight"), he says.

I can tell the natives to the left and right of Lance are getting restless. They're fidgety and coughing a lot.

"Have you seen Tommy around, Lance?"

"Tank?"

Whatever.

"Yeah, he's about to skate."

"Oh! I don't want to miss him. It was great seeing you again, Lance. And hey, come to church and bring your friends. We miss you."

His expression softens a little. "I'll think about it."

Lance may look like something out of a vampire movie, but he's someone's kid. He has parents who adore him, who took him to church every Sunday and Wednesday. He's a good kid. Or he has goodness in him.

I sort of glance over my shoulder just as he lights up a cigarette. My heart sinks a little. Poor Lance. I hope he finds himself soon.

I squeeze into the crowded concrete building. Kids are all over the place. Laughing, pushing. I elbow my way forward. Heat rises up my spine and I can feel the redness on my neck. Dread creeps through me. I know this feeling as the beginning of a panic attack. I stop a minute, close my eyes, and take some deep breaths as my heart speeds up.

Slow, even breaths. Come on, Claire, don't freak out. You're here for Tommy.

I lean against the wall and fight to regain my composure. Slowly, my heart resumes its normal rhythm, and relief floods me. I've warded off this one.

I open my eyes and take in the wall I've been leaning against. This one, as well as the others, is painted to look like graffiti. I guess they want this group to feel welcome. Thankfully, there's nothing obscene. It takes me a few scans of the crowd before I spot Tommy. He's sitting on his skateboard, watching the current contestant.

The fluorescent lighting bathes his face just right, and I see the concentration tensing his jawline. He's gearing himself up for his coming task. Nervously, he pulls at his lip. He . . . wait. What exactly is he pulling on?

I don't want to be a big fat false accuser, so I look closer, hoping I didn't see what I'm almost sure I saw. In a moment of utter shock I suck all the oxygen from the room. That little twerp. He has a lip ring.

He must have gotten it done this weekend, which means Rick is solely responsible. Consolation, yes. But not enough to offset the mother's rage I feel coming on. I send him a glare to beat all glares, fully expecting the force of my wrath will capture his attention. Instead, I hear his name announced over the speakers. Okay, time to set aside my anger and concentrate on prayers for his safety. Any pain he feels today will come from me.

Applause follows him as he takes his place. I hold my breath. He skates doooown then up. Twist around. Kickflip (I know that one). Oh, my word. The boy has got some moves! The crowd is going crazy now. On their feet.

My son is flying, his body crouched above his airborne board. That looks dangerous. I don't think he should be doing it. What if he breaks a bone?

He lands perfectly. I clap as loudly as anyone and whistle my two-fingered whistle.

"Claire?"

I turn. It can't be! "What are you doing here, Greg?"

"Shane's competing in the older division."

"Shane?"

"Vale."

"Our new youth pastor is a skateboarder?"

"Yep. He's making a difference down here. The kids love him. I wouldn't be a bit surprised if we don't end up with half these kids in our youth group before school's out next spring."

Joan Devine's going to love that. Of course, what can she do about it?

I wonder if having a positive role model with common interests has anything to do with Tommy's change. Before the lip-ring incident, that is. I glance toward my son and see him head off with a group of friends out a side exit door.

"I gotta go, Greg." Suddenly I feel a wave of heat and my heart picks up as I look into the throng standing between my son and me. I take deep gulps of air. The room is spinning. Not again! I have to get out of here before I'm in a full-blown panic.

"You okay?" Greg whispers close to my ear. Now I'm not sure if the heat I feel is panic or a natural response to the nearness of a gorgeous guy who always seems to come to my rescue.

"Let's get you out of here."

"But I want Tommy to know I was here and saw how great he is. And that I'm gonna kill him for getting a lip ring."

Greg smiles. Sort of a sexy smile that tells me he's probably interested. Either that, or he likes my hair. Who knows with guys? "We'll find him. But you need some air. Trust me. I am the current expert on taking care of panicky women."

I'd like to offer a quip, but my heart is thundering in my ears and my tongue feels too big for my mouth—which, according to Rick, is as big as the Grand Canyon. But who cares what he thinks?

"Have you seen a doctor about these attacks?"

I shake my head. "Not yet. This is only the second one. I'm just under a lot of stress right now. I'm going to talk to him, though, if they don't stop."

We open the red-metal door and slip outside. The sidewalk is littered with tossed paper cups, napkins, nacho containers. Most disturbing are the teenagers smoking along the side of the building, and boys and girls, some of whom look no older than Tommy, making out like they're oblivious to their audience. I'm repulsed, really. But also a little jealous. I haven't had a good make-out session in a long time.

I cast a sideways glance up at Greg to see if he notices. His eyes are straight ahead. Face like a rock. Unreadable.

"Where are we going?" I manage to ask, trying to look away from his full lips that are just asking to be asked for a kiss.

"Tommy went out the side door, so we're going that way."

Oh, duh!

"How are you feeling?"

"Better, but still heavy in the chest."

We round a corner, and for one brief instant I realize that I do not know my son. There's a boy standing there in my son's body, but that is *not* my son! Tommy hasn't seen me yet—the impostor, that is. He takes a drag from a lit cigarette and I see red. I mean big, bold *red*.

"Thomas Richard Frank, I'm going to beat you within an inch of your life." The panic is gone now and I'm running on sheer adrenaline. My son looks around the three other boys he *thought* were blocking his path; horror widens his eyes and I can see he'd like to bolt. But fear has him frozen to the ground. The smoldering ground where he just dropped his cigarette.

"Mom!"

"Don't *Mom* me, young man. March it to the van. *Now!*"

"Calm down, Claire."

No longer feeling the love, I whip around and pin Greg with an icy glare. "Don't tell me to calm down, choirboy. My son is *smoking*! Cigarettes. Cancer-causing, smoke-expelling—" I give Tommy a pointed look over my shoulder. "—*illegal*, foul-smelling garbage."

"All right. Yell then, but kids are coming around the corner. I think they're looking for a fistfight. Are you planning to give them a good show? Or how about taking this home?"

I can just see the headlines: "Local, sort-of-celebrity, Christian romance author Claire Everett showed some not-so-Christian behavior by starting a brawl at The Board on Saturday."

I whip around like I'm Neo and Tommy is Agent Smith from *The Matrix*. "What the heck are you still doing standing there with those bad influences?" Oh, brother. Poor choice of words. I recognize this to be the case when one of those bad influences turns his scraggly face away and snickers like a seven-year-old.

Incensed and in no mood to be made fun of by tacky boys, I take a couple of steps toward my son and jam my hands on my hips, only vaguely noticing they don't sink in as far as they used to. "What are you laughing at? Does your mother know you're giving thirteen-year-old boys cigarettes?"

His pierced eyebrows go up in surprise as though he's

just been asked to take a bath. "Tank gave *me* a smoke, lady. Not the other way around."

I feel a hand grip my arm. "Claire, come on. Let's go." Greg's voice is stern, commanding. I kind of like that. Since I'm done here anyway.

I hurl the thugs one last ticked-off-mama glare and stomp after my son, who is Toast with a capital *T*.

19

I f a teenager doesn't want to talk, there's not a thing a parent can do, short of telepathy, to wring out his thoughts. I face this unfortunate truth right now as my sullen boy sits as far as he can from me, pressed against the passenger-side door.

"Tommy, don't lean, you're going to fall out."

"Good," he snarls.

"Well, you might not have a problem with it, but I don't need the cops thinking I pushed you out for mouthing off, so get away from the door like I said."

He seems surprised by the force of my God-given right to order my children to do what is best for them. Frankly, I wasn't sure I had all this grit in me. Could have been leftover adrenaline from the mild panic attack I experienced at The Board. Actually, I'm still feeling as though the panic attack isn't quite over. My face is tingling a bit. And my heart is still racing.

Still, a great sense of satisfaction shoots through me as I watch him shift closer to center and slouch down in the seat. Okay, I know he wouldn't fall out. First of all, I'm pretty sure modern vehicles are reasonably safe. Second, he's wearing his seat belt. But I can't get my mom's voice out of my head from the days before "Click it or ticket" laws. *Stop leaning on that door, Claire Everett. What if it flies open while we're driving down the road? Do you want to fall out?"*

Of course, at the moment, I have a much deeper issue to deal with. My son has been smoking. My son! The boy whose dad is a doctor, for crying out loud. "Am I going to have to get your dad to bring over the lung cancer videos again?"

"No," he snarls.

"Watch the tone!" Man, I am really on a roll.

He shrugs, and I admire his restraint. A week ago he would have said, "Whatever." Of course, that grounding is going to look like a ditch of punishment next to the Grand Canyon I'm about to inflict on his life. He's going to be lucky to see the light of day for the next six months.

But since this is a health-related issue, I have decided to contact Rick and ask his opinion about what we should do to this one. Our efforts didn't work so well with Poem Boy. But we're going to be extra tough with this one.

I turn the van toward Rick and Darcy's house.

"Where are we going?" Tommy asks.

"Your dad's."

"I want to go home."

Yeah, I bet you do. Rick's going to go ballistic when he hears about Tommy lighting up.

"Too bad. You belong to Dad on the weekends."

"Don't you think I'm old enough to decide if I want that whole visitation thing?"

"Not really."

His throat emits a growl.

"Take the lip ring out, by the way. I don't know why you thought you could get that pierced after I said no."

"It's not even real."

"What isn't real?"

He slips off the lip ring. Other than a red spot where it was pinching his lip, there is nothing permanent. No holes.

I laugh in spite of myself. "They have clip-ons?" I picture my aunts with their clip-on button earrings from the sixties.

"It's not funny, Mom. I have to wear it or everyone will think I'm a baby. 'My mommy won't let me get my lip pierced.'"

"That's right. Because it's *stupid*."

"No more stupid than those legwarmers you used to wear when you were my age. It's just a style."

"Okay, I understand what you're saying about the difference in generational ideas of what is or isn't a dumb style. But let's get something straight. Legwarmers didn't leave holes in my legs. And my parents didn't object to my wearing them. Believe me, there were things in the eighties my parents would have freaked out about just as much as I freaked out when I thought you really had a lip ring."

"Like what?"

"Mohawks, purple hair. The punked-out look. Madonna CDs."

"Madonna writes kid's books."

Yes, things have certainly changed in twenty years. I feel so old.

We pull into Rick's long driveway. I stare at the home he's given Darcy. A beautiful white colonial with pillars and everything. Like he's a plantation owner and she's the belle of the ball. I put up with him for eleven years, so how come she gets the good house while I'm still living in the one we bought five years into our marriage? Jealousy is an ugly thing.

I slam the gearshift into park and kill the motor. Tommy's eyebrows shoot up. "You're coming in with me?"

"Yep." His surprise is understandable. I have never stepped foot inside Tara, but this is one time when the situation warrants the humbling of my principles.

On the porch, I ring the bell and Tommy looks at me like I've lost my mind. "I live here, too, Mom. I don't have to ring the bell."

My head is beginning to feel fuzzy. My heart is picking up and I feel heat crawling up my spine and around to my neck and face. Sweat is already beginning to bead on my forehead. Should have known I couldn't get off that easily. "Well, I don't live here so I do."

He shrugs, opens the door, walks inside, and closes it in my face.

Indignation shoots through my veins like a shot of red-hot chili peppers. That kid isn't exactly in the position to be a smarty. And I plan to tell him so just as soon as someone comes to the door. I ring the bell again.

A flustered Darcy appears seconds later. "Claire, I'm so sorry. Come in, please. Tommy should have let you in."

Tommy's standing beyond her. "Hey, you can bring a horse to water, but you can't make it drink," he says, shrugging and turning like he's heading up the steps.

"Where do you think you're going?" Rick's voice is stern, and I recognize the underlying anger. Has he somehow heard about the cigarettes? His next words leave me speechless. "You get your behind over here and apologize to your mother."

"What for?"

"First you leave her standing on the doorstep, second you use extremely disrespectful wording to justify your behavior. I want to hear some apologizing beginning right now."

Boy-o-boy. Where'd this guy come from?

I breathe in through my nose, out through my mouth—which, by the way, is beginning to go numb. "Look, deal with this later, Rick. I need to talk to you about something more important. Toms," I say, turning my attention to where my oh-so-in-trouble kid is standing on the third step. "Go on upstairs so I can talk to your dad about what happened today."

He gives me a scowl. The kid is totally ungrateful that I've diverted his dad's attention. I mean, sure, he's in big trouble, and I'm going to have to decide on a punishment for smoking *and* disrespect, if not out-and-out rebellion, but not now. I'm feeling so weird.

He turns and stomps up the steps.

"I can't believe you just undermined me in my own home." Rick's face is red with anger. "And I was defending you!"

Something about the way he said "my own home" and "defending you" translates to "Even though you weren't a decent enough wife to keep my attention and thus deserve a gorgeous home like this one, I am still showing off to my beautiful, sexy current wife by showing her how I will always take up for her when we have children of our own."

I see red again.

Red like Rick is holding a scarf and I'm a snorting bull about to charge.

Except, Rick isn't quite finished. He has to drop the last

bomb. "It's no wonder none of the kids respect you; you don't demand it of them."

"Rick, that wasn't very nice." Darcy, ever the peacemaker, steps next to Rick and slides her hand into his. He relaxes instantly. I swear Darcy is a snake charmer. But something about the entire situation raises my ire. I don't want him to take up for me; I don't want her to take up for me. I don't want to be here! Oh, Lord, please . . . My chest is growing heavy, my breath is coming in short bursts.

Greg . . . I need Greg.

"Claire?" I vaguely recognize Darcy's voice as in a distance. "Rick, come help me. Something's wrong."

Rick sprints into action, like he's vying for Doctor of the Year. He grabs my hand and presses his two fingers to my wrist. Which hurts, for what it's worth. "Does your chest hurt?"

Gasping for air, all I can do is nod.

"Darcy, go call 911! I think she might be having a heart attack."

Idiot! Some doctor he is.

I grab Darcy's arm and gather enough breath to force a word. "Don't."

"Claire. Don't be stubborn. Something's wrong. We need to get you medical attention immediately." Rick's irritation feeds mine.

I give him the full force of my glare. Any fool could see I'm having a panic attack. Nerves. Greg recognized it for what it was immediately. Twice. And he's not even a doctor. "Panic attack," I say with difficulty around the tightness in my throat. A surreal wave is overtaking me. I know where I am and yet time means nothing.

"Help her into the living room, Rick." I hear the concern in Darcy's soft voice. "I'll get her a washcloth for her head."

Rick's arm, slung around my shoulders, isn't helping my tension one little iota. But once I'm stretched out on Darcy's plush, white, pillowy sofa, I start to relax. At least I know that the spinning in my head isn't going to land me on the ground. Next thing I know, Darcy is standing over me, administering a cool cloth to my head. I sigh and close my eyes.

"Everything will be okay, Claire," she soothes as though I'm a child, and I feel comforted. "Just lie there and it'll pass."

"I still think we should call an ambulance. Her heart rate is high."

"Claire knows if she is having a panic attack or not, sweetheart. And she asked us not to call. Let's see how she does and if she continues to have symptoms, we'll call. Okay?"

In a full-blown panic attack—at least from my limited experience—life sort of happens around you. That's how I feel. If I tried really hard, I could get up and participate in the conversation, but everything is so surreal, I just don't want to. All I want to do for the moment is keep my eyes closed, the cloth on my head, and possibly go to sleep now that my heart is beginning to slow to a more rhythmic beat. I am only vaguely aware that under normal circumstances I'd never consider resting on Rick and Darcy's couch. But now it just . . . doesn't . . . seem . . .

My head is pounding. I open my eyes slowly, resisting the light that I'm almost positive is going to slice through my sockets and cause even more excruciating pain. Instead, darkness greets me. For a second, a chill runs down my spine. Have I gone blind? Then my eyes begin to adjust and I recognize Darcy's living room. I relax for a second until reality strikes me. Did I really sleep on their couch all day? The house is quiet. It's got to be past ten.

This is crazy. I stand on legs that are a little shaky—my hangover from the panic attack. I look around and find my purse. My feet slide a little on the waxed tile and I realize I'm not wearing shoes. No doubt Darcy's doing. I glance around, hoping to spot them without being forced to switch on the light. A thought comes to me as I get on my hands and knees and feel around along the bottom of the sofa. Surely, she wouldn't have hidden my shoes just to keep me here. Would she?

I'm not finding anything here. The light's going to have to go on.

As if by magic, it does just that. The light. Comes on. I gasp. That's just too weird. "Claire, what are you doing on the floor. Are you okay?"

The sound of Darcy's voice does two things for me: grants me a measure of relief that my mental processes didn't cause that light to come on, and heaps on humiliation because I'm on my hands and knees facing away from her, so I can only imagine the view she's getting.

I close my eyes and shake my head. There's nothing to do but get up off the floor, turn, and . . .

Greg is standing above me, once again offering to help me up. He's probably starting to wonder if I see him coming and hit the floor just so I can hold his hand. He grins that adorable, lopsided grin. "You're either the most praying woman I've ever met, or you've lost something."

His silly comment eases the tension from the awkward moment and I take his hand. He eases me to my feet and hangs on to my hand just a little longer than necessary. "What are you looking for?"

Oh, honey. I've been looking for you. Where have you been all my life?

He's looking at me with a little confusion creasing his brow. Is he feeling the same thing I am? That attraction that sometimes causes the mind to balk in its intensity?

"I know what she's looking for." Darcy's bubbly voice breaks the spell, and my cheeks begin to burn with the understanding of exactly what it was that Greg was confused about. He asked me a question, and I got caught up in his brown eyes and totally lost my focus.

"How are you feeling, Claire?" Rick enters the room and my whole body tenses. We still have things to discuss. "Greg told me about Tommy's incident in the alley."

I turn to Greg. No accusation, just wondering if he came all the way over here to tattle on my son. His face colors a little. "Tommy won the skateboard. When I didn't see your van at home, I took a chance he might be here."

Pride shoots through me as I remember the skill Tommy displayed. Then I notice the angry determination creasing every line on Rick's face. I nod. "I don't suppose we ought to let him keep it."

20

Y ou're not serious, right?"

My defenses rise in the face of Ari's horrified query.

"Mother, please tell me you aren't actually coming to the carnival."

Whoosh. The sound of my deflating pride.

I'm standing in my kitchen, wearing my "On the eighth day Eve created chocolate" apron, proudly holding out my pan of perfectly baked brownies for Ari to observe, sniff, and rave over. The brownies that were supposed to make up for all those birthday cupcakes I didn't make for her classes at school. But far from the undying gratitude and promises of perfect behavior, my newly turned sixteen-year-old stares at me as though I'm offering tainted food—possibly sprinkled with rat poison.

"As a matter of fact I *am* coming. I'm manning one of the booths."

Not to mention the fact that I burned my fingers (the ones sticking out from the end of my wristband) on this stinking pan of brownies. She could show a little appreciation for not only my pain but my efforts in the first place. There's no way I'm missing out on that carnival after all I've been through.

"I wish you'd just leave it alone." She flounces across the

room and throws herself into a kitchen chair in an Oscar-winning performance.

"What's wrong?"

"Nothing, Mother, I just don't see the necessity of you showing up at the carnival."

"Mother?" Ari has three words to address me (I don't even want to think about how many she has to describe me). Mom, which she uses most of the time. Ma, which she uses when she's trying to weasel something out of me or weasel out of a chore or punishment. And Mother. Mother always signals a problem. She's upset and gearing up for a fight.

I slide the pan of brownies onto the burners to cool.

If there was ever a time I needed Tough Chick, it's now. In the face of Ari's rejection of my sacrificial efforts, I may just melt into a messy puddle of tears. I draw a deep, cleansing breath and turn as I exhale.

"The necessity of my showing up is that I gave my word to the committee that I would be there to oversee the baked goods booth. I couldn't very well do that without bringing a contribution to the effort. Now could I?"

"How about writing a check? That's the kind of contribution we need the most."

"You're the one who said you wished I was more involved."

"When I was little, Mom. It's not necessary anymore. As a matter of fact, it's not wanted."

"Ari," I say, grabbing her arm as she stomps by, thus thwarting her retreat. "Why is it so terrible that I'm coming? Are you ashamed of me?"

Her jaw drops. "Are you kidding? How could I be

ashamed of this hole-in-the-wall town's only claim to fame? Why do you think I'm so popular? I get it, okay! Without you, I'd be just another wannabe following after the cheerleaders and football players."

Shock fills me as I listen to her little speech. She never wants me around because I steal her thunder? So the truth is she thinks I made her popular. Father, how can she not see her own worth?

"Ari, honey."

"Please, Mother. Don't start trying to be nurturing. It's too late. Besides, Paddy's going to be here any sec. I need to go upstairs. I forgot my purse."

She jerks away and I let her go. I'm too stunned to do otherwise. She honestly thinks no one would even notice her if she didn't have an author for a mother?

But I do suddenly understand where she's coming from. She wants to stand out. To be noticed for her accomplishments. That's why she works so hard to be the best at everything she does. It's the reason she gets up at 5:00 a.m. to exercise, why she struggles to make A's, why she, as a sophomore, is already taking steps toward becoming head cheerleader in two years.

Her drive astounds me, inspires me, and induces respect in me. I admire her as an individual who makes goals, sets out to meet those goals, and if she doesn't achieve them, comes pretty darn close. She's an amazing girl.

I know I must tell her so. I can't stand the thought of her living one more second under the false impression that she has to live up to standards I set by mere public perception. But as I walk through the living room to head for the stairs, the doorbell rings. My heart nearly bursts from my chest. That will be Patrick Devine. My Ari is having her first date.

She skips down the steps, smiling brightly as though our conversation never happened. She even kisses my cheek as she breezes past.

"Be home by eleven, Ari."

"Yes, Mom, I know."

We've had extensive negotiations during the past couple of weeks. I originally told her 10:30, she pushed for midnight (of course), I settled for 11:00. She tried to push again, this time for 11:30, but I wasn't budging. So that's a hurdle we don't have to deal with tonight. A good thing, given the spirit of our last conversation—which still has me spinning a bit.

A cool wind puffs through the foyer as the door flies open, then slams shut in a beat. I'm left standing here, alone, like the Rapture happened, only I must have overestimated my position with God.

I quickstep into the living room and hurry to the window. I am dying to watch her beginning her first date. I push the drape aside just enough to see out. A ten-year-old Mustang sits in my driveway. Mustang? No one said anything about a Mustang. What kind of a pastor lets his son drive a Mustang? A make-out car? Oh, no. My daughter is not going to drive away on her first date with a boy behind the wheel of a car that wasn't designed to inspire control and respectability in anyone, let alone a hormone-ravaged teenage boy.

Panic drives me back to the foyer. Another burst of wind accompanies the opening of the front door just before I reach for the knob. I jump back. Red-faced, Ari precedes Patrick into the house.

"Is everything okay?" I ask, trying to slow the rush of adrenaline storming through me.

"Patrick wanted to come in and say hello before we leave."

Hmm. I'm not sure what to think about that. I know boys. Is he trying to get on my good side by pretending to respect and honor me while he's thinking about unbuttoning my daughter's shirt? Okay, no. That's not fair. I think back to all the times I've seen Patrick, hands lifted to God with tears streaming down his face. Tears that I can't believe he faked. "Thank you, Patrick. I appreciate your thoughtfulness." I raise an eyebrow to Ari in a pointed look. She knows what I mean.

"My parents made it a rule." He grins. "I can't go on a date without picking the girl up at the door and saying hello to her parent. So if they ask . . ."

"I'll be sure and let them know." I can't help but laugh. Suddenly, I don't feel like forbidding the date anymore. 'Stang or no.

"Please, drive carefully."

"Don't worry, I'll get her home safely."

Now, I know he's too good to be true. "Eleven o'clock."

A flush spreads across his adorable face. "My curfew is ten-thirty, so I'll have to have her home by ten."

Ari's eyes widen. But I think she's happy enough to be dating Patrick that she'll take whatever time she can get.

"All right then. You kids enjoy yourselves. Got your cell phone, Ari?"

"Yes." She's a little subdued. Hopefully, it's because

Patrick's respect and politeness are penetrating her consciousness and causing her to see the error of her ways where her attitude is concerned.

Patrick reaches for the door, opens it, and waits for Ari to step out first. She walks past, and I barely detect a muttered whisper. "Ten o'clock. Sheesh."

Saying a little prayer for safety (and chastity), I close the door after them. Kids. You can't put them in a tower, locked away until the craziness of those teen years subsides, can you? As much as I'd like to hide her away now, I realize Ari has to walk it out like everyone else, enduring the pain and heartache, the joys and successes, everything that goes along with stepping out of childhood and into adulthood. Tears form in my eyes. Where did the years go?

I see her face as I held her for the first time—completely overwhelmed by lack of experience, and yet loving her with a fierceness I've never known. Her precious head, swollen from her trip into the world. She barely cried. She just looked around as if to say, "Well, Mom, here I am. Don't screw me up, okay?" I've tried to do right by her. But deep inside, I know I have failed in so many ways. The pain of regret slices through me. And suddenly the heat from the oven seems to have instantly created a sauna. I figure it's perimenopausal.

"Boys," I call upstairs where they're playing, "I'm going outside for a while, if you need me."

No answer, which, even on a good day, usually signals trouble. "Boys!"

I hear scrambling. "Yeah, Mom?"

"What are you doing up there?"

"Playing."

"Playing what?"

"Lord of the Rings Risk," Shawn calls down.

Hmmm. I don't believe it. If there's one thing I've learned from parenting these four children it's that they do not play games together until I make them do it during the occasional game night. My skepticism spurs me up the stairs. Hey, I'm not proud of my lack of faith in the boys. Really. But come on. I smell trouble.

I quietly slip down the hall. I'm a mouse. Unheard, unseen. The little boys' door is wide open, so I get a view of the empty room. I slink forward in my crime-stopping venture and halt at Tommy's room. "I'm attacking the Shire." I hear Jakey's voice pipe in.

"You better not." The warning in Tommy's tone is unmistakable. Is he bullying his little brother over a game? I'm about to fling the door open and confront him. But I stop short at his next words. "Look, if you attack Shawn's Shire, you're going to leave yourself wide open on the other side. He's going to take his Shire back and probably wipe you off that territory altogether."

"Thanks a lot," Shawn grouses. "Stop helping him. That's cheating."

"He's just a kid. I can help him if I want."

"Yeah." Jakey's one-word response brings a smile to my lips. Okay, they're getting along, after all, for the most part. Still, I tap the door and enter.

My heart swells in my chest as I take note of the three of them, seated Indian style on the floor around the game board. I'm suddenly feeling proud, maybe a little optimistic that perhaps the attention—and/or the family counseling—

is paying off. Certainly, they wouldn't have been caught dead playing a board game three months ago.

"Having fun?" I ask as three expectant faces turn to me.

"Yeah."

"Sure."

"Whatever." It's been over a week, after all.

"I'm going outside for a little air."

They look at me with disinterested acknowledgment and then back to the board as Jake and Shawn roll the dice simultaneously.

I close the door and stop off at my room for a jacket.

Outside, I sit in the coolness of the autumn night, watching the last of the fall leaves sway in the breeze, as though fighting to hang on just a little longer. The hint of a chill in the air alerts me to the fact that winter will soon be upon us—images of the coming rush of events play like a slideshow across my mind. First Halloween, then Thanksgiving, then Christmas. Plus the little events accompanying each holiday. Parties at church, family dinners, Christmas luncheons (*Ugh*—don't want to think about the Christmas luncheon at the ladies' meeting).

Ladies' luncheon notwithstanding, I'm eagerly anticipating the fun of the next two months. This will be my first holiday season in several years without the stress of a deadline. I look forward to it with relish. I intend to decorate more lavishly—albeit tastefully—than ever before.

I turn to the glow of headlights coming my direction. As the vehicle draws closer, my heart skips. The motion light above the garage pops to life as Greg's Avalanche drives by. He's rolled his window down. He waves and smiles. I wave and smile back. Greg's officially my neighbor now. He and

Sadie have moved in. As the kids say, "It's weird for anyone else to be living in Granny's house." But you know what? It's exciting, too. I have this feeling about Greg. I think he really likes me.

On a whim I make a decision. I am going to get a plate of those brownies for Greg and Sadie. I'll just cut the rest of them a little smaller. I stand to do just that when I notice another set of headlights coming down our quiet street. As a VW passes I strain to see who's driving. I watch as the unfamiliar car drives a few more yards and pulls up behind Greg in his driveway.

In the light of Mom's garage light, I recognize the driver as her long legs pull her from the car.

Ms. Clark. She gives a throaty laugh as Greg walks toward her car. She clutches his arm and they walk together to the house.

Oh, Greg.

What is it about women like that? Men fawn over them, want to take them to bed (not that Greg is likely to do that), but they don't want to marry them. Why can't they take a hint? The women, that is? Don't they have any pride at all? I mean, loosen the clothes and lighten the makeup, sweetheart. No wonder little boys are writing obscene poetry.

The porch light goes out down the street and I get a sick feeling in my gut. He can just forget about getting any brownies from me.

I think about Ms. Clark walking into my mother's house. Poor Mom, she'd never approve.

21

At ten o'clock on the dot, I hear Patrick's car pull into the drive. I'm curled up on the couch, a burgundy chenille blanket thrown loosely across my legs. Since eight, I've been sketching my plotline for the new series. I'm getting more and more excited about this idea, and I'm wondering if my commitment to take off work includes writing up a new proposal. Technically, new proposals are fun. Entertainment. Only after they sell—and money, editors, and deadlines are involved—do they become work.

Of course once I hear the car pull in, my whole demeanor becomes studied pretense. I am no more concentrating on the new Great American Novel than I am playing the flute. The deception is necessary. I don't want Ari to think I am even the slightest bit interested in her date. Not sure I can pull it off, but I plan to try my best.

I wait. Still not hearing the sound of a door. I bet he's kissing her. As a matter of fact, I'd bet my three-thousand-dollar computer with a 19-inch flat-panel screen against his Mustang that he's kissing her. Not sure how I feel about that. Or maybe I do know how I feel about it. As a matter of fact, I don't think it's a very good idea at all. I better hear a car door soon or—

Okay, there it is.

In the amount of time it takes to travel a slow pace from the driveway to the door, Ari opens the door. From my spot on the couch, I can't quite make out her expression. Is it one of joy, hurt, passion, pain? Come in here so I can see your face!

She walks to the doorway between the living room and foyer. Close enough. I peer, determined to find the slightest flicker of emotion. Nothing. My daughter has the audacity to remain stony faced. Completely closed off. Unreadable. How fair is that?

"Patrick isn't coming in?"

She shakes her head. "Curfew."

"Oh, yeah. Do you want to come in here and sit with me for a while?" I sort of hold my breath as I wait for her answer. I've placed a brownie for each of us (since Greg didn't need them), on a plate and have homemade hot chocolate simmering on the stove. We've waited for her first date since she started thinking about boys.

Sixteen. That magic age. Driver's license, first date. It's a scary year. Full of changes. I want her to know that I'm here for her. I want to help her transition if only she'll open her heart to me.

"What do you say?" I ask my daughter, who still seems to be weighing her options. "How about a brownie and some hot chocolate?"

Her eyes alight with hope, and I have a second of joy until she opens her mouth. "You're not going to the carnival?"

Deflation. Here we go again. Well, what did I expect?

"Yes, I am. I just didn't think it would hurt anything to let us each have a brownie."

Her expression drops. Now I feel like a slug. A slug that just got salt poured on it.

I'm melting. I'm melting.

As it turns out, Ari gets her wish. The carnival has been postponed for a month. A freak fall storm blew through last night and destroyed or damaged too many of the booths. It's going to take a while to rebuild. Thankfully, several of the town's businesses have stepped up with donations of necessary materials.

Ari believes God answered her prayer that I'd just stay away. Did He? Surely He isn't sympathizing with her. Regardless, her belief that He did had Ari suddenly reading her private devotion this morning. So that's good, I suppose.

Trish showed up in her mom's car and the two girls went to the mall. Their first outing together since Trish yanked off the shackles tying her to her mom's schedule. One day she's completely dependent. The next, voilà, a laminated card with a false weight (or it will be false by the time she has to have it renewed) and a bad picture makes her free as a bird.

Shawn has finally started his chores (I pray this is a sign of compliance and perhaps a positive result of counseling). Tommy is still grounded, so he's hanging out in his room— possibly thinking over the negative consequences of smoking. (Yeah, I can only dream.) And Jakey is playing Nintendo. It's hard to break him from this drive to play. He is at loose ends and quite frankly drives me a little nuts when he isn't in front of the video game. Still, I'm the mom, right? Am I not supposed to help him find other things to do? Maybe we should get a horse. Or a dog.

I watch his eyes grow wider and wider as he leans forward, getting his body movements into the game. When his character moves, Jakes moves the same way. It would be cute, really, if it weren't so disturbing.

"Hey, Jake, I'm going for a walk. Wanna come with?"

He stays focused. His eyes never leave the screen. "Jake!"

"Huh?" Still no head movement.

"Okay, that's it." With purpose, I stomp forward and flip the power button on the game.

The sound that comes from his throat can only be described as the sound of an angry bull about to gore his victim. From the look of fury in Jakey's eyes, I have a feeling I would be that victim if he thought he could get by with it. "I didn't get to save it, Mom!"

A little bit of guilt tries to entice me to relent. Apologize for messing up his game. But that's it. His eyes are bloodshot. *Bloodshot!* From playing that stupid game.

"Son, playing that game so much isn't good for you. You go wrap it all up and put it in the cabinet."

"Mo-om! I have to finish this level."

"No. You have to do as you're told. Now. And come for a walk with me."

"I don't want to go for a stupid walk. I want to play my game."

I've never really seen this side of my baby before, and I'm not liking that I'm seeing it now. Methinks perhaps I've left him with his electronic babysitter a bit too much during the formative years—his and my career's.

Recognizing that his dependence on the games isn't entirely his fault, I take a deep breath and pray for patience. "Jake," I say in a voice any counselor would be proud of (hear that, Dr. Phil?), "you may finish your game tomorrow. Right now, I'd like for you to wrap it up and put it away like I said."

He shoots me a look of panic, then turns back to the game. I mean, he turns back and *keeps playing*. As though I haven't said a word.

"Jake?"

"I know! Just a second. I have to finish this level."

Okay, now I'm starting to lose the Dr. Phil voice. "Buddy, get your behind up and put away that game."

He shoves up to his feet and drops the controller. Or a more proper description might be he *throws* the controller on the floor with as much force as his weakling arms can muster.

"Okay, buddy, that just got you grounded for a week from your game."

His mouth drops open. "A week? What am I supposed to do around the stupid house for a whole week?"

"It wouldn't hurt you to read a book. And stop saying 'stupid,' can the attitude, and do as I say or I'm going to make it two weeks."

I sit down on the chair and beckon him to come to me. He does, albeit with clear reluctance. I put my arms around his little body and look him in the eye. "Jake, there's nothing wrong with playing Nintendo as long as you don't overdo it. After your grounding is up, you can play for one hour a day."

His eyes cloud with tears. "Mom, don't do this to me. It's not fair."

I can so relate to his feelings. Discipline hurts. Changing habits hurts. Diet, exercise, Pilates. All these things hurt. But do you know that a kid can get blood clots from sitting pretzel-legged for all those hours a day? I wonder which would hurt worse? The reminder of this news article strengthens my resolve (which can easily be crushed by a teary pair of baby blues).

"It's fair. It'll be hard at first and you'll have to learn to do other things, but in the long run, you'll have a blast."

He groans and slaps his hand to his forehead in true B-grade-movie-actor fashion. "I'll die without my Nintendo."

I smile at the theatrics and draw him closer into a hug. He lays his head on my shoulder and I revel in the smell of his shampoo. The feel of his warm little body. If I could bottle and sell the joy obtained by holding a child, I'd be richer than the Donald-Apprentice.

"Go put the game away and let's go for a walk."

He pulls out of my arms. He sighs a sad little breath. "Okay."

I help him wrap cords and find boxes for the game cartridges and we put them away in the cabinet. He seems to be perking up by the time we head outside and trot down the front steps.

"Where are you going?" Shawn calls. I look around at the semi-leaf-free yard and smile.

"For a walk. Wanna come with us?" It might do the little chub some good to get out and exercise.

"No. I want to finish the yard."

Hmm. All this compliance . . . I'm wondering if I landed on some parallel universe. Or maybe God is doing something in my family.

I don't even look at Greg's house as we pass by. Jerk.

"How come Sadie gets our tree house?" Jakey asks out of the blue.

I wondered when the question might come up. That tree house was one of the main reasons the kids used to love to go to Mom's. "Because it went with the house, bud, and Sadie's daddy bought it from Granny."

"I wish I could sit in it."

"I know. Maybe in the spring we'll get someone to build one for you in our backyard. Would you like that?"

His eyes light up as though I've just given him the moon. "Yeah. Can it be just mine?" Poor kid. When you're the youngest of four children, rarely is anything just yours.

I toss out a laugh. "'Fraid not. It'll be for all of you. But guess what?"

"What?" His voice is pouty, but curious.

"Shawn will probably be the only one who wants to get in it besides you, and after another year or so, he won't be interested anymore."

I see the wheels of his mind turning behind his expressive eyes. "Okay. I guess I can put up with him that long."

I roll my eyes and ruffle his hair. "That's big of you."

"Mom! My hair."

Before I can answer, a rumble of thunder in the distance catches my attention. "We better head back, Jakey. Looks like rain." And the sky-to-ground lightning doesn't look so comforting either.

Raindrops are beginning to fall by the time we pass Greg's house. I hear the sound of my name. I guess I shouldn't be surprised that he's calling out to me. But I am. I don't know how he has the audacity to face me.

Now, if I were alone, I'd walk on by, but considering my little boy is with me, and he's tugging on my sweat jacket, I have no choice but to stop and paste a fake smile on my lips.

"Hi, Greg." I can hear tension, but gee whiz, what does he expect?

"Do you two want to come in out of the rain?"

"Oh, thanks, but it's not far."

A crack of thunder reverberates across the sky.

A scream tears from Jakey's throat and he beelines for Greg's porch. He doesn't stop running until he lands in Greg's arms. Helplessly, I follow my son at a decidedly slower pace and try not to be affected by the sight of my little boy cradled in this man's arms.

"Sadie is in the family room painting on her easel," Greg says to Jakey. "You want to go join her?"

Cocooned in safety, Jake's courage returns. He nods and we enter my childhood home just as a bolt of lightning slices the sky, too close for comfort. "I need to call my sons and tell them to stay away from the windows."

"I'd feel better if you let me call."

"You don't want me to use your phone?"

Greg shakes his head. His eyes scan my face with a bewildered frown. "I'm not being stingy, I'd just hate for you to get electrocuted through the phone line."

"Oh! I hadn't thought of that. I'd best run home."

"I'll go for you." Greg heads for the door. Just like that. SuperKnight to the rescue. Not this time, bud. Don't do me any favors.

I follow and stop him before he can turn the doorknob. "Really, I appreciate the offer, but I think I should go. I can't leave my boys home alone in this. Will you look after Jake until this is over?"

"The strikes are getting closer. I don't think either of us should leave the house."

His concern is kinda cute. I'll give him that. But I can't cozy up to the boy down the block while my two sons are sitting ducks. Besides, wasn't he just cozying up to someone else last night?

"I'm not arguing anymore." I pull open the door and step onto the porch as another jagged slice of light splits the darkened sky. He reaches for me, but I evade his grasp and sprint down the stairs and into the driving rain.

I keep running at a pace I'm sure has never been accomplished—not even by an Olympic runner. Never have I been more grateful for the fact that I've been on an exercise program. My heart pounds—from fear that a big fat lightning bolt is about to slice me in two with a blade of electricity. I'm soaked when I arrive home. My teeth are chattering and the noise is drumming in my ears. "Boys!" I jog up the stairs and find the boys playing with their board game on Tommy's bedroom floor. "Oh, good. You're okay."

"Yeah, Mom. We unplugged the TV and your computer just in case lightning strikes." Tommy says it nonchalantly, like responsible behavior is commonplace for him.

"Thank you. I appreciate it."

A shrug lifts his shoulders. "It's okay." The boys are engrossed in their game. They could care less that I'm about to burst with pride in them. Even Tommy, who has been pretty subdued since he got his skateboard taken away. His new one-hundred-dollar skateboard was awarded to the decidedly less talented second-place winner. I expected days and days of sullen bad attitude coming from him. To my relief, only the first couple of days were tense while he came to grips with the reality of his punishment. But now it's been a week, and all seems to be going well.

"I'll be downstairs. If the storm gets any worse, I'll want you down there, too."

"We've been listening to Shawn's weather radio."

"Oh?" Amazing how the most irresponsible kid can suddenly step up if he thinks he's the man in charge.

"The storm warning is only supposed to last a few more minutes. No tornadoes have been spotted with this one. It's basically just a lot of lightning."

"Let me know if that changes." The wet clothes are starting to make me shiver. By the time I grab my SpongeBob loungies and a T-shirt and slip inside my fuzzy slippers, I'm feeling a little better about the storm in general. True to Tommy's prediction, it's all over a few moments later.

The phone rings. Smile. Has to be Greg.

Sure enough, his voice, low and lazy, reaches through the phone line and sends warmth through my belly. "I wanted to be sure you made it home okay."

"Yeah, I was soaked, but fine otherwise."

"That was pretty risky going out in all that lightning." His tone reaches me, a bit concerned, perhaps even a little irritated. But not enough to raise my defenses.

"Making sure my boys were okay was worth the risk."

"Okay, I know better than to dispute that sort of argument. A mother protecting her young is always right."

I laugh. "Very wise man. Should I come back and get my other son?"

"The two of them are playing. Can he stay for a while? Sadie hasn't had anyone to play with since we moved in. I think she's having a great time."

"Does Jake want to stay?"

"Hang on, I'll ask."

I hear a muffled "Jake! Your mom wants to know if you want to stay and play with Sadie for a while."

I can't quite make out Jakey's response. But Greg clears it up when he comes back to the conversation. "He says yes. I'll bring him home later."

"Okay. That'll be fine."

"Before you go . . ." He hesitates as though trying to locate his next words. "I know you saw Ms. Clark at my house."

My cheeks warm and indignation begins to build. Does he really think I give a flip who he has at his house at nine-thirty on a Friday night until only God knows when? Just in case he's under that mistaken impression, I feel I need to set him straight. "Greg. Who you invite to your house really isn't any of my business. So don't think I'm the kind of nosy neighbor who will be watching out my living room window every time you have female company."

"Well, that's certainly good news," he says wryly. "And I appreciate your utter lack of curiosity concerning Ms. Clark. But the truth is that I didn't invite her. She saw me at the grocery store and followed me home."

Wave after wave of relief washes over me in soothing tides. But words elude me. After all, if I sound relieved, he'll know I was jealous. But I can't just say nothing.

"So she followed you, huh? That was pretty nervy."

"She's a pretty nervy woman. Aggressive."

Hmm. How aggressive? I wonder.

Nice words. Be polite. Say nice words. Be polite. I've been giving myself this little pep talk for the twenty-minute drive from my house to Dr. Goldberg's office. The last person I want to see today is Rick. Especially since the doctor plans to delve into our past relationship and has asked us to come without the children. Darcy, however, will be there as an observer.

I'm skeptical about the whole thing. I mean, how honest can Rick really be about his ex-wife when his current wife is in the room? But I agree to give it a shot. What harm can it do?

Darcy and Rick are already sitting in the waiting room when I arrive, a bit breathless, but relieved to be two minutes before our appointment.

Darcy's smile is tentative at best. I never really thought about how difficult this must be for her. After all, she's in love with Rick. I can understand if she is resentful. Much of his time has been taken up lately with counseling. Counseling where, for the most part, he is not cast in a very pleasant light. I try to feel sympathy for him, but if the truth hurts, don't cheat. Still, Darcy also has to put up with the sessions, most of which she is excluded from.

For some reason, the doctor felt Darcy should be present for this particular session. My stomach has been tied in knots since last week after our family session when the good doctor dropped the bomb. "Just the parents. Including you, Mrs. Frank." He was talking to Darcy, of course. But I was this close to responding to the comment as though I were the current. Too many memories are coming back. If Shawn weren't benefiting from these sessions, I would have ended them after the first one, but how can I?

All this so-called counseling isn't doing me a bit of good. As a matter of fact, I think it's making me a lot crankier lately. And today I'm definitely feeling the resentment. I think I might have a bit of a chip on my shoulder.

"Are we ready to delve into the deep recesses of our failed marriage?" I make my eyes go wide. "Gee, I wonder how long it'll take him to figure out why we broke up. Shouldn't we just tell him up front and give him the rest of the hour off?"

"If you're going to go in there and blame it all on me, there's no point to this."

I'm shocked into total silence. In all these years since our divorce, it never occurred to me that Rick thinks there's any reason behind our breakup other than his inability to keep his zipper shut. Now he's going to walk into that office and pretend that *he's* the victim? And of course Dr. Goldberg, being a man, will fully sympathize with the toad-sucker.

"What do you mean?" I finally manage to eke out through my desert-dry throat.

He leans forward, elbows on knees, hands loosely clasped—like he has all day. "I know you firmly believe that I'm the only one to blame here, Claire. But it takes two to make or break a marriage."

"Oh, is that so? Well, remind me again; how many of us cheated?" I press my finger studiously to the side of my chin and make like I'm calculating. "Gee, sorry, Rick, I'm still just coming up with one answer—you."

"I don't believe this." Rick shoots to his feet and walks to one side of the room, gathers a breath, whips around and comes back. "Are you telling me you don't think you bear any responsibility in our breakup?"

Anger boils my blood. I feel the steam rising. "You bet that's what I mean, buddy boy, and furthermore—"

Dr. Goldberg's door opens. I look up, dread slithering through me like a snake. I don't want to do this. I can't . . .

My head is spinning. I feel the tingling and numbness beginning in my face and hands, feelings all too familiar lately. I hear the doctor's voice through a tunnel. "Are you all right, Ms. Everett?"

Somehow I stumble to my feet. I hear myself vaguely apologizing. I make it to the van, with no clue about how I will drive it home. Warmth floods my shoulder.

"Give me the keys, Claire." It's Darcy. "I'll take you home."

Sweet, faithful Darcy. The kind of woman no man in his right mind would ever cheat on.

Somewhere in my angst-ridden mind, a horrifying thought rises to taunt me. If Darcy's the kind of woman no man would cheat on, and I'm the kind of woman a man obviously would cheat on . . . then if I'd done something differently, maybe my husband wouldn't have gone elsewhere for comfort.

Nausea rises inside me, and I think I'm going to— "Darcy, pull over quick!" The wheels screech to a halt and I scramble out the door.

Isn't that just the way it is? You're going along, living your life—a semi-bestselling author with four semi-great kids, a semi-supportive mother, a semi-bearable ex-husband and his semi-sweet new wife, then suddenly, one day, you try to make things better and guess what? You end up losing your lunch right there at the side of the road with the whole world watching.

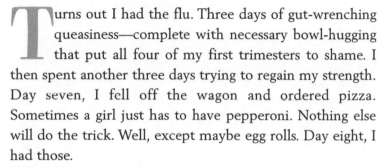

22

Turns out I had the flu. Three days of gut-wrenching queasiness—complete with necessary bowl-hugging that put all four of my first trimesters to shame. I then spent another three days trying to regain my strength. Day seven, I fell off the wagon and ordered pizza. Sometimes a girl just has to have pepperoni. Nothing else will do the trick. Well, except maybe egg rolls. Day eight, I had those.

Sad thing is that several days of Chinese takeout and pizza have put back on four of the twelve pounds I've lost. I resolve to stay off the scale. But I resolved to stop eating pizza and Chinese, too, and look what happened to that, so chances are, tomorrow will find me once again removing every stitch of clothing and hesitantly climbing onto the instrument of torture that just won't lie.

Today is the tenth day since I ran away from counseling. I'm fine physically, except for those extra pounds, but I still can't bring myself to leave the house. From the bed to the couch to the kitchen to the bathroom and back to bed. I'm in a rut. I think I'm depressed. Cheesy, pathetic, and weak of character, but I can't help myself. Rick has once again ruined my life.

First he cheats and leaves, then he gets saved and goes all Husband of the Year-ish, and now, just when I'm on the verge of forgiving him, what does he do? Accuses me of being partly to blame for our breakup. How does he expect to help our son get through this pervy stage he's entered if he refuses to accept responsibility for his own actions? (And for the record, I still think Ms. Clark is at least partially to blame for the poems. I mean, the cleavage—come on.)

The most disturbing thing about Rick finally having the guts to admit what he truly thinks is that for the first time, I'm starting to have my doubts. Visions of temper tantrums and sullen silent treatments and, yes, even "cutting him off" as punishment have sort of been threatening my memory. Despite my attempt to push them away, they keep coming.

Okay, so I admit I wasn't the easiest person to live with, but hello, did he endure the hours of grueling labor to bring forth offspring bearing the name of Frank? Those hours alone should have elevated me to some kind of exempt mode whereby I am not responsible for anything I might say or do. And I endured the excruciating pain four times! I should have been treated like a goddess.

I mean, even if I wasn't the greatest wife a man could hope for, there are never any good reasons to break a vow, right? Anyone can justify anything. Just because a person is hungry doesn't give them the right to steal food. And just because a man is . . . Well, you get the point.

It's all too much. Besides, I have a headache and I just want to stop thinking about it.

The alarm buzzes in my ear. My signal to get up and go pick up the kids. Darcy and/or Rick have been picking them up and taking them daily since my flu. But Rick has committed himself to nastiness and put his foot down, declaring me fit to do my own chauffeuring of the kids. Sheesh, I didn't realize they weren't his kids, too. Whatever. Who needs him to do me any favors anyway?

I haul myself out of bed, grab my slippers, take a second to run a brush through my hair, and head for the van. Ari attends the high school, but rides a transfer bus to the rural K–8 school the boys attend. So luckily I only have one stop to make.

In the pickup line, I hunker down while I wait, hoping that no one will notice me. I have a book, pretending to read. That usually helps people take the hint. Okay, so far so good. Kids of varying sizes, ages, and nationalities are beginning to stream from the school. I crane my neck trying to locate mine. I'm looking the other way when a knock at my window nearly sends me through the roof.

Horror of horrors. It's Greg. I check out my reflection in the rearview mirror, knowing full well I won't like what I see. Why can't I just leave well enough alone? Now I know what he's going to be looking at. Slowly, I turn back to the window. I really don't want to roll it down. Why didn't I even consider this scenario? I'm usually so good at thinking a step or two ahead. Well, maybe not. His brows go up and he points to the wall of glass between us.

Okay, fine. Might as well get it over with. I fire up the engine and press the "down" button.

"Nice to see you out and about," he says. Gotta give the guy credit. He doesn't look a bit scared. Even his eyes are smiling.

"Thanks, Greg. How do you like the house?"

"Love it. So does Sadie."

"Good." And that's where my ability to make nice ends. I've become rusty in my solitude. I'm not fit company for anyone right now.

Finally, he gives a nod. Like he gets that we have nothing more to say. "Hey, do you think Jake wants to come over and play with Sadie after school?"

I shrug. "He might. If he does, I'll send him over when you get home."

He nods and backs off. "Talk to you later." He walks two steps then comes back just as I'm starting to roll the window back up. Leaning in ever so slightly, he sends me a wink and grins. "Cute slippers."

I give in to my first instinct and take a walk down a little road called "cynicism." "Sure they are. Just as cute as the proverbial bug in the proverbial rug." I'm just not in the mood to be all giggly and flirtatious. Besides, giggly and flirtatious is what got me in this funk in the first place. I should never have looked twice at Rick. Never mind that he was a football player and I was the nerd who was supposed to get him through the season with a high enough grade to keep him from getting kicked off the team. Come to think of it, he's always been a cheat. I did most of his work for him. Our entire relationship is just too cliché.

"Okay, then. You're not in a good mood."

"Yeah. Sorry to be rude."

"It's all right. I was married. I remember those days."

Okay, now I'm really embarrassed. So do I let him chalk it up to PMS, or do I tell him it has nothing to do with that?

He smiles again and places his hand over mine. The kindness in his eyes almost breaks me, but Tough Chick emerges, and I steel my heart against him. I've decided to adopt a hands-off policy when it comes to men, which will begin just as soon as Greg's lovely warm hand leaves mine.

"We all have our days. If you want to talk, you know where to find me."

He pats my hand as a farewell gesture and I watch him stride back to the school. Now that guy is definitely too good to be true.

I'm lying on the couch, watching my Nick at Nite, when I hear rustling on the stairs. I pretend I don't hear it and keep my gaze on the black-and-white Dick Van Dyke rerun. From the corner of my eye, I see a head peep over the banister. Whispers follow.

I try to ignore it, but my curiosity gets the better of me. "What are you kids doing?"

Jakey's giggle brings a smile to my lips.

"Come down here." I sit up as he and Shawn file into the living room, followed by Tommy and Ari. "Now, what are you up to?"

I see Shawn is hiding something behind his back. "Cough it up," I say, holding out my hand.

With a sheepish grin, he slowly produces our copy of *Purpose-Driven Life*. Okay, this is not what I expected. I feel myself tearing up. I had to practically force these kids to come downstairs for our nightly reading of this book. Now they're bringing it to me?

"What's this all about?"

"Come on, Mom." Ari sits down at the end of the couch, forcing me to draw my knees up. "No one has the flu for two weeks. We want to know if you're really sick."

"Are you going to die, Mommy?" Jakey's frown shoots straight into my heart.

They're worried? *Remorse* is a mild word for what I'm

feeling. I am such a slug. "You guys thought something was seriously wrong with me?"

"You don't go for walks anymore." Shawn shoves the coffee table out of the way and sits on the floor in front of me.

Tommy sits next to him. "You barely get out of bed. And you don't try to cook anymore."

Try to cook? Hey, now. Show a little appreciation.

Ari pulls her knees to her chest. "We want you to feel better. So we're willing to sit and do the chapter in the book without complaining. If that's what you want."

I roll my eyes. "Your sacrifice truly touches me."

She blushes. "No, we really want to do it, too."

"You do?"

"Yeah, we sort of got used to having you around again since you've been off work. It's nice to have a family devotion."

I grab the book and open it to the bookmark.

Time to snap out of it. Time to face the truth. It's time.

"It looks beautiful on you, Claire."

Linda is weepy, typical of a bride-to-be-again. And well within her right. She presses a tissue to her perky little red nose as she watches me with moisture-sparkling eyes. Clad in a little black dress that comes just to my knees, I'm standing in front of the three-way, full-length mirror at Tammy's Bridal. And I have to say . . . not bad.

For the first time in the history of bridesmaids, the bride has allowed her matron of honor to wear a decent dress. Thankfully, there is no pink, yellow, or even burgundy in this wedding. The whole color scheme is black and white. I'm digging that.

"You're so pretty in that little black number. And the great thing is that you can wear it again when you go out for a nice dinner sometime." She gives me a look that says, "I just know there's a guy out there for you, and that dress is going to reel him in."

I shrug and concentrate on my hips. Which, although smaller than two months ago, are definitely not a size 4. Sigh. Or a 6. Barely even a 12, and that's only if I'm wearing control-top panty hose. I'll be okay. Unless I fall off the wagon again—then I'd have to go with a size 14. It's been a week since I had pepperoni. I'm not doing too badly, but I have to prepare myself for the possibility of a few holiday pounds. Who in their right mind gets married between Thanksgiving and Christmas? I look at the little black number hugging my hips. I hope I don't have to up-size. Control, Claire. Control.

"Looks like this is the one." Linda's optimism is a little infectious and I envision myself walking down the aisle carrying a bouquet of white carnations. Linda is carrying white roses.

"Yes, I think you're right."

"Great. Now that's settled. Are you up for a latte at Churchill's?"

"What time is it?"

Linda glances at the clock over my head. "Just after one o'clock."

My pulse picks up at the thought of my one-thirty appointment. "Wish I had time."

I slip into the dressing room and lean against the wall. Today is the day I have to pick up where I left off last time we tried to have a counseling session with Darcy and Rick and me. It's been two weeks. Funny how in all that time I haven't had one panic attack. But now just the mere realization that I'm twenty-five minutes from being forced to listen to Rick con the doc into believing it's all my fault he cheated, and my hands are going numb.

Why is it that I can't let this go? I know it's a problem. I've prayed and cried and have forgiven until I'm blue in the face and still, it's not taking. I just want to be over it. You know? I want to stop feeling the pain.

I say good-bye to Linda and leave the bridal shop behind. Ten minutes later, I'm on time and doing deep breathing exercises in the minivan before I subject myself to this blame game.

Wariness fills Rick's eyes when I walk through the door and greet them with as much enthusiasm as I can muster. "Hi."

Darcy comes to me, determination in her eyes, that familiar look that pretty much bodes for no argument. "Everything is going to be all right. You'll get through this. We," she says, with earnest appeal, "will get through this. Together." Her smile is trembly, and I know this is hard for her, too.

I give her hand a little squeeze and the door opens.

"Everyone ready?"

I gulp in some air. Am I ready for this? Probably not. Is anyone ever really ready to face a painful past? But I know it must be done. So I forge ahead. I'm determined to be graceful, polite, and by taking the high road show this doctor just how much to blame Rick really is.

Dr. Goldberg bids us to sit. We do—Rick and Darcy in the burgundy love seat, me in the overstuffed chair across from them, separated by a large, square coffee table. I wonder how long it would take me to leap across that table and grab Rick around the throat. Because one word out of line . . .

"Thank you all for coming. I believe the final step in fully helping your son is going to come from your commitment to work things out between you."

"Well, that's why we're here." I give him the fake smile I've perfected from my years of doing book signings.

"You two were married for how many years?"

"Ten." Rick pipes up, practically before I can process the question. He must have been anticipating what the doctor would ask.

"Wrong. Eleven."

"No. Ten."

I scowl and give the doctor my see-what-we're-dealing-with-here look. "Our daughter is sixteen, we've been divorced five years. I got pregnant on our honeymoon." I peer at Rick. "Ringing any bells?"

Rick's face colors. "Oh, yeah. Eleven."

Clearing his throat, Dr. Goldberg makes a note. "So, eleven years is a long time. What caused the marriage to end?"

I snort. I have already decided I will not be the one to answer this question. Apparently Rick has come to the same decision, because we're just sitting there, while time ticks away.

"Oh, come on, you two. How are things ever going to get better if you won't even tell the doctor?" Darcy sighs. "Rick was not a Christian back then. And he sort of . . . cheated."

"Sort of cheated?" Okay, how do you sort of cheat? I pose the question.

"Lay off her, Claire. She's just trying to get the ball rolling here."

"Well, then you answer. How do you sort of cheat? Is that what you told her you did?"

"For crying out loud. I don't need this." Rick shoves up from the couch and heads for the door.

Typical.

"Rick, you knew this wasn't going to be easy." Darcy's small voice speaks so much into the small room. "For any of us. Including Claire."

His shoulders rise and fall. He turns and comes back to the couch.

"Thank you for returning, Mr. Frank. Let's talk about why you had the affair."

"Affairs. He just—"

"He asked me. Not you." Rick shifts forward and I clam up. So much for taking the high road. "Sorry."

"I don't really have a good excuse," Rick says. "Claire and I were just not right for each other. We married too young."

The memories flood back. Years of dating through college and med school. I knew Rick dated other girls. We had an agreement (his suggestion, of course) that we could if we wanted as long as we told the other one. He went out often. I never dated anyone besides Rick. Come to think if it, I never have.

"I felt guilty because I took her virginity," Rick is saying. "I guess I knew we shouldn't get married. But Claire was the 'girl back home.' The one I'd dated through high school and on breaks. When I came home to do my residency it just seemed natural that I would marry her. And I did. Despite my doubts."

Worm! Toad-sucker! Jerk!

I rise on shaky legs. Visions of the years I sacrificed trying to please him slam me like a line drive to the head. My mind is spinning. "You selfish pig! I wasted my youth on a man who didn't love me? Because I was the 'girl back home'? What right did you have to deny me the chance at love?" I'm so filled with outrage I can't think straight. How dare he? How dare he have the audacity to sit here and make me feel so undesirable, so unlovable?

"I know." And that's all he says in his defense. "Claire, I'm sorry. I'm so sorry. I did love you. The first couple of years of our marriage were good. Remember? When Arianna was a baby? I couldn't wait to come home to be with the two of you."

"But you were never there."

"I was on call most of the time. You know what those years were like. First my internship, then residency. I had no choice. At first you were my haven. But when you got pregnant with Tommy you became so demanding that I didn't know how to please you. You pushed and pushed. For more than I could give."

"So it's all my fault. Is that what you're saying?" I hear the tremor in my voice and I'm ashamed. I will not cry. Where's Tough Chick when I need her?

"Claire. This isn't about assigning blame." The doctor's annoyingly objective voice breaks through the emotional scene. "We have to get through the anger to healing. Being willing to consider two sides of the issue is essential to getting rid of the hostility that is most certainly affecting your children."

I nod but really don't trust myself to speak. Because do they really expect me to accept responsibility for the breakup of our marriage?

"Claire. It wasn't your fault that I broke our vows."

Okay, then. That's more like it.

"Until I started going to church and gave my life to Jesus, I blamed it on you. But there was no excuse for what I did. I tore our marriage apart." Tears fill his eyes. "I've never asked for this before. And maybe I don't deserve it now . . ."

Oh, God, please. Please . . . Don't . . .

"No. I won't ask for forgiveness."

My stomach roils within me. I wanted him to ask. Why didn't he ask?

"Forgiveness is something you have to give of your own free will. I know that now. I've been waiting all this time for you to admit to your part in our breakup. But I forgive you. For all the pushing, the fighting, the bitterness during and since the marriage."

Rick's blue eyes are glistening with unshed tears. A week ago, in the same situation, I would have sworn he put them on for effect. And even now I'm not 100 percent convinced that he's not. Still, he says he's forgiving me? What am I supposed to do, fall into his arms and kiss away his tears while thanking him from the bottom of my heart? Pul-lease.

What happens next was probably inevitable. I mean, Rick's going all sensitive on me, so of course he was bound to do it.

"Claire. I'm not asking you to forgive me. I broke my word to you over and over."

And over and over and over.

"All I want to say is that I'm sorry. I'm sorry that I caused you pain. I'm sorry I caused our family to fall apart." Tears slip down his cheeks. And suddenly he's sobbing into his hands. "I'm sorry."

The moment I've waited for since the fourth year of our marriage when I knew for sure he'd slept with another woman. I've wanted to see him cry. Apologize. Grovel, if you will. Now I sit here watching him, a broken man, and I'm numb. I've always thought that if he'd just admit he was wrong, if he'd just tell me he was sorry, that all the bitterness would be gone. I was wrong. If anything, now I hate him more than ever.

Nausea churns my stomach. "I'm sorry," I choke out. "I have to leave."

No one speaks, and no one tries to stop me. I hold back the sobs until I'm halfway down the street, then they come in waves. Droves.

How can I hold a grudge against him now that he's broken down in front of me? What kind of a person does that? What kind of a person am I?

God help me, I can't forgive him. I want to. But I can't.

23

The thing about crying is that, when the reason is this close to home, something you've held in your heart for a really long time, it's hard to stop the tears from flowing. I've been crying for the better part of two days.

Thankfully, the tears have dried up, for the moment. I'm rushing around trying to get everything ready so that we can be at the school grounds on time when Ari—sweet, self-serving thing that she is—makes a kindly gesture. "Mom, really. If you aren't up to going, I'm sure they can find someone to fill in for you."

I roll my eyes at her obvious attempt to keep me from that carnival. They've finally gotten all the booths rebuilt and found a date to reschedule. A week and a half before Thanksgiving. It's a little colder than it would have been last month, but that's okay. We can wear jackets. We've also added a chili booth and apple cider. It works. There's always a way to make something fit.

"Nice try."

She gives a huff.

"Look, let's not go through this again. I'm going to help out at this carnival and that's that. You are going to shine like Venus in the night sky with or without me there."

"Sure. Everyone will be asking me if I can talk to you about getting them published."

I have to laugh at this. It's hard enough for me to get my own next contract. Even with a hotshot agent. Yet, every so often, a new writer asks me if I can get them "in" with my publisher. Do they really think I can just talk to the right people and boom, here's a contract for the new author? Oh, and while you're cashing that million-dollar advance check, how about heading down to the Reality Check Detective Agency and getting a clue!

"All you have to do is tell them they'll have to ask me."

"Oh, sure. Then I'm a snob who doesn't want to talk."

"Well, Ari. You *are* a snob who doesn't want to talk. Aren't all cheerleaders?" I give her a wink-wink.

She rolls her eyes. "That's so stereotypical."

"You're right. I'm sorry. I was just trying to get you to lighten up."

"By accusing me of being stuck-up?"

Oh, brother. This conversation is going absolutely nowhere. "Did you remember to put your duffel bag in the van?"

"Yes. Are they coming to the carnival?" "They" refers to Rick, Darcy, and the boys, who started their weekend with Dad last night while Ari stayed to do last-minute preparations for the carnival.

"I don't know. I didn't have a chance to talk to your dad." And by "I didn't have a chance," I mean I hung up on him the one time he's tried to call since the counseling session.

"Don't worry about it. If they don't come, I'll drive you over to his house for the rest of the weekend as soon as the carnival is over."

We arrive at the school amid a flurry of mid-afternoon

arrivals. I'm wearing jeans. And ladies, my shirt is tucked in. Yeah, baby! I'm not ready for the Levi's. I'm not getting a pair of 501s until I fit into a 29/30 short. But I'm getting there.

My net weight loss is finally up to fifteen pounds. So my size 12 jeans are looking nice. Not too tight. Not loose by any stretch of the imagination, but definitely better than the 16s I was wearing before I started walking and watching the sugar and fast food. I'd love to be in a 10 by Christmas. But again, I have to consider holiday candy and cookies. Summer sausage and cheese. I mean, there's a month of that stuff coming up. What, I'm supposed to just sit there while everyone else is munching on goodies? Well, okay. I guess I know the answer to that.

Mrs. Lincoln greets me with a toothy smile. Ari's cheerleading coach is wearing shorts and her legs are tanned. It's fifty degrees out. I just don't think I need to comment further about that. Except to say she is wearing a sweatshirt, too. And a beanie with a Chiefs logo across her forehead.

There's an exhibition football game this evening and Ari is cheering. It's a fund-raiser between the faculty and the football players.

Within thirty seconds of our arrival at the check-in booth, the masses sense her presence and suddenly Ari disappears amid a crowd of admirers. Yeah. She really needs to worry that I'm going to upstage her. I plaster a smile and try not to stare at Mrs. Lincoln's tanning-boothed legs.

"Any new books coming out?" Mrs. Lincoln asks. I know this woman couldn't care less if I have a new book coming out or not. It's the common question anyone asks when they don't have a clue how to start conversation with me.

Still, I smile, trying to be conscious of the fact that this woman spends every Friday and Saturday night at the lounge connected to the local Mexican restaurant. She hangs all over any man who will show her a little attention and, I suspect, make her feel like she's still prom queen. My heart aches a little for her. "Not for a few months," I reply. "Where do I take the brownies?"

"Oh, gosh. Sorry. Just take them over to that booth. You'll share with Darcy."

I nearly drop the platter. "Darcy . . . who?"

Her face goes blank "Um. Darcy Frank. Ari mentioned you wanted to share the booth?"

"She did, huh?" So Ari is either (a) trying to heal the rift between her stepmother and me, or (b) getting me back for offering to help. "I wasn't aware that Darcy was even planning to be here. I thought the mothers of cheerleaders were supposed to do this."

Mrs. Lincoln gives an airy laugh. "We'll take all the help we can get."

"That's fine, then." I mean, what else can I say, really? Shall I throw a temper tantrum? I could, but I won't. "I'll just go get set up."

I set the individually wrapped brownies on the booth. There are already a few other baked goods on the counter. I assumed they were dropped off by mothers manning different booths. As I start arranging things in an appealing, tasteful manner, a tantalizing aroma wafts over to me from the next booth.

Man. No one told me they were selling bratwurst. I can feel my jeans getting tighter with every sniff, and I feel the urge to untuck my shirt and let it hang over my hips.

My stomach responds to the scent and suddenly I feel the tug of gravity, pulling me toward that booth.

Before I make it that far, I see Darcy coming toward me. My appetite leaves as nerves replace hunger in my gut. She gives me a tentative smile and sets a platter of . . . oh, dear Lord, is that fudge? With walnuts. "You brought candy to a bake sale?"

"I thought with the holidays, people might be in the mood to get a head start."

She's a genius. I'm sooo ready. I give a nonchalant shrug and nod. "Good idea."

Tension is thick between us—thicker than the saturated air. I'm so relieved to see Linda pop up to our booth that I grab her in a tight hug.

"Mmmm," she says, eyeing the brownies, cookies, pies, and cakes and zeroing in on the fudge. "If I didn't have a wedding gown to fit into in a mere two and a half weeks, I'd buy up a little bit of everything."

"Be strong, my friend," I say, knowing full well she could eat the entire booth and not gain an ounce with that fourteen-year-old-boy metabolism of hers.

"Do you have all the wedding plans finished, then?" Darcy's small voice pipes in. I suspect, more than anything, she just wants to remind us she's present.

Linda turns an affectionate smile on the younger woman. "Almost. I just need a singer to croon a sappy love song, and I'm all set."

"How about Greg?" I say, a little faster than I wish I had. Greg. Like we're some super couple and I can just speak for him.

"Greg . . . There's a good idea," Linda agrees with a nod.

She turns to Darcy. Pod Girl gives a chirpy giggle and I have a sneaky feeling Linda gave her a "look" that sings, "Claire and Greg, sittin' in a tree, k-i-s-s-i-n-g . . ."

I shrug. "Whatever."

Linda laughs. "I'll catch you two later. I'm manning the dunk tank. Can you believe we're having a dunk tank in this weather? How busy do you think I'm likely to be?" She turns to leave, then steps back. "Okay, wait. I have to have some of that fudge, dress or no dress. But don't let me come back for more."

I feel a little hung out to dry when she leaves, mainly because now I have no choice but to face Darcy. Someone has been thoughtful enough to provide chairs for us to sit on behind the booth, so we sit. Darcy nearly blinds me with a bright smile. "When Ari told me you wanted me to come, I almost couldn't believe it."

Wow. I can't believe it either. When I get my hands on Ari I'm going to wring her scrawny little neck.

Darcy gives a little gasp, and I can tell by the look on her face she's figured it out. "You didn't ask for me, did you?"

I shake my head.

"Why would she lie?"

"I guess she wants us to talk it out." Or quite possibly she just did it for sport.

"She knows what happened?"

Irritation slams me. What kind of mother does she think I am? "Of course not. But she does know we aren't really talking. I don't have anything against you, Darcy. So don't take this personally. I have things I just need to work out. And right now . . . you and Rick go together . . ."

She nods in understanding. "Do you want me to leave?"

"No, I don't want you to leave. It was sweet of you to come in the first place. Let's just try to act normal for the rest of the evening and we'll get through this."

Turns out, Darcy and I are quite the team. Our booth sells out fairly early. By seven, though, snow flurries are flying around in a hint of early winter. It won't last. It probably won't even dust the ground, but somehow it makes me feel good. "Hey, Darcy. Let's go get a bratwurst and some apple cider."

"Really?"

I nod. "We can watch the rest of the exhibition game."

Her eyes brighten in the glow of the generator-controlled lights. "That sounds like so much fun. Let's do it."

We each buy a juicy barbecued brat, then make our way to the cider counter just as the players begin filtering in from the field. We look at each other. Darcy wrinkles her nose in a cute, disappointed frown.

Darcy Frank, I miss you. And I'm fully aware that the very fact that I miss her, given the circumstances, is just . . . wrong.

"Oh, well. I guess we missed it." I take a bite of my brat. then wash it down with cider. Hmm. When did they get so greasy?

I pull out my cell. "Let me call Ari and get her up here so she can ride home with you."

She nods. "Sure."

Her voice mail answers. I flip my phone shut. "She must have forgotten to turn it back on after the game. Do you want to walk down to the football field with me?"

She nods, taking another bite of her brat. We start the walk across the damp ground. We're quiet at first. I mean, we agreed to get through tonight, right? Our future friendship is sort of in limbo. And what is there to talk about, really? *"Oh, did you hear Rick apologized? What a toadsucker."* See? I can't talk about the stuff that's really going on. Still . . .

"Listen, Darce. We don't have to let this come between us, do we? What if we just forget about that dumb counseling session? I have to work this out on my own."

"Oh, Claire. The counselor has really helped Rick deal with some things. If you'd only give it a chance . . ."

Utter lack of understanding. This is what I get for holding out the white flag. "I have given it a chance. And it didn't work for me. Maybe it worked for Rick because he had deeper issues."

She chews her lip. I know she's holding in her opinion. And I'm not going to pry. I don't give a flip what Barbie thinks about it. Well, I care a little. "All right, what do you want to say?" I blurt.

"That was really hard for Rick. I just thought if he finally apologized it might help you deal with it."

If she's saying what it seems like she's saying, I think I'm going to barf. It means that whole session was a lie. "Are you telling me you made him apologize to me?"

"Come on. No one makes Rick do anything he doesn't want to do."

Well, she's right about that. No one can make him do what he doesn't want to do and no one can make him stop doing something he wants to do. But that's not the point here. And she knows that. I can tell by the quiver in her voice that she's hiding something. "But you are the one who suggested it?"

"Oh, all right, Claire, if you're going to pin me down. Then yes, I told him it would be a gesture of goodwill. And that you needed to hear him apologize for closure."

How did she know? How does she always know the right thing to do? My breath leaves me in a cloud as I give a sigh. "If you had to tell him to do it, it wasn't real."

She stops walking and stares at me. In the lights glowing above the football field, I see anger. "You're too hard to please, Claire. You want everyone else to do the giving, but you're not willing to budge. I might have suggested to my husband that he apologize for the pain he caused, but no one could have faked those sobs. You left and he cried for another half hour. And you know what? Those tears weren't for him. They were for you." With that, Darcy whips her five-foot two-inch frame around and leaves me standing there in the cold.

"I just bet they were for me," I mutter into the night. I stomp toward the abandoned field. Only a few stragglers remain. Mostly kids, goofing off. I spot Trish.

"Hey, Trish. Have you seen Ari?"

She looks a little nervous, which instantly raises my suspicions. I'd like to give her the benefit of the doubt, but when a kid says "uh" in response to a direct question, there's no getting around it. Someone is doing something they're not supposed to be doing. And by "someone" I mean my precocious daughter. "All right. Spill it. Now."

"She'll kill me, Ms. Everett." Like that's supposed to induce sympathy.

"Spill it."

"She's by the bleachers."

"Thank you." My gut clenches as I conjure up all the stuff

she could be doing "by the bleachers." Drugs, drinking, smoking . . . the possibilities.

I think about calling out so she can stop whatever she's doing, thereby relieving me of the necessity of confronting yet another issue. But I'm starting to get mad enough at the thought of her doing any of those things that I want to catch her red-handed.

I walk around the side of the bleachers. I'm tempted to close my eyes. Hear no evil, see no evil, stay sane another day. But I keep them open and face my daughter's truth. I stop short. A wave of dizziness washes over me. There, at the end of the risers, I see my cheerleader daughter, leaned back against the bleachers in what has to be the most uncomfortable position in the history of make-out sessions. Patrick is practically on top of her. I see red. As if things aren't bad enough, now I catch my daughter being groped in public by the preacher's son.

24

There are times in a girl's life when she wants her mother. And right now, I want mine oh-so-badly. But the phone is ringing off the hook and Mom's not picking up. I try Charley's line and a teenage girl answers. Just what I'm *not* in the mood to talk to. I get my information as quickly as possible. The girl happens to be a fan of my books, and it's not easy to get off the line with someone who thinks you're a celebrity.

Here's the scoop: Mom's out to the theater with Charley and Marie. The theater. They have culture in Texas. Can you believe it?

Good for Mom, bad for me.

I hang up, dejected, and head upstairs.

My hands are shaking by the time I reach for the ibuprofen in my bathroom medicine cabinet. The tension in my head is reaching the point of explosion. I'm relieved the kids are staying at Rick's. I was really tempted to drive Ari home, march her upstairs, and lock her in her room until kingdom come. But I think Darcy sensed I might not be in the best frame of mind to handle my daughter's indiscretion in the wisest manner. Despite our earlier disagreement, Darcy was able to convince me to let it go for the weekend.

I slide on my SpongeBobs and a ratty old Chiefs sweatshirt and pad into my bedroom. I've made a quality decision. Tonight I am going to finish *The Mirror Has Two Faces*. I've avoided romance in books, movies, music, and Hallmark cards for three whole weeks. Now it's time to face my demons.

I am just crawling beneath my fluffy quilt when the doorbell rings. Shoot. Why didn't I go ahead and pull the van into the garage? Now there's no way to pretend I'm not home.

I shrug into my blue terrycloth bathrobe and slide my feet into my leopard-spotted slippers.

This better be good. And it better not be Rick or Darcy or any of the kids, because I'm just not in the mood. Well, unless one of the kids is sick. What if that's it? My footsteps pick up and my heart is racing as I fling open the door. The second time in a week Greg has seen me looking my utter worst. What's with this guy? Does he have radar?

"Hi." His lopsided grin does nothing for allowing my heart rate to return to normal.

"Greg. What are you doing here?"

He holds up a pizza box. I think I love this man.

"Sadie's with Mom for the night, and I saw Rick with the boys this afternoon so I figured you'd be home alone."

Okay, if you want to know the truth, I'm a little insulted by the assumption. I mean, what makes him think I don't have a date? I mean, besides the ratty robe and SpongeBob jammie bottoms and leopard-spotted slippers. Oh well, who am I kidding anyway? He figured right. I shrug. "Yeah. Here I am. All alone." Looking at your pizza box.

So why is he standing on my porch with pizza in hand, anyway? A sudden urge to share his pizza with me? I'm starting to catch a glimmer of hope. Still, I don't want to assume. He hasn't made any kind of declarative statement to make me believe he is in fact suggesting we spend the evening together. He may just need to borrow a paper plate or napkins for all I know.

"Have you had supper?"

If you call that bite of greasy brat supper—which I don't. "No. I wasn't all that hungry."

His expression drops. But I refuse to read too much into it. "Oh, well, I guess I can go on home. I just hated to eat alone."

"Are you kidding?" Just the medicine I need to brighten my general outlook. I take the box from him and motion him inside with my head—which, amazingly, is feeling all better. "Who says you have to be hungry to eat pizza? Pizza is fun food. Comfort food. A food for all occasions and any situation. This *is* pepperoni, right?"

"Is there any other kind?" He laughs and follows me inside, shutting out the cold behind him. "A girl after my own heart."

Really? Stop it, stupid. Hands-off policy. Remember?

"So what do you have planned for tonight?" He's looking at me in my PJs and asking me what I have planned? Hmm. Cute, picks the right kind of pizza, good singer, not so quick on the uptake.

Apparently he makes the connection himself, because his ears go red. "You were going to bed early? Do you want me to leave?"

Try to take this pizza, bucko, and you will lose most, if not all, of your fingers.

"This is a better idea," I say. "I was just going to watch a movie upstairs. I wasn't exactly planning to sleep."

"Oh, really? What movie?" He goes right to the cabinet by the stove and grabs a couple of plates. Now, never in the history of someone going to my cabinets have I ever, ever had someone nail it the first time. I mean, what's wrong with him? Doesn't he know that's where the cooking stuff like salt and garlic powder is supposed to go? That's just too weird.

But I don't ask and he doesn't offer so I'm assuming he just opened the closest cabinet and got lucky.

"It's sort of a chick flick." Why am I apologizing? *"The Mirror Has Two Faces.* Ever seen it?"

"No. You offering?"

"You'd watch it with me?"

"Thought you'd never ask."

Okay, is it any surprise that I'm melting into a pile of mush?

After dinner I trot upstairs to grab the movie. While I'm at it I put on a bra and change my shirt so I don't have to sit around in my bathrobe. I wonder where his sense of propriety went, anyway. Only a few weeks ago he didn't want to come inside to get a house key for fear of the neighbors talking.

Should I ask him, or leave well enough alone? I watch him sitting all cute and manly on my sofa, and the choice is pretty clear.

"Shall I start a pot of coffee before we watch the movie?"

"None for me." He smiles, his eyes sliding over me, registering the fact that I changed out of my bathrobe. When his gaze returns to mine, I see appreciation. I practically swallow my tongue as unspeakable joy leaps to my heart. Imagine if I had another ten pounds off.

No more pizza for a month! And I mean it.

I slide the movie into the VCR and take a seat on the sofa, next to Greg.

The movie is a little embarrassing in parts, but I'm totally able to identify with the Barbra Streisand character. I mean, gee whiz, I want that heart-pumping, orchestra-music-hearing, passion-filled relationship. Funny how the Jeff Bridges character is also named "Greg." How's that for providence?

When the credits roll and the two of them are dancing in the street, two unlikely lovers finally finding their way to each other, I gather the nerve to cut a glance to Greg. My heart plummets. This movie definitely didn't inspire an ounce of romance in the sleeping hunk.

One thing I can say for him. At least he doesn't snore. Information that might come in handy some day when he's on his knee and I'm trying to decide whether or not to take the ring.

"Wake up, slugger," I say, shoving his shoulder. I'm a little ticked off. We finally spend an evening together. And I'm so boring he falls right asleep.

"What happened?" he asks, blinking, trying to focus.

"A tornado hit New York and they both died." Which is just as well, because why even try to have a relationship.

I stand up and move toward the kitchen with him following me. "Hey, are you mad at me?"

I whip around to tell him "No." But he's . . . there.

His arms reach out to steady me. His gaze captures mine, and I feel all the things a woman is supposed to feel when she's in the arms of a great-looking guy with charm, wit, a strong sense of who he is in Christ, a job. I'm blown away by emotion. I think he might be about to kiss me. I want to raise my chin just a little so he knows it's okay.

Instead, I burst into tears.

He doesn't seem surprised. I find that, in and of itself, to be surprising. Suddenly I'm tucked into a warm embrace, my head settled against a firm, broad chest. I feel his hand stroking my hair. The gentleness of the action makes me sob even harder. I want a man like this to love me. Or do I want *this* man to love me?

"I'm sorry," I gulp when I'm finally able to gain enough control to pull away.

"Don't be." He hands me a tissue from the counter.

After making good use of the thing, I gather in a breath, trying to screw up the courage to look him in the eye. "I never break down like that."

"Then maybe it's time you did." He smiles tenderly, and I'm shocked that he's not bolting out the door with the speed and grace of a gazelle.

I shrug. "Maybe."

"If you need to talk, I'm good for more than just a shoulder to cry on."

I know darned well that if I start, he's going to hear the venom in my voice when I mention Rick. That alone will likely run him off. Not to mention Ari's exhibition of practically sexual activity right in front of the whole world. What kind of mother will he think I am?

"If it's any help, I already know some of what might be troubling you."

"Oh?"

He nods. "Rick is my friend."

"I see." I knew they were friendly. Didn't realize they were friends. Awkward.

"Rick told me what happened at the counselor's office."

"You know what? If one more person tells me how sorry Rick is and how hard it was for him to—" I use my fingers for the quote/unquote sign. "—'apologize,' I think I'm going to blow my top."

"I wasn't going to do that, Claire." His hand slides down my arm until it reaches my hand. He laces his fingers with mine.

Okeydokey, then.

With my heart in my throat, I allow him to pull me toward the couch. He sits, and I follow. He doesn't pull away, so I try to be inconspicuous just in case he hasn't really noticed we're holding hands.

"I'm not here to talk about Rick. I know you've gone through a lot lately. I just thought you could use some company."

"You fell asleep," I accuse.

"I never said I was good company."

I laugh.

"That's more like it." His eyes hold fondness. Fondness for me? Is that the little-sister kind of affection? Or the I-must-have-you-lest-I-die kind of affection?

I can write romance to make your toes curl, but don't ask me what's really in a man's mind. I'm totally clueless. But then, I'm sure that's not real news.

His eyes are on my hand, my wrist, which bears a scar that makes it look as though I tried to end it all. "When are you getting the other operation?"

"Monday, as a matter of fact." More than ready to hop off

the emotional roller coaster, I immediately warm to the new topic. "Only I'm not getting the same type of procedure. The surgeon did more X-rays, and the left wrist isn't as bad. We can do a less-invasive procedure. Lots less pain and a much shorter recovery time."

"That has to be a relief."

"It is. I'm ready to get back to work." No. that's only par- tially true. I am ready to be creative again. I'm ready for a routine. But I'm afraid, too. I'm still having trouble with the kids. What if I go back to the way things were before? Like Ari said to Mom on the phone that night? Only before, I al- ways knew Mom was there to buffer my head-in-the-clouds neglect. Now, I'm all they have. Besides Rick—but it's not the same.

I know it's my choice. But old habits die hard.

"What's going on in that head of yours?" Greg asks. "You've grown a little pensive."

See. Every writer needs a man who understands words like *pensive* and uses them correctly. This guy was made for me.

Can I have him, God?

Hmm. God's not answering. Guess I'll just have to wait and see.

25

om finally calls me back on Monday night. A full weekend after I left my message. I'm feeling a little groggy from pain medication, but this outpatient surgery was so much easier than the first one. Thank You, God.

"How'd it go, honey?" she asks.

"Much better. I should be ready to get back to work in a couple of weeks."

"I thought you were taking off until New Year's." Her voice is slightly stern.

"That's what I meant." I smile to myself. Unless you count getting my new proposal typed up and sent off to my agent. But like I mentioned before, proposals are fun. Not work.

"So, how was the theater, Mom?"

"Fun. We saw *Cats*."

"*Cats*? Like the Broadway *Cats*?"

"It was a college production. The president of the college bought an SUV from your brother and invited the three of us to go."

"That's nice."

"Yes. Bob's a very nice man and he's a real cowboy."

Bob? Something about the familiar way she says "Bob"

raises my suspicion. Not to mention the fact that I'm wondering how a college president can be a real cowboy.

But I don't have to ask, because Mom's coming right out with it. "Would it bother you if I started dating Bob?"

Wow, what am I supposed to say to that? Yes, Mother, I think you should remain forever true to the memory of my father. Which I guess I actually do think, sort of. I guess I'll have to lie.

"Of course not. You're a big girl. So this Bob guy. Pretty neat, huh?"

She gives a slight laugh. Embarrassed, I think. "He's a wonderful Christian man. Goes to my church, even."

Well, there you have it. "What's Charley think?"

"Oh, you know your brother."

Okay, suppose I don't. "Likes him, huh?" I take a chance.

"Of course. Charley likes everyone. He just wants me to be happy."

Oh, the guilt.

"Me, too, Mom. I'm happy you've found someone to have a little fun with."

"Thank you, hon. I was hoping you might bring the kids and come for Christmas."

Now, my mom knows that's not going to happen. I don't even know why she would bring it up. "You know I can't take the kids away from Rick on Christmas. He's been very good about letting me have them every year, despite the fact that he could have them every other Christmas. I want him to at least get to see them on Christmas Day."

"I understand. I was just hoping to introduce you to Bob. And of course, I ache to see you and the kids."

I can't help the warmth of emotion filling my chest.

"We'll try to get there soon after the first of the year for a weekend at least."

We hang up, and it's not until later that I realize she wants me to meet Bob. What exactly does that mean?

Two and a half weeks after my surgery, I make an executive decision. It's time to wow the neighborhood by decorating for Christmas. I still can't carry anything heavy, so I enlist the kids to drag all the decorations from the attic.

I like my attic. It's a walk-in, and I find it so spooky and full of things to trip the imagination. Jakey, however, strongly disagrees. He refuses to help, and no amount of threatening will change his mind. The attic terrifies him.

"Leave him alone, Mom," Ari says. "I'll bring down his share. The kid's scared."

I'm so pleasantly surprised at this moment of empathy and rare support for her brother that I don't even scold her for mouthing off.

"Okay, Toms, go out to the shed and bring up the ladder, will you?"

"What do you need a ladder for?"

"Outside lights."

"All right!" Shawn pipes up, the first sign of excitement I've seen from the kid in a while. "Can we use icicle ones like Granny uses?"

At least someone has the Christmas spirit. "Yes, we can. Granny left hers. They're in that bag in the hall closet. Bring it out, will you, Shawny? I bought some garland and a few more ornaments, too."

Ari trudges into the room and drops a box onto the floor.

"Sheesh, Ari. Careful. You're going to break all of your Hallmark ornaments."

She rolls her eyes. "What a tragedy." Nice attitude. Grinch.

"Well, one of these days, you'll be glad to have them."

She saunters back toward the hall where the stairs to the attic are tucked into a little alcove. "I could use a little help, here." Her gaze spears Shawn. He looks away like he's suddenly been stricken deaf. "Mom, tell Shawn to help me. Will you?"

I look at my son, who is looking back with pleading eyes. Of all my children, he likes busywork the least. I hesitate just short of calling him lazy. Still, in all fairness . . .

"Sorry, buddy boy. Gotta do your fair share."

"Nuts!"

I ruffle Jakey's hair. "Want to come help your mom stretch out the lights along the porch?"

He nods and his mouth stretches into a grin. My heart thrills to the sight of his two missing front teeth. My favorite stage of childhood. The "All I want for Christmas is my two front teeth" stage. So cute.

"Go get your coat and hat," I say to my youngest. He hops to it. I suspect he's just glad to have something to do. It's been a little hard on the kid, adjusting to limited Nintendo playing. But he discovered Junie B. Jones books at Sadie's house, and I bought him the entire kindergarten year and most of first grade. We read, we laugh, I love it.

We grab the new lights and step onto the porch. Tommy is just coming around the side of the house carrying the ladder.

"Just right there, Tommy," I call when he's at the corner. "And hang around; I could use some help."

"Can't, Mom. I have band practice."

"Band practice? Since when are you in band? What are you playing and how much is it going to cost me?"

"Not the dorky school band. The guys and me got up a band."

Oh, please, Lord, not a *band* band. In my mind's eye I can see it clearly. Long-haired, headbanging, electric-guitar-playing rockers. And my son is one of them.

"Wait. Where are you practicing?"

"The garage. They'll be here any second. Can I order us a couple of pizzas?"

Okay, on one hand, this is my chance to be the cool mom. To make my son happy and support his new endeavor. On the other hand, this is my chance to nip this whole fiasco-waiting-to-happen in the bud before I get a ticket for disturbing the peace. With a sigh I opt for the former.

"All right, go ahead and order. But get the special. I'm not made of money, you know!"

"Thanks, Mom!"

"Send Shawn out to help me, will you?"

"Can't. Shawn's playing keyboard for the band."

Oh, good, then it's not heavy metal. Suddenly I'm picturing 'NSync, and I feel better about the whole "band" idea. My sons—perhaps they'll launch the next era of boy bands. Shawn's had lessons for four years. He's a natural and will probably be the only band member with an ounce of musical ability.

"Fine. Don't sing any nasty songs or I'm putting a stop to

the whole thing!" I call after him. Like I have any chance of knowing what the words are, if his band is anything like the music he listens to in his room. Every so often I grab his CDs and do a lyrics check. *Oy.*

I look at Jakey as Tommy flies on out of the vicinity. "Looks like it's just you and me, bud."

"I'm cold, Mommy. Can I go in?"

"You don't want to help me with the lights?"

"Can't I just look at them after you get them on the house?"

His lips are trembling and maybe tinged just a little blue. I guess it is pretty cold. "Sure, slugger. Go inside and ask Ari to make you a cup of hot chocolate to warm you up."

His gap-toothed grin widens his mouth once more and I laugh, despite the fact that I am about to be forced to hang lights all by myself. And I've never done it before.

I sing "Have Yourself a Merry Little Christmas" as I string the lights across the porch, then plug them in. Something about plugging in the little white icicle lights steals my breath. This is going to be the best Christmas season ever. I am going to put all my worries behind me and just celebrate the birth of Jesus.

I have more time to get into the "'Tis the season to be jolly" frame of mind since I've stopped the family counseling sessions. The doctor agreed that he's done all he can do with us as a family. I guess he means until I'm ready to face things. Or maybe he just figures it's all out there now and, really, it's my choice.

Regardless, Shawn will stay in one-on-one counseling. The doctor feels it will benefit him to have someone to talk to outside the family. Shawn has always been the most sensitive of the children. I can't help but wonder what is going

on behind those expressive blue eyes and his ornery grin. I'd
love to hide a bug in that office and listen in to what he's
telling the doc. But then, maybe I don't want to know. He's
been laying pretty low, not getting into trouble in school—
as in no more nasty notes lately. I can only hope the therapy's doing its job and he doesn't have something else up
his sleeve for Ms. Clark.

I unplug the Christmas lights and grab the little plastic
hangers to stick along the frame of the house so I can hang
the lights without hammering nails. With the package in my
hand, I ascend the ladder. Okay, have I mentioned I do *not*
like heights? Now I remember why I don't hang Christmas
lights. I definitely need two hands to climb this thing. I stop
my ascent and slide the package between my teeth. Then I
grab the ladder with both hands and continue the climb.
How come this awning is so high up all of a sudden?

A gust of wind blows out of nowhere, sending a jolt of
fear through my stomach. I grab the ladder tighter and give
a little yelp. The package of plastic hangers falls from my
mouth. Shoot! Now would be a great time for a little help.
But of course the kids are doing their thing and wouldn't
hear me if I screamed my head off.

Now I'm going to have to climb all the way down and get
those hanger things and climb all the way back up here.
Only, you know, this is really a lot higher from this angle
than it appears from the ground.

Gulp and a half.

I'm not budging. Couldn't if I wanted to. Which I don't.

So I hold on for dear life and pray. "Lord, if You will get
me down from here, I'll—" Okay, I'm thinking. Already attending church regularly and doing my Beth Moore Bible

study, not to mention my daily reading in *Purpose-Driven Life* with the kids. I'm doing my exercises almost every day. Hired someone to clean, spending time with the kids— seems to be going well, this week anyway. Have made a friend and was willing to wear fuchsia if necessary to be her matron of honor (thank goodness she's on her second time around and has developed a little taste in her maturity). I will even be taking my shrimp pasta salad to the ladies' Christmas luncheon for Darcy despite the circumstances.

I don't mean to go all Mary Poppins on God, but I've been working on me pretty hard, and hey, I really am practically perfect in every way.

Another gust of wind. I know, I know. The whole Rick thing. But come on, God, Rome wasn't built in a day. I mean, okay, it was eventually built, so I can't use that one forever. But you and I both know I'm going to bite the bullet and let this thing go someday. I'm trying, Lord.

Mom always says, "You can either say Yes, Lord, or No, sir," I remind myself, in a very Forrest Gump–ish sort of way.

But I'm not saying no to God. I'm trying in a subtle way to find it in my heart to say to Rick, "I forgive you." But not yet. Not even to get down from the ladder. But I have another idea. "All right, Lord, here's the deal. I will fast for one we—"

"You okay, Claire?" Greg's voice comes out of nowhere.

Okay, does that bargain actually count if I didn't get the last word all the way out?

"Greg. I'm scared." I feel like bawling. But I refuse to do it. I cried last time I saw Greg, and I'm not doing it again. And that's that.

Oh, sure, *now* Tough Chick shows up. Now that I have to be rescued like a maiden in a tower.

"Shall I let down my golden hair?" I'm trying really hard to control the tremor in my voice.

"Leave your hair just like it is. I'm coming up to get you."

"Greg Lewis, don't you dare step one foot on this ladder. There's not room for us both."

"Sure there is. I'll be there in a minute. Hang on."

"No! Greg. I'll get down on my own."

"Think you can do it?"

Uuumm, nope. Not a chance. I squeeze my eyes shut and shake my head.

"All right. I'm coming to get you."

I'm not even bothering to protest. If he doesn't climb up and get me down, I'll be here until I die from hunger. I keep my eyes shut and try not to panic as the ladder shakes with every step he takes. He stops when he's two rungs below me.

"All right. Take one step downward."

I shake my head with gusto. "I can't. I really can't, Greg. I mean really, really."

"Claire, if I come up any higher we could slip. Take one step down. If it looks like you're going to miss, I promise I'll tell you."

I have to do this. It's not going to be easy. But it's not impossible. People have been climbing ladders forever in the history of ladders. The fact that they've also been falling from them as well slips through my mind, taunting me with its horrific images. I hang on tight with both hands while I take one step down.

"There you go. You're doing great. One step at a time."

His encouragement sounds just a tad patronizing at this point. And even in the face of almost certain death, I find myself rebelling. Inwardly. But the stubborn streak I inherited from my dad serves me well and gets me all the way to the bottom of the ladder.

Greg's chest is puffed out and he's sort of strutting in that "Me man, you woman" kind of guy thing. He grabs the lights from the porch and the hangers from the ground. "Let me do it for you."

"You don't have to do that. I've actually never put up outside lights before. I don't know why I thought I'd start this year."

But he insists. So I watch him go up the ladder like he's a big heroic fireman. It strikes me that Greg rescued me from a tower. And if there's one thing I've learned from watching *Shrek* and *Shrek 2*, it's that when a prince rescues a maiden (or a matron, as the case may be) from a tower, he must marry her. It's just the way it is. He doesn't know it yet. But hey, I didn't make the rules.

26

Ice balls from heaven. It's like the world has been hit with some ultra-freeze ray gun. Two days ago the high temperature was sixty-two. Who would have thought that today I'd be standing in the freezing cold, wearing a black spaghetti-strap bridesmaid's dress and trying my best not to break my neck in the three-inch strappy heels Linda insisted would be sexy?

It just so happens, I'm not real concerned with sexy at the moment. I just wish the bride and groom would stop taking their time and get out here so we can blow our bubbles and get out of the arctic air, which slid down from Canada overnight.

And just for the record, I think the whole concept of blowing bubbles at a winter wedding is kind of dumb. I mean, what happens to liquid at thirty-two degrees? Exactly. Just what we need—more ice balls pinging our windshields.

But then, tossing birdseed on the happy couple is kind of dumb, too. In my opinion. I guess I can understand banning the age-old tradition of tossing rice. Besides the painful experience of being chunked in the head by some smart aleck teenager who decides it might be funny to *not* open the bag before throwing it, there is that humane factor of preventing bird deaths. You'd think a bird would know better than to eat something that is going to cause it to bloat up until it dies, but then you never can tell about birds, can you?

Funny where my thought processes are taking me as I shiver beneath the lacy shawl Linda thought would be oh-so-elegant. Too bad she didn't like the idea of a nice elegant parka. We've only been out here for about five minutes. But if those two don't come on pretty quick, they're going to have a coup on their hands. Instigated by a disgruntled and half-frozen matron of honor.

I am looking at the doors, willing the happy couple to hurry already when, amazingly, warmth envelops me. I turn to find Greg standing next to me, his coat draped across my shoulders. "You're freezing," he says.

"I passed freezing about two and a half minutes ago," I shoot back in my oh-so-clever quippy way. "I'm frozen solid."

He smiles and I feel myself thawing. "Put your arms through the sleeves. You'll be warmer."

"I can't take your coat." Of course I can. And I'd like to see him try to take it back.

He smiles. "I still have on a jacket. I won't miss my over-coat nearly as much as you would."

I grin through my chattering teeth. "Thanks, you're a life-saver."

Finally, the door opens and the couple arrives on the steps of the church. They wave like a king and queen making a showing for their subjects. I take one look at my friend's face and all of my irritation slips away. My breath catches in the light of such radiant happiness as they walk hand in hand. I'm so mesmerized, I forget to blow my bub-bles. Linda reaches for me as she passes. I take her hand and she squeezes, looks not so subtly at Greg, and then gives me a wink before letting go.

I'm not sure if he saw the exchange, but Greg slips his arm around me. I try not to read too much into that. Most likely he's just trying to warm me up. And, if that's the case, boy, did he ever meet his objective.

I stare at the buffet line. My spirit wars with my flesh. I'm down seventeen and a half pounds. The question of the day appears to be: Do I want to forfeit the half pound for a wedge of Mrs. Devine's magic cookie bars?

I give it serious thought and I'm coming up with a resounding, "You betcha."

I reach, I touch—too late to put it back now. I take a decadent bite with relish. I have to force myself not to close my eyes and let out a "Mmm."

Darcy breezes by. "What do you think?" she asks in a needy sort of way that I completely understand.

My mouth is filled with the heady delights of coconut, pecans, chocolate chips, and graham cracker crust, so I give her a hardy thumbs-up. Her luncheon is an enormous success. She's won over every woman between the ages of eighteen and eighty who attends the church. Before we began the gluttonous part of the day, we heard a wonderful lesson about Mary's response to the angel Gabriel when she was told she would bear the Messiah: "Be it unto me according to Thy will."

Chills, and a few tears, made the rounds in the room. It was a message of surrender divinely inspired and taught by none other than Pastor's aunt. Which I thought was a stroke of genius on Darcy's part to even ask her. I mean, come on. It also just goes to show you how God can use anyone.

"Oooh, give me one of those before they're all gone," Darcy says, nodding toward the magic cookie bars on the buffet line. I grab one and hand it over.

"So, you think the Christmas tree is offending anyone?" she asks as we walk to a table with a couple of empty seats.

I glance around at the groups of laughing, talking, stuffing-their-faces women and I have to be honest. "No way."

The decorations are a hodgepodge of traditional and modern. Beautiful poinsettia candle-ring centerpieces with fat red candles add a soothing atmosphere to each table. In one corner of the room, she has set up the nativity. Somehow she's fixed the baby Jesus and the shepherd's staff and it looks brand-new. "It's perfect, Darcy. You've done a fabulous job."

Her face pinkens with pleasure. "Thank you, Claire. I was so nervous." She leans a little closer. "Mrs. Devine hasn't frowned at anything so far."

I pat her hand. "I think she chilled out once she saw most of the women backed your idea. She's not a bad woman, you know. She's just got some funny ideas about what is or isn't proper. Maybe this is a new phase of her life, her 'Be it unto me according to Thy will' stage."

"Claire, I think you are so wise in so many ways." Her eyes well up with tears. "Thank you for coming today and supporting me. I know it's not always easy for you right now."

For crying out loud! Why can't she just leave well enough alone? Here we are, all getting along, and she has to go and bring up that of which we don't speak. I am about to tell her to take a chill pill when her eyes go wide with horror. Alarm shoots through me. "What's wrong?"

Without a word she bolts from the table. I bolt after her and into the bathroom. "Darce? You okay?"

Her response comes from the stall, but not in words.

I hope I don't catch her flu the week before Christmas.

She emerges moments later, pale and shaken. I hand her a wet paper towel.

"Do you need me to finish up here for you?"

She spits out a mouthful of water and shakes her head. "I'll be okay. I think that cookie was just a little too rich. Thanks for coming after me."

Her heels *click-clack* on the floor as she dries her hands and heads for the door. I lean back against the sink and try to figure out how she can go from happy-go-lucky to Barferella then back to fine-and-dandy in a matter of minutes. A cookie? That's ridiculous. The only time anything rich like that made me sick was when I was preg—

Oh, dear Lord.

Somehow I manage to fake my way through the rest of the day and get out of there with my dignity intact, despite my suspicions that Darcy is pregnant. As I walk up the steps toward the second floor of my home, my safe place, I hear sniffling coming from Ari's room. In the middle of a school day?

"Ari?" I tap and enter.

My daughter is flung across her bed, tears streaming down her swollen face.

"Baby, what happened?"

"Nothing, Mother. I don't want to talk about it."

"Well, I'm sorry, but you are crying your eyes out in the middle of the day when you should be in school. You're going to have to talk about it." I don't want to be insensitive, but I think sometimes a parent just has to demand answers. I mean, did she get into a fight and get expelled? Did someone say mean things about her? Did her panties fall down in the middle of a cheer? It could be anything.

She sits up and leans back against her headboard, clutching a stuffed rabbit she's had since her fourth birthday. Oh, boy. If she's hanging on to Fluffy Bunny, this is bad.

I get a wad of toilet paper from her bathroom. She makes use of it and hugs the bunny to her chest.

"All right. Now tell me what happened."

Her lower lip trembles like she's about to burst into tears again. "Patrick. He's seeing someone else."

I'm not sure I heard that right. Does any boy have the audacity to choose someone else over my beautiful Ari? How foolish is he? "I'm sorry, honey. What happened?"

"Trish told me she saw him with Shelley at the movies last night. Only stupid me, I got mad at Trish. Then today—" She shudders as another sob shakes her slight frame. She gulps. "Today I saw him actually *kissing* Shelley."

"He did *what?*"

"Can you believe that, Mom?" Her tearful eyes meet mine. "I thought he liked me. He was so cool."

Her anguish is palpable and I move in, taking her in my arms like I haven't since she was a little girl. She resists for only a moment, then relaxes against me. Her tears soak the fabric of my shirt, and my own tears run freely down my cheeks—totally feeling her pain.

I'd give anything to spare her this.

She pulls away. "Why can't men just be satisfied with the women they have?" she asks as the anger part of this process kicks in. "It just doesn't make sense. Shelley isn't prettier, she isn't skinnier, she's not funny, and Mom, she's dumb as a box of rocks. She's just different. And Paddy has nothing whatsoever in common with her. Why do guys have to get tired of one girl and move on to the next? I really thought he was going to be the one."

"What do you mean by *the* one?"

"Yeah, you know—*the* one."

"Oh." I can't help but be a bit disturbed that my sixteen-year-old daughter is thinking in terms of *the* one about the first boy she's dated.

"I know you probably think I'm too young, but I really love Paddy, Mom."

"I believe you, Arianna." After all, I loved her dad when I was her age. Maybe if Rick had shown his true colors back then I would have been spared my heartache. Of course then I would have lost out on four amazing kids as well. "Ari, the two of you didn't go any farther than what I saw that night on the bleachers did you?"

Horror lifts to her eyes. "Mother!"

"Don't act like you don't know what I mean."

She scowls and acquiesces. "We've never had sex, if that's what you mean."

Yep. That's what I meant.

"We really both wanted to do what's right. Paddy wants to be a youth pastor. He does want to wait until marriage. But he's just . . ."

"A teenage boy and sex is everywhere he looks."

She shrugs. "Something like that." Her soulful eyes capture mine. "If I tell you something, you promise you won't flip out?"

"I never flip out." But I will if she says she was lying and they actually have had sex.

She rolls her eyes. "Forget it."

"Come on, Ari. You can't set me up like that and then just say forget it."

A shaky sigh leaves her. "We didn't have sex, but we did more than kiss."

Oh, Lord. I feel my breath coming in bursts. I know I don't want to have this conversation, but somehow, I know I need to. If only I'd been able to speak to my mother about these things, I might have been spared a lot of heartache myself. Because Rick and I definitely didn't wait until marriage. I lost my virginity in the backseat of his dad's Delta 98 after his senior prom. I was Ari's age. "Okay."

"It's just . . . I wish I hadn't done so much. I mean. To me it was special and I only let him because I loved him. But the thought of him doing those things with other girls . . . just tears me up."

I really want to knock this Patrick kid upside the head and tell him what a creep he is. "I'm sorry, honey. I'm sorry you have to deal with adult feelings now. You know, spending time with God helps. When you feel weak, the Bible says to run away from youthful lusts. Even those of us who are not so young have to run sometimes."

"Oh, gross, Mother. TMI, okay?"

"Too much info. Got it." I chuckle. I guess it's just as well we don't go there.

"Love really stinks." She hugs Fluffy Bunny tight. "I'm

never falling in love again as long as I live. Guys are all the same." She gives a bitter snort. "Just like Daddy."

My gut clenches. As much as I'd like to tell her they're all alike, I know this isn't true. Even her dad isn't the same as he was when I was married to him. I know that. I really do. I guess it's time to suck it up and admit it.

"Ari, honey."

"I know, Mom. We're in the same boat, aren't we?"

I shift around on the bed so that I am face-to-face with her. "No, we aren't."

"But we were both cheated on."

"Not really. Your boyfriend broke up with you and started dating someone else. That's not the same as a husband cheating on his wife."

A look of betrayal slides across her face. "I should have known you wouldn't understand."

I stand. I know better than to try to reason with her when she's all full of no-one-understands-me indignation. "For the record, Ari, I think it's you who doesn't understand. You can't compare an eleven-year marriage to a few weeks of dating. You can't compare a husband and the father of your children to a seventeen-year-old boy you barely dated. What your dad did, he did to me. Not you."

"It affected me." The kid has her mother's stubbornness.

"That's true. But he never stopped being your father. And whether you'd like to admit it or not at the moment, he is a good father."

"I can't believe you're taking up for him."

Yeah, you and me both, chickadee. "Can I tell you something?"

"Is it about sex?"

I grin. "No."

She grins back. "Then go ahead."

"Your daddy apologized to me."

"When did he do that?"

"During our last counseling session. You know when it was just Darcy and Dad and me?"

She nodded. "Wow, I thought you two must have fought during that one since you won't even talk to him on the phone."

"I have issues. But that's not the point." I give her an even look so that she can see I mean what I'm saying from the bottom of my heart. "Your dad is truly sorry for the way he treated me. He cried and cried about breaking our vows, breaking up the family." I swallow hard past a sudden lump in my throat.

Her eyes widen. "Really?"

I nod. "He isn't the man he was all those years ago, Ari. So don't compare him to someone who hurt you. He didn't do anything to you but leave your mother."

She gives a grudging nod.

"By the way. How did you get home?"

A sheepish grin tugs at her mouth. "I knew you were at the luncheon, so I called Dad."

"He left work to come get you?"

"He was heading home anyway. Darcy has an appointment of some kind today, and he said he wants to be there with her."

"Did he happen to say what kind of appointment?" Like I don't already know.

"No."

"Okay. No big deal."

Very big deal. Enormous. Ari has no idea how much her life is going to change in the next few months.

"Hey, you want to go see a movie?"

"Really?"

"Sure. I'll call Greg's cell and see if the boys can ride home with him. And Jakey, at least, can go to Greg's house and play with Sadie until we get home."

"Thanks, Mom. I should ditch school more often." She tosses me a cheeky grin.

"On second thought, maybe I should march you right back to school."

"Have a heart." She jumps off her bed like she's never heard of Paddy Devine. "I want to put on makeup first."

"Okay. You fix up while I call."

"Hey, Mom."

"Yeah?"

"Thanks."

"You're welcome, Ari. I'm sorry I haven't been there for you much the past few years."

"You were as much as you could. And at least you were in the house. Most of my friends have practically raised themselves. We had Granny, and I knew I could always come into your office if I wanted to."

"So you're not scarred for life?"

She laughed. "Not for life." A serious expression passes over her face.

"What?"

"You know what I miss?"

I shake my head.

"Hearing you type at night. I knew something was missing. But I just put my finger on it the other day when you were at your desk for a few minutes."

"So it's not going to bother you when I go back to work after your Christmas break?"

"No. Because I think things are different now."

"You got that right."

And she does.

27

I'm leaving Wal-Mart with a vanload of Christmas presents, including Mom's TV/DVR combo player, when I happen to glance across the street. A growl rumbles in my throat when I see Patrick's love-mobile parked in the video store parking lot. On a whim, I drive over there and pull up next to the Mustang. I'm thinking it's time for a little chat with Casanova.

He's behind the counter. A blush spreads across his face and neck when I stare him down. My stomach twists and churns with nerves as I'm forced to wait while he attends to the lone customer in the video store. The middle-aged woman smiles at the good-looking seventeen-year-old, clueless to the fact that he's a groping, two-timing jerk. She leaves with her movie.

I set my purse on the counter and clear my throat while Patrick pretends to be attending to something in the computer. He bites his upper lip. Lips that kissed my daughter. And Shelley, and no telling how many other girls.

"Let's get this over with, Patrick," I say, suddenly infused with courage.

The kid takes a deep breath and looks away from the computer screen, meeting my eyes.

"How are you, Ms. Everett?"

I know he's about to throw up, but I'm having a hard time feeling sorry for him. A vision of Ari's swollen eyes and red nose haunts me as I stare him down. "Well, Patrick, I'm not doing very well, to be honest." I lean in. "Tell me why I shouldn't go to your parents and tell them how I caught you handling my daughter on the bleachers, or share some of the information Ari's given me about your dates. You can do a lot before ten o'clock can't you, Paddy?"

His face drains of color. "I care about Ari, Ms. Everett. If she'd just talk to me, I could explain."

My anger rises. "According to Ari, there's nothing to explain. And don't try to con me. I know all the excuses."

"I swear to you, I'm not lying. It wasn't the way Ari thinks."

He looks so miserable I almost believe him. Against my better judgment, I fold my arms across my chest and cock my head. "Convince me that you weren't on a date with another girl or kissing the same girl the next day."

"I wasn't. At least not the way Ari thinks."

"Okay."

"My mom has been ministering to Shelley's mom for the last couple of months. She knows Shelley has a crush on me and asked me to be nice to her."

I can't help the harsh expulsion of laughter that pushes from my throat. "Come on, Patrick. Don't yank me around."

"I'm not. I swear it."

"All right. Tell me why Trish saw you at the movies with this girl."

"Her mom is messed up. A druggie. Shelley was at the movies with some friends and got sick. She tried to call her mom to come get her, but she was so high when she answered the phone, she wasn't making any sense. Shelley called my house and my Mom asked me to go get Shelley

while she went to check on her mom. That was all there was
to that. Trish saw us leaving together and assumed we were
on a date. Ms. Everett, I'd never cheat on Ari. I care so much
about her. I promise."

Call me crazy, but I believe him.

"All right. I can verify this with your mom." And I fully
intend to do just that. "Tell me why you were kissing
Shelley where my daughter could see you."

"Shelley interpreted me being nice to her as me being interested in her. I just didn't know what to do about her. She
sort of cornered me in the hall and kissed me. I didn't kiss
her back and I didn't have my arms around her. If Ari really
thinks about it, she'll admit that she saw my hands on
Shelley's arms, pushing her away from me."

"I've heard enough."

"My parents know everything, Ms. Everett." His eyes
shine with earnest appeal, drawing me in. "They know Ari
and I went too far physically. They prayed with me and I
feel like God's forgiven me. If Ari will believe me and take
me back, my parents have said we can only date in groups."

Okay, for the record, I'm not crazy about my pastor
knowing these things about my daughter, but I'd bet my
laptop he's telling the truth. "I'll second that. If she takes
you back, group dates only."

His eyes widen. "Will you ask her to call me?"

"I'll tell her what you've told me, and if she believes your
story, I'm sure she'll call."

Relief spreads across his face. The bell over the door
dings and a customer enters, effectively ending our conversation.

I give him a tentative smile as I leave. Amazing turn of events.

The smell of gingerbread cookies wafts through the house on what should have been the last day of school before Christmas break. But a northern air mass collided with a southern storm system, dumping twelve inches of snow on our city and forcing the superintendent of schools to announce a snow day. So Christmas break started one day early. The kids'll pay for it at the end of the school year by having to make it up, but they're not thinking about that. Right now, the boys and Greg's Sadie are outside playing in the snow. Ari has spent the entire day on the phone with Paddy sorting out their love life.

My big idea to make gingerbread men is paying off in a great-smelling house, and the cookies, cooling on the stove, actually look good enough to eat.

I'm feeling very June Cleaver–ish, with Christmas music playing throughout the living room and kitchen. I'm getting that picture of Greg and me again. The one where we are married and I'm cooking for him. He adores me. Adores my children, adores that I need to hire a housekeeper (this is *my* fantasy). Adores my cooking.

The front door slams, pulling me from the unlikely dream.

I hurry to the living room. "Tommy, don't track snow in here. Take off your shoes in the foyer."

"Whatever."

Uh-oh. "What's wrong, Toms?"

"Nothing," he mutters, but slides down the wall and sits on the floor, his knees pulled up, forearms resting on his knees. His shoes are making puddles as the snow slides off and melts when it hits the floor.

I sit on the third step from the bottom. "Come on. Talk to me."

He scowls.

"Jenny Wellington said something that made me mad, so I came in."

"The girl you like?"

He nodded.

"What did she say?"

"I'm a freak."

"You're a freak?"

He nods. "That's what she said."

"When?"

He jerks his head to the door.

I get up and go to the door, look out through the little square security window. Holy cow. My yard is swarming with kids of every shape and size. Gulp. "What'd you do, invite the whole school?"

"They live around here. We started a snowball fight and they just started coming."

"Who all is out there?"

"The Willards from down the block. All three of them. Sam and David from across the street. Jenny and her friend Melody live a block over and heard us. Plus Sadie Lewis, unfortunately."

"Oh, be nice to her."

"Believe me, I try. It's not that easy."

Sadie is demanding and a bit spoiled. For some reason, Jake puts up with it and they've become the best of friends.

"Well, I think it's kind of neat that so many of your friends showed up."

A shrug lifts his shoulders. "I guess."

"So why did this Jenny call you a freak?"

"Promise not to flip out?"

What is it with these kids? "I never flip out."

"Is that your promise?"

"Oh, all right. I won't flip out." Probably.

He pulls that fake lip ring from his pocket. "I wear this. And sometimes I wear eyeliner at school. But I'm not gay or anything."

Sheesh, who thinks that? I am, however, about six seconds away from flipping out about the lip ring and eyeliner, both of which I've forbidden.

But wait . . .

"So this Jenny doesn't like the whole look?"

He shakes his head. "She said she'd be my girlfriend if I didn't look like such a freak. Her mom won't let her go with me."

Okay, maybe as a mother I should be ticked about anyone calling my boy such a name. And the girl's mom? She should be so lucky my son even wants to date her snooty daughter. But back to reality. If his feelings for this girl will wake him up to the error of his ways, I'm all for the little snot calling him a freak.

"Well, I guess that's that," I say, totally trying a little reverse psychology.

"What's what?"

"You'll have to start looking at other girls. The kind who like that sort of thing."

He gives me a dubious frown. "Mom, I'm not four. I know what you're doing."

Shoot.

My cheeks warm. "I don't know what you mean."

"Yeah, you do." He stands and heads back to the door. "I just needed some time to cool off. I'm going back out there. I might stop wearing the lip ring and eyeliner, but I'm not giving up my skateboard. And that's final."

Yes!

If I had a dime for every Christmas present I've ever gotten from my kids, I'd be . . . really poor. But for some reason, this year, they put their money together and bought me a DVD edition of *Gone With the Wind* with special features, including interviews.

My children know it's my all-time favorite movie, so it makes it that much sweeter—that they made sure what they bought for me would be something I love. That speaks more to me than if they'd let their granny pick out something and put my name on it as usual. Although I always appreciate the sentiment, this is different. It proves that God is healing our family.

Christmas morning leaves me all weepy. Tommy is so excited over his skateboard that he actually hugs me and kisses my cheek. Then tells me I'm getting skinny. If he'd have told me that a week ago, I'd have sprung for the board that cost twenty-five dollars more. But how was I to know?

Ari laughs when she opens her book *I Kissed Dating Goodbye*, which I bought mostly as a joke and before she got back together with Patrick. She does love the diamond stud earrings she's begged for each of the last three years. Not only did I not have the money for such an expensive gift before, I didn't think she was grown up enough. Things have changed, and that was a little last-minute gift.

The little boys got their usual games, toy guns, remote-control cars, and books.

The morning goes by way too fast and I want to hold on to every minute I can. I fix blueberry pancakes and link sausages. I've been planning the Christmas breakfast for a month, and I'm so excited I can barely contain it as I call them into the kitchen.

"Wow." Ari's eyes are wide. "Mom, this is great."

My heart swells as they scarf it all down in fifteen minutes flat. "That was good, Mom," Shawny says with his chipmunk-cheek smile. "We should have that every Christmas morning."

Tommy pipes in, agreeing with his brother for the first time that I can remember in recent memory. "Yeah, we could have a tradition."

Jake frowns and rains on our parade. "I don't like blueberries."

Oh, well, can't win them all.

"Then maybe I should make you some chocolate-chip pancakes next year."

A grin splits his mouth, making it clear he did not receive his two front teeth for Christmas.

Finally, at ten till eleven, I give a reluctant sigh.

"It's time?" Ari is getting pretty good at reading me.

I nod, trying to hold back tears. Rick has always conceded Christmas Day to me. I don't know why. Guilt, maybe? Because he wasn't married? Who knows why? But this year, he's decided to take his court-ordered holiday. It's only fair. I know that.

But that doesn't make it any easier.

We pile into the van and as if by unspoken agreement between themselves, the kids give an effort to contain their excitement, as there's no way I can hide my dread over spending Christmas Day without them.

"You could stay and have dinner with us, Mom," Ari says, breaking the silence. "You know Darcy wants you to."

Yeah, I know she does. I've told her no at least ten times. "This year you need to be a family with Dad and Darcy. Without me."

"You're not running off, are you, Mom?"

I nearly swallow my gum. "Tommy! Good grief, where'd you get such an idea?"

He shrugs. "Just making sure those pancakes weren't a guilt breakfast. Losing all that weight, wearing makeup. I don't know. It just seems like you've got something going on. Like a trip to Mexico to get married or something."

I laugh. I can't help it. The kid is too clever for his own good.

"Hey, I told you I'm turning over a new leaf. Besides, I would never get married in Mexico."

"Mommy's going to marry Sadie's daddy, anyway. Aren't you, Mom?"

At Jakey's question, a tension fills the air.

"You mean Lewis?" Tommy's voice is filled with a hostility I don't really get. "There's no way I'm living in the same house with that little brat of his." Ah, now I get it.

"My teacher? That's not a good idea, Mom. Conflict of interest."

Good grief, Shawn. "Where'd you learn 'conflict of interest'?"

"I'm not a baby." The child has no idea how smart he is. It's rather disturbing.

"So answer the question, Mom," Ari says. Partly, I know, as a joke. But partly because I can see she's starting to put two and two together.

"I'm not marrying anyone."

"Never, ever?" Jakey asks.

Well, never say "Never, ever."

"I promise there would be a family discussion before something like that ever happened. And besides, I'm not dating anyone."

"Do you *want* to date Mr. Lewis?" Shawn asks.

"That is my private business, Mr. Conflict of Interest."

We are pulling into Rick and Darcy's circle drive and for the first time since they married, I don't feel a bit of jealousy. Hmm. Methinks perhaps I've come to a little intersection we like to call the Building Blocks of Character Development. Next I'll pull onto a road named Moving on with My Life.

"Are you going to be okay all by yourself, Mom?" Ari asks after the boys have bounded toward the house and are already descending upon poor Darcy. The kids are maniacs on Christmas Day. Between the excitement of new gifts, the sugar-filled, carb-loaded blueberry pancakes they had for breakfast, and all the chocolate Santas they found in their stockings and ate before breakfast, she's going to have quite the time trying to corral them.

"I'm going to be fine. Don't worry about me."

Ari's just closing her door when I see Rick coming to

greet me. You've changed, I keep reminding myself. You can face him now in a spirit of forgiveness.

I watch his ears and nose go red from the cold. I roll down my window. "Merry Christmas." It's halfhearted at best. But I'm putting forth this effort. Faith in action. Determination to heal from my wounded past.

His eyebrows lift as he returns my greeting. "Did you have a good morning with the kids?"

"Try to beat my gift to Tommy." I give him a cheeky grin.

"You got him the skateboard, didn't you?"

"Yeah."

He tosses back his head and gives a hardy laugh. "Claire, so did I!"

"No!"

"I guess we'd better confer from now on."

To his credit, he doesn't mention that he's tried to reach me at least a dozen times in the past month. And no way I'm bringing it up.

"So, I'll let you get in and enjoy your day with the kids."

"Uh, Claire. Before you go. We want you to come in for a minute. We have something to tell you."

Oh, Lord. Here it comes. I open my mouth to take a rain check, but his hand covers mine.

"Please."

I gather a steadying breath and nod. "Let me roll up the window." He steps back as I do so. I kill the motor.

As I follow him into the house, I try to rationalize. Maybe they're not going to tell me Darcy's pregnant. Maybe they're building a new house and given my reaction to this one, they've decided they need to break it to me gently.

Perhaps they're moving to Indiana or Chicago or anywhere besides here.

Darcy is radiant as we step inside. She is wearing a gorgeous red-silk pantsuit with a poinsettia-decorated scarf. I look down at my jeans and Rudolph sweatshirt, and once again I feel like the nerdy chubbo next to the gorgeous cheerleader.

She hugs me enthusiastically. "Merry Christmas! I made apple-cinnamon muffins. Do you want one?"

"No thanks." I am finding it difficult to muster any responding enthusiasm. "We had blueberry pancakes."

Her expression drops a bit. "Oh, then the kids probably won't want any either."

Oh, why do I always love her so much? Forced laughter finds its way to my lips. "These are my kids, remember? They'll find a place for your muffins. You'll be lucky if there are any left for you and Rick."

She smiles at this and I feel Rick squeeze my elbow. Okay, hands off, bud. I move away oh-so-subtly. I have to congratulate myself for not recoiling and jerking from his thank-you gesture.

"Well, then. What's this you need to tell me?"

"Let's go into Rick's study." Darcy leads the way, her heels clicking on the ceramic tile.

Once we get inside the room, she moves in close to her husband. *Her* husband. Rick slides his arm around her and draws her ever so slightly closer. I steel myself.

Darcy's eyes fill with tears. "Claire, I'm pregnant. We're telling the kids today, but we wanted you to know firsthand from us."

The tunnel is dark, and even though I knew what was

coming, I still find myself sliding toward that place of obscurity. My heart is racing. I drop to the closest seat, which happens to be Rick's office chair.

"Claire?" Rick moves toward me. "You okay?"

I hold up my palm and he halts.

The shock is wearing off and anger has risen to the surface. The past couple of weeks, I've known she was probably pregnant. I've waited for the announcement and imagined my cool and levelheaded reaction. But faced with the reality that Rick is getting a second chance at a great life with a beautiful, perfect wife and most likely a perfect kid, I blow a gasket. I stand. "Congratulations, Rick." The venom flies from my tongue as everything on my mind spews into the room. "It isn't enough that you ruined one family. Here's a good idea. Why don't you start another one?"

I turn to Darcy. "Enjoy him until you lose your figure, honey. Because that's about how long he'll stick around. One consolation. At least you'll have a baby to love. And the child support will make a nice little nest egg for Junior's college tuition."

I fly past the black-leather chair and maneuver around the couple as they stare, dumbfounded. I yank open the door and beeline for the exit. If I don't get out of this house . . .

"Claire Everett, you stop right there!"

I do. Because I've never heard Darcy's voice trembling with anger and outrage. I whip around. She stands before me, her face bright red, tears streaming down her face.

"Take it easy, sweetheart," Rick says.

She turns on him. "Don't tell me to take it easy. Will you go away and let me deal with this? Your kids are waiting to spend Christmas with you. Go feed them muffins and stop hovering over me."

I think Rick's more shocked than I am. Regardless, he meekly obeys her order and disappears toward the kitchen.

"Well?" Inside I'm feeling nerves I never knew I possessed. I don't like being confronted. I do the confronting. I turn to mush when it's reversed.

"I know it's hard for you to be the one who got left behind. The one who was cheated on. The woman scorned. But once and for all: I DID NOT COMMIT ADULTERY."

Sheesh. Tell the whole neighborhood.

"I know that, Darcy." I'm proud of my calm response, spoken in an even tone that will elicit a calm exchange from her.

"You know, but you don't act like it's true. You treat me like the other woman. *I'm not* the other woman. I am married to the man I love, baggage and all."

Hey. Now I'm baggage? Besides, that wasn't the calm reply I was going for with that whole "even tone" thing.

"I've tried and tried to be your friend. I've been nice to you, loving to your kids, gone the extra mile because I understood your feelings. I knew you were hurting and I wanted you to know that it's okay.

"Do you know how difficult it is to follow in your footsteps, Claire? You were the childhood sweetheart. The mother of his four kids. The smart woman who worked two jobs so you could bank every cent of child support. The gritty ex-wife who not only tried to write a book but finished it even while working so hard. And then you even got published. For the love of Pete, Claire, who does that? The one who is now a bestselling author. A local celebrity. Do you know what I'm considered? The doctor's arm piece. Eye candy. The stupid blonde midlife-crisis bimbo. And you have the audacity to reduce my wonderful pregnancy to something less than the single most amazing event in the history of the universe?"

I can't even speak. I can't defend myself. I haven't got a leg to stand on. How can I explain to her that it's Rick, not Darcy, that I'm angry at. That if Darcy were married to anyone else, I'd be the first one to congratulate her on being pregnant. The fact is, I just can't stand the thought of his happiness when I'm all alone, raising the four kids we had together before he walked out. Darcy sees none of this inner struggle. And now that she's finally letting it all hang out, I find she's not quite finished.

"Do you think I don't feel hurt? All my life I've been the bastard child. The result of my mother's affair with a married man. Oh, yes. You didn't know that, did you? I grew up in a town with two thousand residents. My mother was a wild child, my dad a local realtor. He wanted excitement, she wanted love. He got what he wanted. She didn't. She got pregnant and ostracized. I never had a chance in that town. So don't tell me I don't understand. Every time I passed my father's wife on the street, I saw the pain in her eyes. Pain that I caused her because every time she saw me, she remembered what her husband did. I see that pain in your eyes every time I look at you, too.

"But I am not to blame here. I didn't even know Rick until you two had been divorced for three years. Why can't you just give me the chance to love my husband, love my sweet baby, and yes, Claire, love you."

I start to speak this time. But Darcy doesn't give me a chance.

She stomps past me and opens the door. "I want you to leave my house, Claire. Until you can treat me with some respect, you are not welcome here."

My jaw drops. My stomach churns. I step outside with my head high.

The door slams shut behind me. Time stands still as I wait on the porch, trying to make sense of what just happened.

I hear Darcy's heartbroken wail on the other side of the wooden door that separates us. My own tears form and come fast. I make it to my van amid sobs, crank the motor, and drive away. I stop at the park a block away. In the parking lot, in front of a deserted pond, I weep. I weep for Darcy, for her father's wife, for her mother, for me. For all the women of the world who have been the victims of infidelity. I cry for hours. It's Christmas Day, and while the rest of the world celebrates family and friends, I'm all alone.

28

It's lightly snowing as I pull into my driveway. Normally, I adore a soft *It's a Wonderful Life*–ish snow. But right now my head is aching and my nose is stuffy from the tears. Not much could lighten my mood.

The last thing I want to do when I walk inside my house is talk on the phone. It's ringing. I try to ignore it, but even in my state of depression I can't resist the urge to peek at caller ID. Greg.

"Claire? What's wrong? Your voice sounds funny."

"Just an emotional morning."

"Sounds like you need to come be with people. Mom and Sadie and I want you to come down and have Christmas dinner with us."

I feel my eyes well up again. How sweet of them to think of me.

"Greg, I'm so sorry. I would love to any other day, but I need to be alone right now. Okay?"

"I understand. If you want to come by for dessert later, you're more than wanted."

"Thanks. I'll keep it in mind. Good-bye."

I hang up and flop onto the couch. I look around my messy living room. The wrapping paper and gifts the kids had to leave behind are still lying all over the place. The remnants of our morning together.

Anger shoots through me. I hate that I had to give up my babies today. I hate that I don't have one family member to have Christmas dinner with. I'm so angry with Rick at this moment I could just yell. So guess what? I do. "I HATE THIS, GOD!"

I picture them sitting around the dining room table, Darcy radiant and perfect, Rick carving the turkey or ham or whatever they're having. The black-and-white TV sitcom family. "Gee whiz" and "Oh, golly."

I kick at a pile of wrapping paper. What's the point of even trying to make a decent home? I can't give my kids what Rick can. Not anymore. They're going to have a little brother or sister now. Are they even going to want to live with me when they can be a family with two parents and a baby over there? I wouldn't put it past Darcy to go get a puppy. From the Humane Society, of course.

The Christmas decorations are really bugging me all of a sudden. The kids are staying at Rick and Darcy's until New Year's. So what's the point in leaving the tree up? And it's not like I really have much else to do.

In a split-second Grinchy decision, I stomp up to the attic. The kids tossed everything everywhere. No rhyme or reason to how these decoration boxes are thrown around. I head to the corner of the attic to grab first the boxes for the ornaments. Under the boxes I find my old wooden rocking chair. The one my mother handed down to me when I was pregnant with Ari.

I drop the boxes and pull the chair from the corner. There are some scars from four babies' worth of use. I can't resist the urge to sit. Memories move across my mind like a slideshow as I rock back and forth. I wrap my arms around me and longing washes over me in waves. A longing for that American Dream life I'd so hoped for as a girl in love with the captain of the football team. I almost had it all. Almost.

We were so proud when we brought Arianna home from the hospital. I rocked her until late into the night. Then I laid her gently in the cradle Rick made for her.

The cradle. Where is that? I need to see it. In a frenzy, I toss boxes and keepsakes here and there. If anyone saw me in such a state, they'd think I had lost my mind.

I expel a relieved sigh when I spot the wooden cradle tucked between an old bookcase and a footlocker my grandfather used during the Korean War. I kneel beside the little bed and run my hand along the curved headboard. It rocks a slightly crooked arc. I remember how proud Rick was when he showed this to me for the first time. His baby would sleep in something he made with his own hands. Something that cost him more than money—which was good because we never could have afforded to buy a cradle back then.

Rick's new baby will have anything he or she could possibly dream of. I can only imagine the layette Darcy is planning.

A twinge of something akin to pity pinches me. Darcy won't see the joy of a young husband presenting her with something like this.

I'm still feeling sorry for them when a thought comes to me. I reject this unwelcome scenario immediately. But it returns with more force.

Let it go, Claire. It's time to let it go once and for all.

I know that sweet, still voice. And I'm filled with a sense

of awe to be on the Lord's radar. Still, He's asking me to do something I don't know that I have the strength to do.

My grace is sufficient.

I rest my head on top of the cradle and tears slip down my cheeks as I picture each of my babies lying there. In the cradle made with their daddy's hands.

My heart softens toward Rick. He truly did set out to be the best husband and father he could be. Life happens. Hurt happens. We say things we don't mean. Things we regret but are too stubborn to take back.

Yeah, yeah, yeah. It wasn't just Rick. I get it. I was a bitter, angry wife. I didn't support him, and I wasn't even nice to him very often.

When one finally stops and takes a look at one's own heart, it starts a snowball effect. It's like you see one thing after another. Things you didn't even realize were there. But now that I've finally faced my own responsibility, I'm seeing every scowl, hearing every resentful word.

Oh, Father. I was so afraid for my marriage that I pushed Rick away. The truth is, I'm equally to blame for our marriage not surviving. Infidelity isn't the only betrayal. I stopped loving, honoring, cherishing. Rick was right. I might not have been unfaithful sexually, but emotionally I pulled away first.

An invisible hand squeezes my heart and the ache is almost more than I can bear. What right do I have to virtuous indignation? I swipe at a tear and drop to my knees beside the cradle. More tears slip down my cheeks as I cry out my heartbreak and ask for forgiveness for my part in the divorce. Forgiveness for all the nasty things I've thought and said about Rick and Darcy. For what seems like forever, I sit on the attic floor, sobbing tears of repentance and asking God to change my heart.

I wait, feeling God's presence, His tenderness, His love. Knowing I'll never be the same after today, that God is wiping me clean.

As I gather in a deep breath, I hear that still, small voice speak to my heart. *I know My plans for you, Claire. This isn't the end, but the beginning. Your best days are yet to come.*

The thought that I have a future shoots like an arrow into my heart, and I lift my eyes (like God's really in the attic rafters). Hope lightens my heart. Hope that I can move ahead, let Rick and Darcy be happy without my constant sarcasm and venom. How about letting my kids be happy for them, too, and not so afraid of hurting my feelings that they pretend indifference to their new little brother or sister?

I think of Rick and Darcy and the kids again, and my earlier vision of their perfect Christmas fades. I know I've put a damper on their happiness. And I know I can't justify my actions, but I can put action behind my faith that God can change my heart toward Rick.

I lift my children's cradle lovingly, carefully, and start down the stairs. I spend the next hour cleaning it up. Dusting, polishing. It's still old and scarred, but it's clean. Exactly how I feel. A little scarred, old, but clean. I take a swath of wide red ribbon, wrap it around the length of the cradle and fix a large bow to the headboard.

I slip into my coat and carry the cradle to the van. My heart pounds against my chest as I drive over to Rick and Darcy's. I carry my offering to the porch, set it down, and ring the bell before hurrying back to the van. This is about them. Rick will understand. And so will Darcy.

I don't look in the rearview mirror as I pull away. I feel such a sense of peace, closure. I realize this baby is a gift from God. For more reasons than one. Finally, I'm ready to move forward.

Speaking of which. I pass Greg's house on the way to mine and suddenly I remember his invitation. I pull into my drive and try to decide if I want to take him up on it, or just go inside and fall into bed. In a hasty decision, I get out, stuff my keys into my jeans pocket, and walk the few yards to Greg's house. He seems a little surprised when he comes to the door.

"Claire, come in."

"Is the offer for dessert still open?"

His face lights with pleasure. "It sure is."

Mrs. Lewis hugs me and wishes me a merry Christmas.

"How was your Christmas, Miss Sadie?" I say to the little girl.

She melts my heart with the same gap-toothed grin as Jakey's and shows me a CD Walkman.

"Very cool. What are you listening to?"

"Veggie Tales."

I look at Greg and grin. "What else is there?"

The only thing that could have made my evening nicer would have been having my kids with me. But all in all, a rousing game of electronic Clue sure beat spending the evening alone. And Mrs. Lewis's (or Helen, as she insists I call her) apple pie was melt-in-your-mouth delish.

"Sadie, kiss your daddy good night and Grandma will tuck you into bed," Helen says as we put away the game pieces.

The little girl doesn't even protest as a wide yawn stretches her mouth. She hugs and kisses Greg then gives me a shy little wave. "Good night."

"Well, I suppose I should be going, too." I stand and take my hot chocolate cup to the sink. Greg holds my coat as I slide my arms in. "Hang on while I get my coat," he says. "I'll walk you home."

I know better than to protest. I lean against the frame of the door between the living room and kitchen while I wait. I never thought I'd be able to walk into Mom's house and feel as though it truly belongs to Greg. But he's made it his own.

He walks back into the room and a funny little smile tugs at his lips. "What?" I ask. Standing directly in front of me, he slips a finger underneath my chin and tips my head.

Oh. My face flames instantly. Directly above me is a sprig of mistletoe made from construction paper—obviously put together by Sadie as a school craft.

"I hope you don't think that I stood here on purpose." I straighten up and I'm just about to walk away when Greg moves in. He rests his forearm on the wall behind me. My heart rate doubles. He's standing so close I can feel his breath, warm on my face. His eyes capture mine and I couldn't look away if the house suddenly went up in smoke.

"Claire," he murmurs, and his eyes look downward to my lips. "I haven't even thought of kissing another woman since the day I met my wife."

Hey, Romeo, probably not the best thing to say to the woman you're about to make a move on.

Lucky for him, he shuts up and dips his head for the kiss. A firm, steady kind of kiss. I only have one guy to compare him to, and in all honesty I have to say, Greg's kiss was . . . all right.

He pulls back, and I figure he knows I'm underwhelmed because a boyish grin tugs at his mouth. He attempts to explain. "I was being a gentleman." His voice suddenly takes on a husky sort of heart-stopping tone. "But since you mentioned it . . ."

I mentioned nothing, of course, but a little bit of intuition goes a long way in a man. He slides his arms around my waist (thank You, God, for the weight loss) and pulls me tight against him. He doesn't bother to ask my permission as his lips move over mine in a kiss that completely erases what's-his-name from my mind. For that matter, what's *my* name?

I sink against him, and he chooses that moment to remember he's a gentleman.

My eyebrows go up as he gives me that "Now what do you have to say about that?" kind of look. He looks so smug—no doubt caused by my shameless reaction to his mind-boggling kiss.

I shrug. "Better." I grin. He laughs and we head for the door. He catches my hand and laces his gloved fingers with mine as we turn toward my house.

"I thought you said the kids were staying with Rick."

I look ahead to my driveway. Rick's car sits there with the engine running. "They were supposed to. For the whole week."

To my delight, and a little bit of embarrassment, he keeps his fingers tightly intertwined with mine as we greet Rick and Darcy by the car.

"Are the kids here?"

Darcy shakes her head. "Ari's watching the others."

Rick's eyebrows go up when he notices I'm holding hands with Greg. Darcy's eyes are moist and her face is shining. She pays no heed to the fact that we're standing in the freezing cold with snow blowing around us or that I am holding hands with my great-looking neighbor. Instead she rushes toward me, leaving me no choice but to drop Greg's hand and embrace her. "Thank you, Claire. Thank you so much."

My own tears are flowing. "I'm sorry for the way I acted, Darcy. I hope you can forgive me."

"You know I do." We hold each other at arm's length. In a moment like this, there's nothing to do but give in to an awkward moment of laughter.

Rick steps forward. I'm not ready to hug him, so I can only hope he doesn't have that in mind.

He doesn't. Rather, he stands in front of me and smiles. His eyes, too, are moist. "Thank you for the cradle. I'd hoped. But I knew I couldn't ask for it."

"Like you didn't ask for my forgiveness?"

"Something like that."

"It's okay, Rick. You don't have to ask for either. They're yours."

As Greg and I stand on my front porch and watch them drive away, Greg slips his arm around my shoulders and pulls me close. "You're an amazing woman, Claire Everett," he whispers into my hair.

In his arms, I feel like an amazing woman. This day has been just too much. I rest my head on his shoulder and my breath leaves me in a sigh. I finally put my past behind me today. In a way that was more than faith. I walked it out. I felt it inside. I know the work is done.

Forgetting those things that are behind me, I'm pressing on . . .

I look up at Greg. Are you my future, Mr. Wonderful?

He gives me a curious look. "What is going on in that brilliant mind of yours?"

Okay, anyone who thinks I have a brilliant mind is definitely a keeper.

"My thoughts are all my own tonight."

He brushes his lips across my forehead. "I'm going to go home so you can get out of this cold."

I don't go in right away. Instead, I take a moment to enjoy the fat flakes still blanketing the ground. Greg's steady footfalls are carrying him toward home, and I watch his broad shoulders and tall, lithe form. I keep focused on him, and I can't help but wonder if he's part of that future God said was going to be filled with my best days.

I wish I could say I'll never get angry with Rick again. I know better than that, but I think in my desire to make all those changes in my life, I lost sight of what's important—inward change. I believe I've made a great start tonight. But it'll take faith to change my actions. The heart change is quick, and God's grace is sufficient for that. The rest I'm going to have to work on. Be vigilant. Put action to my faith.

And as far as the kids are concerned . . . Well, having a healthy mom who is spending time with them is one thing. They've enjoyed that. But having a mom who is ready to put away her anger toward their dad is going to have major benefits for their own emotional well-being.

The thought of the future is always a little shaky.

Especially when you're not sure where you're headed. And, personally, I have no idea what tomorrow holds. The only thing I'm sure of is where I've come from—the mistakes I've made. I'll forget the past, but not the lessons learned back there.

My pulse quickens as Greg stops in his driveway, which is illuminated by the motion light over the garage. He turns and waves. Even from this distance I can see his smile. "Good night," he calls.

I lift my hand and return his wave.

From where I'm standing, my future's looking pretty bright.

Epilogue

January 2, I drop the kids off at school and come back to the house with a sense of purpose. Time to dig into the sequel to *Esmeralda's Heart*. I climb the steps to my office. Instead of turning on my computer, I glance at the Wal-Mart receipt attached to the top of my monitor. The List. I smile, remembering how desperate I was to change my life. So much has occurred during the past three months that I almost don't feel like the same girl. Okay, let's be honest. I'm still me. No doubt about it. And guess what? At the New Year's Eve celebration when Rick and Darcy announced their pregnancy, I felt a little bit miffed. So I know I have a ways to go. But I also recognize that it's my problem, not theirs.

I'm a work in progress.

So let's take a look at this list of mine. I smirk at myself and lean back in my chair with my legs propped on the desk.

During the next three months I will:
1. Go to church more. (This includes daily prayer time and maybe a Beth Moore Bible study.)

I can safely say I have achieved this one. And more than I dreamed possible, my relationship with God has grown.

I'm a different woman inside. The Word has definitely been a double-edged sword, cutting away the *ick* in my heart.

> 2. *Clean my house. (Or probably hire someone. My wrists, you know.)*

Okay, I read an article the other day about how homes with a little dust in them actually boost children's immune systems against allergies. So I figure I'm actually being a better mother by *not* achieving this one.

> 3. *Reconnect with my children. (Will have to plan further for this one.)*

All I can say about this one is "Thank You, Lord." For the first time since Rick walked out, I feel like I have a real place in my kids' hearts and lives. And I'm staying there. Trust me.

> 4. *Exercise—maybe. (But then again, I will be recovering from surgery. Wouldn't want to hurt myself. Could probably walk on the treadmill. We'll play this one by ear.)*

Lost seventeen pounds before Christmas, gained back four. So I'm still in the black. Time to get serious again. Maybe I should go for a walk now, before I start working for the day. Hmm. Nah, I'll do it later. If I have time.

> 5. *Figure out why my only socialization revolves around my computer. I mean, I love the writing groups, but does*

lunch with the girls always have to involve trying to negoti-
ate a turkey sandwich while instant-messaging one-handed?

Ladies' Bible study has given me a great handle on real relationships, not to mention the friendship I've developed with Linda. (Who, by the way, came back from her second honeymoon, tanned, radiantly happy, and more beautiful than ever. And I still love her.)

6. *In response to #5—Join ladies' group at church. Perhaps read the book* How to Make Friends and Influence People. *Or maybe one of Dr. Phil's.*

Joined ladies, made friends. Without Dr. Phil.

I gather a breath and look back over the List. Technically I achieved my goal. Which is amazing because lists don't usually work for me. If I really want to analyze the whole thing, I recognize that in the past I've always tried to fix my life from the outside in. And it wasn't until the inward change began that I saw outward changes in my life.

When this forced sabbatical began, I didn't realize how far I'd wandered from the things in life that matter most. I hid from the problems, and only when I decided to face things head-on did I finally understand that sometimes God chooses to give us a reason for the tough things in life—like unapproachable kids, mothers who leave town in the middle of a crisis, ex-husbands and their new wives, and a body that looks like a marshmallow—and sometimes He stays quiet and watches as we either follow His lead and grow, or fall on our faces.

I admit I'm not necessarily the fastest learner, but during the past three months, I've learned that there is peace with surrendering to God's dealing in my life. I'm not all the way there yet where Rick and Darcy are concerned. I'm not thin, the kids aren't perfect, and Greg hasn't proposed. But I'm not giving up. I'm pressing on, running my race. God is at the finish line with a "Well done" and a pat on the back.

> 7. *List to be amended as necessary. (amending)*
> 8. *Press on to the goal so that I may obtain the prize.*

With a smile, I power up my computer, open a new document, and begin to write.

READING GROUP GUIDE

1. Approximately 50 percent of non-Christian marriages will end in divorce. Startlingly, Christian marriage statistics are neck and neck with these. How should the church deal with the victims (the children, the divorcees themselves, the new spouses of divorcees) of divorce? Are we doing enough?

2. Claire often uses pop culture, movies, the Internet, and food to deal with her issues. Do you turn to other things besides God for your comfort? Does it work?

3. Claire's relationship with her mother is based on need; she leaned on her a lot following her divorce. What did she learn by letting go and beginning to handle life on her own? How does your relationship with your mother/grown daughter affect your life and decisions?

4. Do you relate positively or negatively to Claire's parenting methods? Is she a good mom? Is there really any such thing? How do divorced couples effectively parent when they're sharing responsibility with someone living outside the home?

5. How do Claire's feelings about Rick affect her relationship with her children?

6. Even though Darcy met and married Rick well after Claire's divorce, Claire still sees Darcy as "the other woman" in many ways. Why do you think that is?

7. When Claire finally surrenders to God, she experiences freedom for the first time in years. Has there ever been a time in your life when God met you at your darkest hour? Were you able to surrender or do you still struggle with bitterness about the past?

8. Is Greg the right kind of man for Claire? Why or why not?

9. Claire starts out to change her life. Do you set goals for your own life? Do you achieve them? Did Claire?

IF YOU ENJOYED
Leave It to Claire . . .

Claire
Knows Best

Book Two in the Claire Everett Series

Claire Everett thought her life was finally on the right track. She's connecting with her four kids and getting along with her ex-husband and his pregnant wife. Now attending church regularly and dating Greg, the cute widower two doors down, Claire's world should be in order. So how come life has suddenly become such a juggling act?

A tornado rips through her roof, forcing a move for Claire and the kids. Greg has suddenly decided on a new career and Claire's not happy with his choice. Adding confusion to an already crazy situation, Van, the local contractor, is suddenly paying her quite a bit of attention; her daughter's rebellion is creating big challenges; and her writing career is cooling off instead of heating up. So when panic attacks threaten to make her a prisoner in her own home, she breaks down and hires a life coach to help her sort it all out. But is a life coach the answer?

Can Claire finally let go and admit that it is God who is directing her steps, or will she try to create her own destiny and insist that Claire Knows Best?

AVAILABLE JUNE 2006